Lost
Eagle

The Untold Story of
HIH Grand Duchess Tatiana of Russia
1897-1926

Lost
Eagle

The Untold Story of
HIH Grand Duchess Tatiana of Russia
1897-1926

Steven Ingman-Greer

TOP HAT
BOOKS

Winchester, UK
Washington, USA

First published by Top Hat Books, 2013
Top Hat Books is an imprint of John Hunt Publishing Ltd., Laurel House, Station Approach,
Alresford, Hants, SO24 9JH, UK
office1@jhpbooks.net
www.johnhuntpublishing.com

For distributor details and how to order please visit the 'Ordering' section on our website.

Text copyright: Steven Ingman-Greer 2013

ISBN: 978 1 78279 079 2

A CIP catalogue record for this book is available from the British Library.

Design: Stuart Davies

Printed and bound by CPI Group (UK) Ltd, Croydon, CR0 4YY

We operate a distinctive and ethical publishing philosophy in all
areas of our business, from our global network of authors to
production and worldwide distribution.

CONTENTS

Dedication
To a very special family...
May their prayers for the Earth and Mankind be answered.

To all those people who have helped me during the writing of this book, I extend my thanks. You all know who you are.

I send my love to My Lady of the Roses. She knows who she is, and what she has meant to me, not only during the creation of this book, but always...

"At night, in the silence of my heart, I listen to the music, and I remember."

Steven Ingman-Greer
February 15th 2013

A note on the dating system used in this book

Before 1900, all dates in the Russian calendar were 12 days behind the rest of Europe because of the difference between their Julian (basically a reformed Lunar 355 day) Calendar and our Gregorian (basically a Solar 365 day) Calendar. In the 20th century their dates were 13 days behind. After February 1st 1918, Russia reverted to our Gregorian dating system. So that day became February 14th in line with the rest of Europe. For convenience, all dates in this book are given in the English Gregorian Calendar.

"Love is Light and it has no end. Love is great suffering. It cannot eat. It cannot sleep. It is mixed with sin in equal parts. And yet it is better to love...If love is strong – the lovers happy. Nature Herself and the Lord give them happiness...All is in Love, and even a bullet cannot strike Love down."

Father Grigory Rasputin (1869-1916)
Transcribed by Grand Duchess Tatiana in her book of sayings and letters from the Siberian mystic.

Prologue - August 30th 1982

A Stop on the Railway Line Between St Petersburg and Odessa

Boris Chernenko did not like his job much. A signalman on the Soviet Railway, he had begun life on the Stalinskaya Collective Farm in his native Georgia. Collective farm life had suited him much more than this boring existence stranded in the middle of nowhere. Every day the same routine, passing the same trains through at the same times. He was convinced he could do it in his sleep. A man of nearly fifty, he still fondly remembered the days of steam and the engines that pulled the old express along this line. With fire in their hearts, it was as if the engines were living beings. It was even possible to imagine them with their very own voices and personalities. He chuckled to himself; a very Romantic Old Russian perspective. At night he would dream sometimes of a mysterious steam train with a very special whistle. One that pierced his heart. It was a little like being in love.

A sound on his board jerked him abruptly out of his reverie. A buzzer had sounded, denoting the presence of an oncoming train. This was very peculiar. It was the middle of the afternoon. The next train through here, the diesel Odessa Express, was not due until 6pm. He lifted the phone to call ahead. No, no train due for another three hours. It must be a glitch in the system. He tapped his board and the noise stopped. Sitting back in his chair, he suddenly felt very tired and put his cap over his eyes. Good job he was both supervisor and sole employee. He could fire himself for this infraction of the rules of work. What would his Commissar of Labour say?

The buzzing sound woke him abruptly again. This time, it sounded more insistent, like an alarm. He had never heard the board make that sound before. The train must be very close and the sounding of that second buzzer denoted the fact that the train was due to stop at his halt. This was very unusual. Scheduled trains had not stopped here in decades. In fact, he seemed to recall his predecessor telling him, when he started work at the halt in 1959, that the only trains ever to stop at this place on a routine basis had done so before World War I. What train could be coming that would break the old tradition? He remembered noticing in one of the old warehouses a dilapidated and broken Imperial Double Headed Eagle. With its spots of gold, it still looked magnificent and, in spite of himself, he had felt his heart stir within him at the sight, until he had reminded himself that he was a true Communist and son of the Motherland. He had always quietly wondered to himself whether his post was an old Imperial Halt. The destruction of the last family and the contempt in which they were still held in official circles meant it was almost treasonous to even think about them. But sometimes Boris wondered. What were they like? He had seen an old photograph once of the Tsar and his family. They seemed so gentle at first impression... His thoughts drifted wistfully.

He was pulled back to earth for the third time by the sound of a train whistle. His heart nearly stopped with fright. It was the whistle of the train he had heard in his dreams. It pierced him like a note of music from a great soprano: elegant, filled with love and longing. Hastily he opened the cupboard at the back of his office and, without knowing why, he put on his best uniform and hat and rushed out onto the platform as fast as he could.

The sight that greeted him froze his blood. In front of him was the most beautiful and elegant locomotive he had ever seen. Its wheels were highly polished black. All the metal gleaming gold in the afternoon sun. Curtains, drawn at the windows, a plush red. Luxury like this was rare in these days of stagnation. But what really made him stare was the marking on the carriage doors. A large, gold, double headed eagle. It was the old Imperial Train carrying the family to their summer hideaway at Livadia.

Not knowing what to do, Boris was rooted to the spot, watching in fascination as one of the doors opened and he saw two girls get out and descend onto the platform. One was tall, blonde haired and very beautiful, the other slightly shorter, with rich auburn hair. As he looked again, he realised she too was an exceptional beauty, with eyes like burning black stars. They were laughing and holding hands.

The taller one spotted him. Detaching herself from her companion, she walked over to him. Unable to believe his eyes, he felt a growing presence and energy moving towards him. It was like a very powerful jolt of electricity and it seemed to make his cells feel more alive. He instantly felt more alert. She was facing him now.

"Do you by any chance have a drink of water? My sister and I are thirsty."

Bowing his head in respect and not knowing why, he said, "Of course, Your Highness, but surely you have plenty on board?"

"There was an accident higher up the line," she said calmly. "Our water holder has cracked. We'll have to wait to our destination to get a proper repair. Meanwhile, we thought we'd stop here and see if you would be kind enough to oblige us..."

"Boris Chernenko, ma'am."

"Thank you for your kindness, Boris."

She smiled at him. Her sister had joined her. They looked at each other and gave him a look which defied description, but he would remember it forever. He fell in love at that moment. A love from which he was never to recover.

Quickly, he got the two Grand Duchesses some water and organised the loading on board of all the water he had on the station in containers. When all was on board, he escorted them to the train and helped them on board. They graciously allowed him to take their hands.

"A safe journey, Your Highnesses."

"Thank you, Boris," said the tall one. "I think it will be."

Slowly, and in a cloud of steam, the Imperial Train pulled away from the station. The two young women fixed Boris with their gaze. He continued to watch until the train was a speck in the distance and lost in the heat haze.

Then, he went to sit back in his office. Recovering his self-possession, he called ahead to the next stop and, without knowing what he was saying, warned them of the imminent arrival of the Imperial Train.

A week later, Boris Chernenko was ordered to take a leave of absence due to ill health. He discovered that the Imperial Train had last stopped at his halt in the summer of 1916 and had been broken up for scrap in 1934 on the orders of Stalin, who did not want any reminders of a decadent past.

He never forgot his experience of August 1982, or the gentleness of the young ladies. He became a secret convert to the Orthodox Church and eventually, following the fall of Communism, a priest. He was present in 2000 at the official ceremony when Nicholas and his family were declared saints. Every year on July 17th, he made a pilgrimage to Ekaterinburg and laid flowers at the cross which marked the place of their deaths. The card with the flowers was always the same. It read:

August 1982/July 1918. In memoriam. All my love forever. Please pray for my soul. Boris.

BOOK 1

MEMORIES OF BEAUTY

Eternity

A jumble of images. Putting on a pair of Pointe shoes. The feel of a woman's breast through a lace dress. Blood and a sharp pain in my back. A pair of soft, warm lips touching mine. Squirrels in a cedar tree, playing. Music swirling through my mind. Choking sensations, not getting any air. Heat, blazing heat and the salt of the sea. Cool breezes on my naked body. A deep voice echoing through my soul, hypnotic and sweet. Horror and panic. The noise of an aeroplane engine, steam trains and boat rides. Magnificent eighteenth-century architecture rising from a lake. Love, deeper than the universe in the song of a robin at my elbow and the gaze of a pair of beloved eyes. The feeling of dancing, dancing, dancing. Suffocation. Entrapment. Arguments and useless pleading. Piano music, melancholy and beautiful and my fingers playing it. Irritation and hopelessness. Slow chanting in a dark cathedral. Cold, bone numbing cold. Shouts in my ear and a small dog squealing in fright. Pain, indescribable pain tearing my spirit to pieces and a loud scream of ecstasy turning to despair echoing down the tunnel of lost time. Loneliness deeper than futility. The icons looking at us with detached pity and compassion. Slowly waking on a bright summer morning. The face, of someone familiar and trusted, turning demonic, as in a nightmare. Bedtime stories and a loud explosion in my ear... blood in my mouth. Darkness. Music. My beloved's voice healing my shattered soul. Floating in the light. Sleeping in the light which surrounds me ever more intensely with each passing second. The softness of her arms around me. I lie on her breast. Peace. Timeless wonder. The feel of the cool breezes again. Home. My beloved home. Melting and dissolving in incandescent beauty, my consciousness fades into an orgasm of blinding, overpowering light...

PART 1

CHILD OF NATURE

JULY 1899 - JULY 1913

July 1899 – St Petersburg

Funeral corteges. Slow moving carriages. Horses in black. Papa and Mama looking sombre. Gloom, all pervasive, yet outside, birds are singing.

I see two squirrels playing halfway up a cedar tree. Time seems to slow to a standstill, until the universe contains only myself and these smallest of God's creatures. I hear a voice in my mind, deep and resonant, as real as any speaking voice. There is no difference between the two.

"Why so sad, Princess?"

"My Uncle George is dead."

"Who told you?"

"Mama and Papa."

"Don't believe them. Death is a trick of the light, from which we all come, and to which we all return. It is only love that is truly real."

"How do you know?"

"I just do. Everything does. So do you. Look not with the eyes of the mind. They see nothing and believe it is everything there is. Look with your heart, Princess, and you will see."

As if my eyes had been opened, I saw a light in his heart, then in the hearts of the birds on the grass and the people lining the route. The light illuminated their forms, making them radiant to the naked eye. Some lights were brighter than others.

"Different shapes in the same light that penetrates everywhere."

Standing in front of the tree where the squirrel had been, I saw Uncle George. Next to him stood a figure in a black cloak with penetrating eyes whom I did not know, yet who seemed strangely familiar. They smiled warmly. I smiled back.

Suddenly, the sunlight burst through the morning clouds and my uncle and the stranger vanished. I began laughing uncontrollably.

"Shut that child up!" exclaimed Grandmamma. "Don't you know this is a funeral, an occasion for solemnity?"

"Uncle George..." I said in my childish falsetto, pointing back to the tree the cortege had just passed.

"Nonsense, child," said Grandmamma, "your Uncle George is not a tree." Turning to my mother, she said, "The child will claim she hears voices and talks to animals when she gets older I daresay. That stupidity runs in your family line."

She gave Mama a sour look and turned away. I still kept laughing. Papa looked at the tree, then at me and gave me a half smile. I have always wondered if he knew. In the distance, the Imperial guns were booming darkly in salute.

26ᵗʰ January 1903 – St Petersburg
Schubert Piano Fantasy in F minor D940.
Soft, lilting lines of limpid green nature, lines of water flowing through a hazy summer greenwood. Trees softly blowing in warm breezes which touch my nose and promise heaven to my soul's heart. Lying in Olga's arms, as we listen to Mama and Mr Rachmaninov playing the piano. Schubert, I think. Black, dazzling darkness, so impressive a trait of young Sergey's soul, he and Mama are playing as one spirit. Between my half-opened eyes I can see a light hovering above their heads, situated between them like a glowing street lamp. The atmosphere in the room is warm, cosy and velvety in the gathering darkness of the orange-sunset candle flames. Papa smokes his pipe, thoughtfully puffing. Long time ago and far away, they seem to be saying. I feel a suggestion of – "home" says Olga, stirring sleepily. Odd sensation, having one's innermost thoughts verbalised. Maybe these are Schubert's thoughts in music. Yet more than this, suggests the glowing light above the players' heads. We all seem part of something greater. This moment. Movement, flowing yet eternal, static and as beautifully proportioned as the statue of Venus I saw yesterday. In the notes, I hear the Goddess speaking. Languages of pictures and light. Before time somehow. Here, yet not. If only I could hold us here forever. Unable to grasp fully, like a searched-for word that will not come fully into my

9

conscious mind, I doze, overwhelmed by Olga's warmth and the feeling of love in the room saturating my being in the joyous, incandescent light of a faraway sun.

11th February 1904 - 2.35am – St Petersburg
Dreaming ... dreaming ... walking through the corridors of an unfamiliar palace ... the walls are similar to ours here at home, but there is something strange, something "other" about these walls. I'm getting a feeling from my surroundings ... it's distant... definitely not a feeling of home. I'm alone and the corridors are lit only by single candles ... so the light is very dim. In the distance, a record is playing ... it is a song I do not recognise... I pick up odd words ... Yankee doodle? Sweetheart ... dandy ... they repeat over and over again ... the distant feeling is getting stronger... the pit of my stomach hurts ... the pain is getting worse ... the sound of the record repeats louder and louder ... over and over. I drift into a room to my right, nausea almost overwhelming ... at the far end of the room I see a woman standing in front of a mirror, her back to me, admiring herself. I feel as if I'm going to black out from the pain ... she turns towards me, sees me and bursts out laughing. The laugh hurts my ears, my head, my whole body ... is on fire... I'm burning in the very pits of Hell or worse. Suddenly she flies towards me; the colours of the woman's dress and room blend like some evil firework. I'm pinned to the floor with fright... Much more of this and I will surely explode. She is standing over me laughing ... laughing ... but the face is that of a man ... grotesque, in make-up, all smeared with tears of laughter ... hysterical, evil... so evil ... the hands, covered in blood and smelling of cheap perfume come towards my throat as if in slow motion... I begin to strangle ... the overpowering stench of blood is in my nostrils ... my head swims with nausea ... as I'm about to black out, I wake up screaming ... screaming...

Softly, in the deep darkness of night, I feel loving arms enfold me. I smell Olga's familiar smell. She wraps me in her arms ... strokes my hair and face ... my cries slow to a whimper ... I fall into my sister's loving embrace. I am safe here ... nothing can harm me now ... I am home ... forever ... I sleep and do not dream...

12ᵗʰ August 1904 – Peterhof
We have a little brother at last! He will be called Alexander after his grandfather and great grandfather. When he is Tsar, he will be Alexander IV. Mama is tired, but overjoyed. We all went in to see him. He has such an angelic little face, and is so good and quiet. I'm sure we all cried a lot more when we were born. Forty-gun salute fired in St Petersburg. Sunny until 10.30pm.

25ᵗʰ September 1904 – Tsarskoe Selo
Mama wouldn't let us play with Alexei this morning. The doctors were here all day. Spent the whole time with the nanny. Didn't even see Papa. Olga tried to find out what was happening, but stopped short of Mama's room when she heard raised voices.

28ᵗʰ September 1904 – Tsarskoe Selo
Mama and Papa away all day in St Petersburg. Alexei is with them. The nanny tried to keep us amused, but we were all feeling sad and afraid. Something is wrong.

2ⁿᵈ October 1904 – Tsarskoe Selo
Morning riding lesson with Olga and ballet practice. Saw Mama at breakfast. She had been crying. No sign of Alexei. Lessons and bed early. Boring day.

6ᵗʰ October 1904 – Tsarskoe Selo
Tea with Mama and Papa at last. And Alexei was there in his cot. We all rushed over to see him. Mama warned us not to touch him, rather sharply I thought. Then Papa explained that the doctors say he has a disease of his blood. He cuts and bruises easily and must be protected from knocks and bangs. We are to be careful around him and not touch him too roughly. We will all

pray for a miracle. I'm sure God will make him well. After all, he is just a child. The disease cannot be his fault.

29th December 1904 – Tsarskoe Selo
First skating lesson. Fell over three times. Bruised my behind. Olga laughed and laughed and skated away, showing off her skills. She is like a ballerina on ice. So beautiful! I wish I had her grace. Threw snowballs at her afterwards and escaped into the park laughing when she threw back.

Sat under a tree. A robin came and sang to me on a nearby branch. Magic!

22nd January 1905 – 4pm
Saw Papa arguing with Uncle Serge. Aunt Ella was here taking tea with us. We were all bored. Olga had a headache. Uncle Serge frightens me. His eyes are so cold. Papa was shouting at him about something. All I heard was:

"God in Heaven, Serge, all those people. They will think the order was from me! How could you? Without asking me!"

Then they went through a door into another room and I couldn't hear them any more. Olga followed discreetly. She said Papa was shouting at Uncle Serge about something that happened in St Petersburg this morning. It was obviously awful, but she can't make out what it was; only that Papa was furious with Uncle Serge about it, as if it was his fault.

23rd January 1905 – St Petersburg
Uncle Serge gave an order to shoot a large number of people who were coming to see Papa in Palace Square. Papa hadn't been asked. Now there is apparently a revolution on, so Olga says. People are not going to work, and Papa is being blamed, even though Uncle Serge gave the order. If only people knew how gentle and kind Papa is. They would all love him. He is in despair. A large amount of money has been given to relief for the

families and children of the dead and Papa has ordered mass to be said for them in our chapel until further notice.

25th January 1905 – Tsarskoe Selo
Olga fell off her horse this morning. She asked it to jump a fence and it refused and threw her over its head. She is still unconscious. The doctors have been called. I am sitting with her. Strange. A minute ago, I felt her standing next to me. I saw her in the corner of my eye, standing behind me and to the right, but when I turned to look, she had gone. How can she be standing behind me, but also be in the bed?

I slept. Dreamed Olga and I were sitting by a lake with pine trees stretching up to the horizon. Glorious sunshine. Very warm. When I woke, I was lying with my head on Olga's bed. She was stroking my hair, and was awake! I shouted for Mama and the others. General rejoicing.

17th February 1905 – St Petersburg
Uncle Serge is dead. Blown up in his carriage this morning. We all felt the force of the explosion, as it shook the windows of the Winter Palace. Mama is very distressed. Her sister, Aunt Ella, is a widow. I can't say I'm sorry. Uncle Serge was horrible.

17th February 1905 – 11.30pm
Woke up screaming. Dreamed of Uncle Serge. He was a body without a head. Coming towards me, arms outstretched. I was forced into a corner. Couldn't escape. Suddenly saw a vision of his disembodied head. It was covered in blood. He was screaming uncontrollably. Then I woke up, screaming too. Couldn't sleep all night.

20th February 1905 – Tsarskoe Selo
Dreamed of Uncle Serge again. As he came towards me, I began to pray for help. Out of nowhere, a tall, kindly, fair-haired man

in a military uniform came and protected me. Lifted me in his arms, and carried me from the room, locking it behind us, leaving the spectre raving impotently. We seemed surrounded by an aura of light which protected us from harm.

"There you are, little one. You're safe now."

There was such warmth in him. He looked so familiar. I'm sure I've seen him before, but can't think where. We walked out into a beautiful garden, full of summer scent and flowers.

"Think of me, if you need me and I will come."

He walked away into the distance. As he faded from sight, I saw another tall, older man in a monk's robe come to meet him and they vanished into the sunlight together. Woke, feeling warm and protected. Who is he? Who was the monk?

31st October 1905 – Tsarskoe Selo

Hide and seek in the park with Olga, Marie and Anastasia. Running round a tree to get out of sight, I fall over a man in long black robes who is sitting under it... He catches me, and smiles.

"There, my child, who are you running from?"

I must have looked shocked. A memory hit me. I *had* seen him before, at the funeral of Uncle George. He was standing by the tree with Uncle George as the guns were firing. The smile in his eyes seemed to confirm this. It penetrated my soul.

"Who are you? What are you doing in our park?"

"Mama summoned me to tend to the little one. The Holy Mother told me it would be so."

"Alexei is sick."

"But not forever. Doctors do not know everything. They have never succeeded in finding a human soul, and they never will."

He smiled. I felt safe with him.

"Do not worry about your brother. His sickness comes from within himself. Mama is not to blame, neither is Papa. His healing will also come from within, when he remembers his connection to the sea, the wind, the sky and his motherland. He is sad. He needs to remember his joy in life. When he does, he will be well. The earth will help him remember. Now go. Your sisters have nearly discovered your hiding place."

"But you haven't told me your name."

"Grigory Rasputin."

I got up to go.

"Goodbye, sir." I curtsied.

"You may call me Father Grigory."

"Goodbye, Father Grigory."

We smiled at each other. I ran back to my sisters for our game. As I turned back to look for my new friend, I discovered he had gone.

24th September 1906 – Alexander Palace

Pipe smoke... Coming to, slowly, I notice Papa seated at his desk. He must have come in while I was sleeping. He smiles at me, that warm, secret smile that I love so much... He knows so much that he tells no-one... I close my eyes and listen to him shuffle his papers quietly, going through the business of the day... Surely nothing can disturb this feeling of utter and complete tranquillity... Silence... beyond thought...

10th June 1907 – Tsarskoe Selo

Birthday cakes! Pancakes! And a little puppy. He's a tiny French Bulldog. I shall call him Ortino (can't think why – the name just popped into my head). Sleeping in the evening sunlight, full of birthday tea. Woke up in bed late. Ortino curled up next to me. Heaven must be like this...

24th June 1907 – Royal Yacht Polar Star

Going to England, to take part in a race, apparently, and to see Great Aunt Alex and Great Uncle Bertie *(Edward VII – Author)*. Papa is very excited to see his cousin, Prince George and his wife, May. North Sea making me feel sea-sick. Olga is taking it much better.

Running about on deck, playing hide and seek. Olga buried in a book most of the time.

30ᵗʰ June 1907 – Royal Yacht Polar Star
Arrival in England at last. Staying at what Mama calls The Barn (Buckingham Palace). Horrible place. Reminds me of the Winter Palace back home, but not anything like as big. Draughty. Cold. Unfeeling. The English are terrible. Great Uncle Bertie is fat and awful and his beard smells of old tobacco. Great Aunt Alex is scary. She sleeps a lot and when she wakes up seems to spend most of her time shouting at us, even when we're only two feet away.

Papa was overjoyed to see Prince George, his cousin. I've not seen him laugh so much before. Mama seemed very pleased to be back in England.

Spent some time with Prince George and his sons Bertie and David. Olga likes David, I think. I don't. He's cold and empty, just like his grandfather. Bertie is nice, but he stammers a lot. David makes fun of him, which frustrates him and sends him into rages.

Met Prince John too. He is the nicest of all of them. Quiet though. Likes birds and plants. Mama says he is ill, so we don't see as much of him as I would have liked.

1ˢᵗ July 1907 – Cowes, Isle of Wight
Yacht racing. Great Uncle Bertie is on the *Polar Star* with us. He sleeps a lot. So does Great Aunt Alex. She woke up and started shouting again, which scared poor Ortino. Olga laughed her head off.

2ⁿᵈ July 1907 – Royal Yacht Polar Star – off Cowes
Papa was made an Admiral of the British Fleet by Great Uncle Bertie this morning. He looks good, if a little weird in his new uniform. He seems proud. Our yacht won the big race. So

Britannia does not rule the waves after all.

3rd July 1907 – Royal Yacht Polar Star
Spent the day with another of our royal cousins. Kaiser Wilhelm II of Germany. It was a boring day. The Kaiser is very stiff. And his jokes aren't funny. At all! In the evening, when he had gone back to his own yacht, Papa treated us to his impersonation of him. It was so funny we all laughed until we were sick.

14th July 1907 – Peterhof
It's so good to be home. England was boring. I would hate to have to live there with Great Uncle Bertie and Prince George. Everyone is so unfriendly. Ortino was having trouble eating. But now he's home, he's eating again. In England, David's stupid cat menaced him. Horrible cat, horrible boy.

11th August 1908 – Tsarskoe Selo
Picked the wrong mushrooms today while out walking. Was violently sick and saw people in my room who could not possibly have been there. It wasn't scary. Just weird. At one point saw Olga, who came to talk to me about Ortino snoring at night. It is bothering her and she wants me to see if I can't keep him more quiet. Later, questioned Olga, who denied ever having come into my room in the middle of the afternoon. Marie confirmed at that time they were both out in the park, riding. I think they are playing tricks on me. I wasn't amused.

12th August 1908 – Tsarskoe Selo
Afternoon. Came upstairs to get away from the heat outside and the noise of Alexei practising his mock parades with his friends. Sat at my dressing table when Olga walked in and complained about Ortino's snoring. It was exactly the same conversation as the one yesterday when I was in bed. To the word! Olga asked me what was wrong.

"I love Ortino, you know," she said, stroking my hair. "I just need him to be a little quieter at night. She paused. I must have had an odd look on my face. "What's wrong? You look like you've seen a ghost."

Perhaps I had. The Ghost of Things to Come.

28th October 1908 – Tsarskoe Selo
Walked past Papa's study this morning. Poked my head in to say good morning and quickly thought better of it. Leaning over the rail at the top of the stairs, I could see that he was reading a letter and muttering to himself. All I heard was, "Unbelievable arrogance. Bloody man thinks he's master of the Universe."

I wonder who he was talking about? He was in a sour mood all day. He didn't read poetry to us after tea, like he usually does, but went back to his study again. I think he works too hard.

15th November 1908 – Tsarskoe Selo
Olga is thirteen today. In celebration, we all (except Anastasia who is soon to have her foot corrected) choreographed a small ballet to music, about the Muses. Alexei was made to sit and look grand as a Young Apollo. Olga, being the only one of us old enough yet to do *Pointe* work, was his chief Muse, Terpsichore, Muse of Dance. The three of us knelt at his feet at the end and kissed his hands. His look was positively angelic. Olga was given another pearl for the necklace she will wear when she comes of age. Mama embraced her after the performance and for once, I think they understood each other. Papa smiled indulgently. He had presented her earlier with a new dress, designed in Paris. It contains an eagle motif in the beadwork at the front. A single, not a double-headed, eagle. Olga is already very fond of it. The eagle is her favourite symbol. She tells me she loves its grace and power, and its ruthless defence of all that it loves, even into death. As she speaks, her air becomes almost beatific. I embrace her, and, for a moment, we are a universe away. In my mind, I see

her dancing, dancing forever in translucent, pure light.

6th January 1909 – Tsarskoe Selo

Orthodox Christmas. To church in the falling snow. As the snowflakes fall around us, we all try to catch these falling stars on our outstretched tongues. The effect of the softness on us is magical. Even more so when we enter our chapel surrounded by the smell and sound and sights of the Divine Liturgy. Truly Heaven has come to Earth. The singing echoes in my mind for days afterward. We must make Earth like this. The joy is indescribable.

Diary Footnote – 1924

I still feel the joy of this service today. My belief has dimmed, but I remember, and my broken heart still sings a long lost melody that vanishes into silence.

30th May 1909 – Royal Yacht Polar Star

Dear Diary... if I hear one more stupid Prussian military march, I think I am going to be sick! Kaiser Wilhelm II of Germany (Cousin Willy) has "graced" us with his "Imperial" presence. Patronised us all with his pompous, strutting stupidity more like. He thinks *he* is the head of this family and wasted no time marshalling us all... for the entire day!

Everything had to accord with *his* wishes. The other yachts had to manoeuvre according to the wishes of *his* Flag Admiral. Everyone accorded with *his* stupid punctual schedule.

Example:

8.00am: Rise from bed.

8.01am: Wash face.

8.02am: Brush teeth.

8.03am: Get servant to dress you.

8.14am: Have servant shot and thrown overboard for giving you the wrong buttonhole (Thursdays instead of Fridays).

8.15am: Fart loudly, comb your handlebar moustache, try on the crown of state and prance about in front of the mirror in your state room looking like a prize idiot. Meanwhile everyone on deck, including the Tsar of Russia, are trying on their best false smiles, trying not to let you know they all see straight through the whole idiotic, useless façade!

Dear Diary... do you think I found it all just slightly frustrating? No? Just my imagination then...

Diary Footnote

Oh yes. One more thing. If you ever see our photograph album for this "visit", look at two photographs. First, Papa and Cousin Willy, stood together on the deck of *The Hohenzollern*. Look at Cousin Willy, notice his expression, then look at Papa. The Kaiser has absolutely no idea how nauseating Papa found him and his whole entourage. Second photo. Cousin Willy, Mama, Anya and all the girls with their dolls. Oh what *fun* we are having! All to order!

"Achtung!"

Short pause in diary entry while author goes to the nearest toilet to be violently sick...

12ᵗʰ June 1910 – Royal Yacht Polar Star

My thirteenth birthday passed two days ago. What a wonderful way to spend my special day. We had a party with cakes and chocolate (not in that order) and dancing afterwards on the covered deck. Papa had hired an orchestra for me especially for the occasion. The weather was wonderful. There was no wind, even here in the Baltic, and the sun shone until 11pm! Olga and I stood together staring at the distant shore in the multi-coloured light of the sunset, marvelling in another of Nature's wonders. I wonder how much beauty there is to see in the world. Such sights make my heart soar with sheer happiness. The sunset was incredible – an unearthly green light filled the sky and we were treated to a shower of shooting stars. Papa stood with us looking over the rail. I know he was as transported as we were. Went below to the sound of our sailors singing an impromptu Kontakion. A Holy end to an enchanted evening.

14ᵗʰ June 1910 – Tsarskoe Selo

I've not told anyone, but I do see real nature spirits sometimes. Papa says they don't exist, but last time he said that, Father Grigory gave me a special smile. We were standing in a clearing in the park at Peterhof and I said I could feel them. After Father Grigory's smile, a small light flashed just over his left shoulder. I laughed. Alexei asked me what I was laughing at and when I pointed to the light, which was now in the tree, he instantly recognised it without my prompting. Papa, feeling very outnumbered went back indoors, muttering something about Nature Madness.

When we were alone, we sat together on the ground and Father Grigory told us stories about the Elementals, how they are Mother Nature's way of protecting the Earth from harm. He said that you should always respect them by keeping the wild wood intact and he told us how the people in his native Siberia manage the forests and the animals by working in harmony with them.

"Honour these Spirits and God will be very happy with you."

He also told us how the various species of animal protect and care for the Earth and that it is all right to eat meat, but only if the animal has made a willing sacrifice of itself.

"Hunting and animal slaughter is abhorrent to God."

"But Papa hunts," said Alexei.

"Yes, but he is an adult and set in his ways, little Prince. It is for the children to enlighten and give grace back to the Earth."

"Why is hunting and animal slaughter abhorrent to God?" I asked.

"Because you are taking the life of a being without asking its permission or gaining its consent. All creatures have free will.

This is the Primary Rule of the Universe. Not even God can interfere with the course a being freely sets itself, although He can guide."

"How?"

"With inspiration and prophecy."

"But," I said, "I thought prophecy was unalterable."

"Only if the people involved do not change their minds about an event before it happens."

There was silence while we marvelled at the tranquillity in this small forest grove. We were so close to home, yet felt so far away.

He gestured to us and we followed him back towards the palace.

18th July 1910 – Royal Yacht Standart

Our summer cruise is a perfect time for me to reflect on our visits with Father Grigory. In these periods away, when we don't see him, I've taken to compiling a small book of what I call "Nature Notes", copying down all the letters he's sent us and the sayings and ideas I can remember from our times together. It helps me to discover more of my "faith". Having brought my book on deck to read, I had wandered over to the side of the yacht and, staring tranquilly over the rail, I remembered our recent encounter and found myself wondering if everything in Nature had a guardian spirit. At that moment there was a loud crash and a sailor hit the deck behind me. He had been felled, I discovered, by a cunningly-placed banana skin. Yet another of Anastasia's practical jokes. Olga ran up behind him, helping him to his feet. The look in his eye was marvellous. And when he looked at me, I saw him blush. I was right. He was in love with my sister. Pausing for a moment to take in this delicious notion, and wondering if I should tease Olga about it later, I mused about the consequences of having spotted the offending article before the man fell and removing it, thus spoiling the joke.

"And changing the prophecy of the sailor's downfall, I suppose," said Olga sarcastically.

"Don't you start. Removing the banana skin would have made me his guardian spirit. Look, I know you are more accepting of fate than I am. But I like to think we can control our destinies and change our fate. Father Grigory was suggesting that, don't you think?"

"Yes, but he also submitted to the will of God. We all have to be submissive to a higher power sometimes."

"You can be if you want, but I'm going to control everything, even God."

Olga gave me a look and slapped my behind.

"Ow! Sorry, that was naughty, but you know what I mean. I just want everyone to be happy."

There was a long pause. She looked deeply into my eyes. Her next words spoke for us both. "I know. I sense it too. Clouds on the horizon."

"But do they contain rain or snowflakes?"

"I prefer the snowflakes."

"So do I. Remember the snow mountain in the park last year?"

"And the toboggan rides."

Hushed together.

"Don't tell mama about Alexei."

"I know. We let him ride headfirst down the hill. I've never heard him whooping so loud."

We both laughed. Father Grigory's healings really did seem to be changing the apparently unalterable facts in our brother's future. It was he who was Alexei's guardian angel. Olga squeezed my hand and kissed me. At that moment, Nature really did seem to be looking after all of us, even the lovesick sailor. He had resumed his watch and was trying to look nonchalant, in spite of the fact that I could feel his seething emotions from the opposite side of the yacht. Olga, unaware of his amorous desires, continued to stare into the far distance, looking, as usual, at something far beyond all our comprehension.

7th May 1911 – Tsarskoe Selo
A balmy day. Breezes from the southwest reminding me of our summer holidays in the Crimea. I stroll in the park alone for once, free from Mama and Papa and the noise that is always in my head. Here among the trees, flowers and birds, I hear a whisper so faint it is almost inaudible. My own voice talking to me in the deep silence of Nature. I swear I can almost see Anastasia's fairy-folk out here, little lights dancing in the gloom of the coppices and groves.

"So, Highness, would you like to learn how to talk to the Earth?"

"Father Grigory! You startled me. I didn't know you were coming today."

"Mama, she sent for me. I have come early so I can be with the animals in the park. They know more about what goes on than you think. They sense that you love them. You have always wondered why you, of all your sisters, could get close, when they could not? That faun you touched, he remembers you and sends his love."

For the second time in only a moment or two I was startled. When I had got close to the faun, it was in Poland, at Papa's hunting lodge. He had come close one summer evening, curious about us and not yet knowing enough of us to be afraid. While Papa and the rest of the family were engaged in conversation, I ventured out onto the lawn where he was grazing, looking up at the house occasionally. It was twilight. The sun had set behind the mountains and the back of the lodge and lawn were illuminated only by large torches. I approached him slowly and quietly. His overwhelming stillness was compelling. I stood, transfixed by this trivial yet beautiful sight. As I reached his side, I paused. Suddenly, all was quiet and I seemed a million miles away from the family lodge. The universe seemed to contain just the faun and me. In the silence, I felt rather than heard his thoughts. I had never experienced anything so beautiful. For only the second time in my life, time slowed to a standstill and we both became as living sculptures in a vast natural landscape, connected by the energy of our being. As I stood, almost as if in prayer, I felt the animal reach out towards me and, for a second, my thoughts merged with his and I understood what it was like to be him. Suddenly it was as if the whole consciousness of faun had invaded my brain. But, instead of being overwhelmed as I usually was by my human family and friends, I was welcomed in. In a gesture of love, I reached out and stroked his head. He paused in his grazing and looked at me, I now realised, with the eyes of his whole species and I understood in a flash.

"What you do to the smallest of My creatures, you do also to Me."

I began to cry. Not just for the pain of the deer as men hunt and kill them for needless sport, but for the ignorance of Man, who does not realise that in hurting the Earth, he hurts only himself. I also realised in that moment that the plants, animals and fish were just different expressions of the whole consciousness of Nature, or, as a friend had told me eleven years earlier,

"Different shapes in the same Light that penetrates everywhere."

A noise from inside the lodge startled the faun and broke the moment. He ran away. I had never told anyone of the experience, not even Olga.

"How do you know about that?" I asked Father Grigory.

"The Holy Mother. She told me," he said, enigmatically. I did not know whether by Holy Mother he referred to the Virgin Mary, or something else, more heretical in nature.

6th July 1911 – Livadia

A day of rejoicing. The new palace Papa has had built here in the Crimea is a replacement for the old one, which, attractive though it was in some respects, was oppressive and holds dark memories for my parents. It was here in the summer of 1894 that Grandpapa, Alexander III, died. Papa suddenly had the weight of the world on his shoulders. He has told me about those awful days, and how he will never forget the smell of death that hung over the palace after his father died. That smell, and the feel of decay that went with it, have stayed with him. It is quite understandable that he should want to demolish and rebuild. Now there is a new palace, made of white marble, done in a Mediterranean style. It is so full of light. Everywhere. How better to banish the old darkness and ill feeling and to overwhelm it in the light of life. We all feel so happy here. We all have our own rooms. Two by two for the girls, and Alexei has a room to himself.

However, even though it has the feel of being on holiday, we still cannot escape our lessons. This morning, French with M. Gilliard. Marie took a picture of Olga and I sitting out on the terrace with him. He's trying to keep a calm look on his face, even though we are precariously perched on the terrace railing. Nothing disturbs his air of calm nonchalance. I wonder if all Swiss are as undemonstrative as he is. Trouble is, he can't hide from me. I've seen the look in his eye when he's teaching us. I know he finds Olga and me pretty, and that he likes us. That gives me a warm feeling, and I feel very secure with him. I know Olga feels the same. We are always delighted with his lessons and things go smoothly, and as serenely as the feel of the Crimean sunshine.

Afternoon trek to the coastline. Swimming in the sea. Tea with Aunt Olga, Papa's favourite sister.

Grandmama is coming here next week. Uughhhh!

14th September 1911 – Kiev
What began as a night out at the opera turned into something chilling and frightening. Papa had decided to go and see a performance of Glinka's *Life for the Tsar*. Now this is not my favourite

opera at the best of times, but Kiev Opera House is very lavish and they always accommodate us with grace and good manners, so an evening out there is very comfortable, no matter how boring the music.

Papa's Prime Minister, Pyotr Stolypin, was there too. He is a lovely man. I have met him several times over the last few years. As a politician, he is one of the very best, so Papa tells me. And certainly, the agricultural reforms he's put through since 1908 have revolutionised things for the small landowners. It was quite a coincidence to find him here, and very pleasant too. The four of us talked during the first interval like old friends and he was very charming to Olga and me. I think I can see why his wife is so fond of him.

As the second interval began, something made me look over at Mr Stolypin, who was sitting in the front stalls. He glanced at me and smiled. I shall never forget it, for I have already wondered if he hadn't been smiling at me, whether he would have seen the danger in time to avoid it. A young man was walking up to him, dressed like a normal student. Unfortunately, he was very far from ordinary, for he pulled a gun on Mr Stolypin, and fired into his chest from point blank range. I froze in terror. The man looked up at me and, for a second, I truly thought he would level the gun at me. If he had, I would have been a sitting target. There was silence for what seemed like an age, then a woman screamed. The scream broke the spell. Suddenly it seemed as if there were twenty policemen converging on the stalls, and the young man was wrestled to the ground and taken away. Mr Stolypin turned to us very slowly, gave the sign of the cross and slumped into his seat. Papa rushed to help him, but by the time he got there, he was already unconscious. Eventually, people arrived to take him to the hospital. The three of us went home; we just couldn't stay after that. Papa was very subdued. Olga and I cried all the way home and for some time afterwards. I can't tell you how I know, but that shooting has changed everything. I seem to recall the opening line of a poem from somewhere, I don't know the original context, but it's horribly appropriate:

"And suddenly it's evening… "

15th September 1911 – Livadia

Everyone was quiet today, in spite of the glorious weather. Even the picnic on the sun terrace seemed to a strange degree devoid of light. Papa was absent too for most of the day, making frantic phone calls back and forth to St Petersburg about a temporary replacement for Mr Stolypin. Then he stayed in his study. He feels the shock of last night very deeply, as do Olga and I. We went riding in the afternoon to try and escape for a while, but it is impossible to escape from yourself. For my part I kept seeing Mr Stolypin smiling at me in slow motion as the man walked up to him with the gun. I feel so stupid. I should have shouted, thrown my programme, or my opera glasses, or anything. But no, I froze like a coward and did nothing. That sign of the cross he gave us will haunt me forever.

18th September 1911 - Livadia

Pyotr Stolypin, Prime Minister of Russia 1906-11, died early this morning without regaining consciousness. Evening has become twilight.

19th September 1911

Had a horrible stinking row with Mama today. She told me that Father Grigory had recommended a replacement for Mr Stolypin and that she would make Papa accept him. It wasn't this that made me flare up; it was Mama's assertion that Mr Stolypin was no good and deserved death for opposing Father Grigory.

"How *dare* you say *anyone* deserves death!" I shouted. "What about his wife and children, how will they live now? And all you can do is crow. I have never heard anything so unfeeling and heartless!"

I stormed out of her presence and avoided her for the rest of the day. I understand that she blames herself for Alexei's illness, in spite of Father Grigory repeatedly telling her she is not at fault. It is this basic insecurity that leads her to trust him so, as a man of God. But sometimes I feel she takes it to lengths that even he would find too much, and it blinds her to any feeling for other people. Papa tolerates it because he loves her so much and although I've seen it before occasionally, I too have turned a blind eye. After all, she is my mother, and Tsarina, and I love her with all my heart. But that insufferable crowing over poor Mr Stolypin's death and with no feeling for his wife and family pushed me beyond the limit of my patience. Papa by contrast has already caused a requiem to be sung, and is determined to make sure his dependents are cared for. For someone who did what he did for Russia, it is the least we can do. Mama can do what she likes to me for the insult, but I shall not retract it. This time, she went too far.

24th October 1911 – Tsarskoe Selo

Piano lesson with Mr Rachmaninov. Today, he allowed us to play for him on the grand piano in the main drawing room here at the Alexander Palace. Of all the instruments we have here, this one is by far the finest; an Erard made in Paris in 1873, the year our teacher was born. Its sound is like liquid black velvet, and, unlike our uprights, you need a very soft action, predominantly from the wrist, to play it well. So it is a great test for us both, and has never happened before in our years of tuition. I felt very nervous. I had presented my pieces to him before, but not on this instrument or in this large a space. Any mistake I made would be instantly audible. I didn't want to make a fool of myself. His approval is hard won, and means a lot to me.

Entering, Olga was in the throes of one of her favourite works, Chopin's Prelude No.15 in D flat. Mr Rachmaninov was sitting by the window, staring out into the park, his expression distant and unreadable. As the last chords evaporated, he turned to me, and gestured to me to sit and play him my pieces. I had chosen one of his own preludes, No.6 in G minor. I trembled at the thought when I chose it, but it was a sincere choice, and one of my favourite works. Beginning, I felt the military rhythms course through me, and imagined myself at one of our parades at Krasnoe Selo. But as the Romance began, my eyes closed, and I found myself lost in a world of nature, surrounded by lakes and forests stretching to the horizon. At the end, he remained staring out of the window, unmoving. Nervously, I began to play the other work I had prepared, a section of Bach's Well Tempered Clavier. As I ended that too, there was silence, and I began to feel upset. Usually if he is this quiet, he is disturbed by our playing, and we will receive a lecture on each one of our faults, which he always knows with incredible precision. Apparently coming out of his own interior world, he walked over to the piano and asked to replace me at the stool. He then proceeded to play all four of the pieces we had prepared, but from his own memory. The performance was transcendent, stunning, and filled the room with sparkling light. Olga and I stood either side of him, marvelling at his utter mastery of form and expression. When he finished, he rose from the stool, and embraced us both.

"Our lessons are finished. You have no more to learn from me. Both of you are now masters of your own expression. Keep practising, and consult me, always for advice, but your techniques are now set and will naturally evolve on their own."

I burst into tears. He embraced me again. "There, there, Tanya, did you think I would scold you? I asked you to play to me here because I felt that the time had come for you both to fly my nest, and I was right."

He kissed Olga's hand and then mine, and then we both sat for him and played for him the slow movement of his own Symphony No.2 in the four hand arrangement he had made especially for us. His look was intense, and I shall never forget the tears that fell from behind his closed eyes as we played his soaring endless melodies in the light of the October sun that morning.

29th December 1911 – Tsarskoe Selo
Christmas preparations are almost complete. There is a tree in every single one of our rooms, all decorated by us (with a little help from everyone else, including the servants, ADCs, and any other unsuspecting people we could rope in when they least expected it!). It is going to be a quiet holiday. Mama is only inviting Lilli and Anya to share table with us. Of course, Father Grigory is going to be there. Hopefully he will tell us another one of the special stories he only tells at Christmas. Last year, he told us again all about St Seraphim of Sarov. He is one of my favourite people, a true example to us all from God. I think all of us could benefit from some time in Nature. Only when I'm there do I feel truly at peace and that nothing can harm us, a sensation that is becoming increasingly rare these days. Olga has said too, that she feels a menace coming. It is distant, but the feeling is real. When I've mentioned it to Father Grigory, he gets a strange look in his eye. He then has an annoying habit of patting me on the cheek and saying, "There, there, my child, all will be well. Keep praying to the Holy Mother for protection and She will always guide us to safety."

The contrast between the comforting statement and the look in his eye when he says it makes me think even he does not entirely believe his own counsel. This makes me feel more worried than ever.

6th January 1912 – Feodorovsky Cathedral
Christmas morning. Church with everyone. Snow, sunlight and the beauty of the sound of the bells always captivating the heart. Feeling happy inside as never before, my spirit soared during the

service. The sound of the deep bass voices in the choir resonating through me like some giant tuning fork. My soul seemed in tune with God afterwards. Home for presents and Christmas lunch. Olga got an edition of Tolstoy's poems. I got a new edition of *Anna Karenina*, signed by the great man himself just before he died. Marie got a beautiful edition of stories by N Taffy and Anastasia got a world atlas, which made her laugh, as Geography is her worst subject, which, as Papa pointed out, is half the point of the present. In addition, we all got the usual jewellery and dresses. We obliged Mama and Papa by dressing in these for the afternoon. Then Father Grigory came and told us stories of the Old Believers, many of whom he has met in Siberia. They tell of long-forgotten links between the Tsar and his people and God. This is a divine trinity that must not be broken, for its truth forms part of the story of the evolution of Mankind. The theory is quite esoteric, but the feeling is good and pure. We feel the truth of his words and later they seem to light us to bed like a candle being held before us by one of God's angels.

30ᵗʰ May 1912 – The Kremlin

30th May 1912 – The Kremlin

All the grand ceremonial of which the Orthodox Church is capable was lavished on the celebrations today of the centenary of Borodino. This was the great battle in which General Kutuzov defeated Napoleon. Or, should I say more properly, fought him to a standstill. My reading of the strategy and tactics suggests that neither side won this contest. What can be said of the battle is that casualties were appallingly high on both sides. What can also be said is that the stalemate, combined with the scorched earth policy and the subsequent abandonment of Moscow by the people resulted in Napoleon being smashed for good. Our ancestor, Alexander I, is rightly seen I think as the victor of that war. Without him, Europe would not have known the freedom it now has. Yes, the world has a lot to thank our family for.

The aura of the service reminded me of something else,

though. Alexander is reputed not to have died in 1825, but to have retired to the countryside and become a holy man. He seems to me to have understood what true spirituality is. Power, as in being the Tsar, is not an end in itself, but simply a vehicle through which great things can be accomplished, that are both temporal and also reach beyond time and space. Alexander I appears to me to have achieved a divine balance between worldly power and divine introspection, and, if the legends about him are right, he is the first of us to have truly achieved grace through suffering. He is a model for all men. Today, in the cathedral, I am sure I felt his presence. But his feeling was oddly neutral. He seemed to be watching everything with compassionate detachment. What does he know? And how unalterable is the Will of God? Just like my ancestors' fate, everything is shrouded in mystery and I left the service feeling disconcerted when I should have felt comfort and peace.

31ˢᵗ May 1912 – Moscow

That feeling of discomfort I alluded to yesterday after the service of thanksgiving was made worse by the visit Papa, Olga, Marie and I made to Aunt Ella's Convent afterwards. Following Uncle Serge's assassination she took the veil and founded her own order at the Martha and Mary Convent. I have never have liked her. She and Uncle Serge were alike, both extremely cold and unfeeling. I'm not surprised the terrorists killed him in 1905. His attitude to those not of his own class was shameful and he and Ella are little short of heartless. A shame, because she is physically one of the most beautiful women I have ever seen. The only one of us who can put up with these visits is Masha, whose placid goodness seems to make her immune to Aunt Ella's coldness... I get bored easily and find her vacuous. Olga gets angry at her lack of feeling and complains of a headache whenever she comes to tea. If she didn't excuse herself, now she is older, I know that she would eventually lose control and tell her what she thinks of her and her nuns in couture gowns. Spiritual? I think not.

5th June 1912 – Tsarskoe Selo
The dancing master banged his stick loudly on the polished floor. All I could think about was the sight and feel of the morning sun as it bounced off the floor and refracted through the dust particles swirling in the still air.

"Highness, you are not paying attention! Lift your leg higher and concentrate on turn out. Here, I will show you again."

He marched up to me with that strange, waddling gait which always made me laugh. Ceccetti didn't look much like a brilliant dancer, but in his youth he had been the toast of the French opera and now he was coach to Pavlova and Kcheshinska. His darting blue eyes never missed a fault and, although he barked loudly, he never chastised us. Behind the mask, he was genial and kindly. I could see why the dancers at the Maryinsky liked him. Gently, he took hold of my leg, turned my foot out to a perfect angle and raised it until the point of my toe was level with my shoulder.

Holding it for a moment in place, he said, "Let your physical memory absorb this. This is where and how your body should express itself in this movement and remember, without perfect technique, there cannot be perfect expression of the soul."

Where had I heard that before, I wondered?

Behind him, Olga was pulling faces and mimicking his gestures. Another tutor would have caned her for less. Ceccetti wheeled round like lightning and caught her at it. There was a stunned silence.

Quietly he said, "Highness, they say that imitation is the sincerest form of flattery. Now, if you will please imitate your sister by repeating the movement I just demonstrated and then show me a perfect fifth position."

Olga turned slowly and positioned herself at the barre. Elegantly she turned her foot out, pointed her toe and raised it effortlessly into position, level with her shoulder. Then having regained perfect poise, she rose up slowly onto pointe in fifth position and as the crowning touch raised her hand, which had been gently holding the barre until both hands touched at fingertip lightly over the crown of her head. I had never seen anything so beautiful. Regaining a resting position, I heard her exhale slowly. There was silence.

After a seeming eternity, Ceccetti spoke. "Bravo, Highness. You will make an adequate dancer in the corps de ballet. We meet at nine tomorrow morning."

And with that he bowed deeply and left, waddling as before. I never cease to wonder at the paradoxes in the human form.

23rd July 1912 – Livadia

A really extraordinary and rare experience today. Olga has, from time to time, annoyed Mama with her manners. She can be very rude to people she doesn't like. She once told a portrait painter, quite bluntly, that he was a silly man with a boil on his nose; this before unceremoniously walking out on him. Mama gave her a spanking for that herself and our tutors have been given permission to discipline us if we stray outside the manners that would be expected of a Royal Princess.

This morning I knew something was wrong. Olga does not like Geography at the best of times. But today, she slouched in her chair even more than usual. Madame asked her politely to sit up straight and pay attention. Olga ignored her. A little later, she repeated the request. Again, silence. The third time, Olga gave our tutor such a look of undisguised contempt that it would have withered a rose at a hundred paces. It reminded me of the afore-mentioned incident with the portrait painter. This time, however, her mood was nothing like as funny. It was her use of language that caused the problem. She uttered a swearword in colloquial Russian that I will not repeat here for fear the page will catch fire.

Madame gave Olga an icy look. "Young lady, you know very well what your Mama and Papa think of that kind of peasant language. If you will not be polite and gentle as a well brought-up young woman should be, you will be made into one by force. You know what I need."

I caught my breath. I hadn't seen anything like this before, although the threat had always existed. Olga rose elegantly from her seat and walked past me to the back corner of the room. As she passed me in the other direction, I saw that she was carrying the long, thin cane that always rested in the same place and that we always saw when we entered the schoolroom, tacit and ancient symbol of the tutor's authority over us. Olga reached the tutor's desk.

"Assume the position, if you please."

Olga bent herself over the desk and reached her arms out to grasp the other side. When she was ready, our tutor put her hand in the small of Olga's back. What was odd, was that I felt that it was done, not with malice, but with love.

There was a whistle sound, and then a loud crack as the instrument connected with Olga's body. No sound else, other than the sound of the birds outside. The room felt extremely warm, almost stifling. A second whistle and a crack. Olga jerked forwards, her head came up, her neck bent, her eyes closed tight, as if she were concentrating hard. A third time. The air felt so stifling, I was finding it hard to breathe. Olga jerked again, this time emitting a small stifled moan through her parted lips. Madame's hand almost seemed to stroke the small of Olga's back, as if comforting her. On the fourth stroke Olga began to cry. A single tear rolled slowly down her cheek, a reluctant letting go of her inner agony. What was strange was that I could feel my sister's pain coursing through my body too. But there was something else as well. A growing Inner Light. Small at first, but growing in intensity, I felt a whirl of emotions at the centre of which was an experience of excruciating pain all mixed up with love, sacrifice, redemption and physical passion. Was this how Christ felt when the Romans scourged him, I wondered. As the last stroke fell, I felt an indescribable feeling of yearning and ecstasy overwhelming me. Olga's tears, streaming down her face, caressing her skin, were my own. It was as if my sister and I were drowning in light.

It was over. Olga raised herself, took the cane from the mistress's proffered hand and kissed it. I have heard that our beloved martyrs and saints kiss the crosses they are to be killed on. The metaphor was small, but telling.

"Thank you, Madame."

With all the dignity and grace of a ballerina, Olga walked past me. Our eyes met. She knew I had felt what she had felt. The experience had been painful, but beautiful. As our Friend was fond of saying, *"Repentance is very pleasing to God, but first we have to sin."*

Having placed the instrument of correction back in the corner of the room from which it came, Olga resumed her seat. She was upright and the look on her face was shining, bright and alert.

17th July 1912 – Livadia

Masha came to talk to me this morning. She was in something of a distressed state. Apparently, she had been walking near Papa's study when she had come upon one of the young men who act as ADC with us. She had been, as usual for Masha, lost in her own thoughts, had rounded a corner and been knocked down by him. Seeing her distress, he had graciously offered both his hand and his apologies. As she had re-arranged herself, she had become aware that she was blushing and had run off without speaking to him. Reaching her room, she had gone and knelt on her bed, aware of sensations within herself that she could not define, but were a combination of fear and excitement. Coming into our room, she engaged us with what was on her mind.

"What do you think it means?"

I began to laugh. "I think you are attracted to him."

"I am not!"

"I think you are. Was he good looking?"

"Well, yes." She slipped into reverie. "He's most wonderfully tall and has such striking eyes that seem to stroke you with their gentleness..."

"See," I said with a smile, "you are attracted to him."

"Oh." She was embarrassed now. "What do I do?"

"What all the rest of us do, my love. You may think about it, but you must do nothing."

Behind my shoulder, I sensed Olga come into the room. I could feel her frustration. She had heard me.

"And why must she do nothing?" she enquired testily.

"You of all people know what our restrictions are..."

"Yes, and I *hate* them," she said vehemently. Her eyes were smouldering. "Don't you think I know what she longs for, even if she doesn't know it yet? The same thing we all do. Don't think I haven't felt your thoughts too, Tanya. Admit it to yourself. You have thought about it. I have seen the pictures in your mind. And we must do nothing? Our souls will die if we do not express ourselves. Have you heard nothing Father Grigory says? Don't tell me you don't feel it in your heart as I do."

She walked over to Masha and kissed her on the mouth. "Feel it."

Masha had now blushed scarlet.

"That's what you felt when you looked at him. You know what you wanted. You felt it."

"Do what your soul tells you that you must." She kissed Masha again, this time on the cheek. Quickly, she rose from her seat and left the room.

Olga turned to me. Her eyes were ablaze. "Always trying to restrict. Control. Have you learned *nothing*?"

"But..."

She walked up to me and grasped my arms, holding them

painfully to my sides. I did not protest. Her voice was low. "Father Grigory says we must free ourselves, or there will be no salvation either for us or for Russia. Let Masha do what she must. You must too. You know what I mean."

Her arms had slipped round my waist. She held me and gently kissed me on the lips, her hand brushing my breast. As if a lightning flash passed through my body, I was struck and passed briefly to another place altogether. I got a sensation of forests and a tranquil lake. But only for a split second. Then they were gone and I was back in the room again. Olga was sitting in the chair where Masha had been. She was smiling at me.

"Let your passions loose, Tanya. You must. Come, let us play together."

She got up and passed by me, so close I could smell the deep, rose scent of her perfume surround and hold me in its tender grip. She walked over to the piano that sat by the fireplace. Sitting down, she gestured to me to come and sit beside her. We sat together as close as Siamese twins and began slowly to play the opening of Rachmaninov's Suite op.5, which he had arranged for us to play with four hands at one piano. Our eyes closed and we ascended by the power of music to that special heaven that was our teacher's domain, while we could feel near us our little sister crying out with deep joy as she felt her soul pierced with the first exquisite pangs of love.

9th August 1912 – Krasnoe Selo
Olga was shouting at me. Around me was a jumble of people, while in the distance, beyond the immense window, the bands could be heard playing the Imperial March.

"Come on! Move faster! If you don't get yourself ready soon my horse will take the salute without me."

"But my helmet doesn't look right. I'm sure it's not meant to be at this angle. It'll fall off and I'll look a fool in front of Papa, not to mention all the men laughing at me. I can't go on like this.

You go without me."

"And do what? Lead your horse out and tell him to take the salute on his own? Don't be ridiculous. Except he probably has more intelligence than you do right now. You look fine. Here, I'll make sure your helmet stays on."

She walked up to me and pulled my helmet strap tight. It hurt and I yelled. She took hold of my face in her hands, gently. "You look beautiful. Everything will be fine, trust me."

At that moment her eyes had a look in them which I cannot describe. She was looking beyond time at something not yet existing. I felt a communion with her soul, as if we were not on Earth, but somewhere indescribably different and deeply strange. I felt swept into her field of confidence in spite of myself.

We came back to Earth with a bump.

"Your Imperial Highnesses, we must take your pictures now. The parade is starting."

"Come on!" shouted Olga running ahead of me. "There is no time!"

Breathless, I ran out behind her and down the ramp to where the photographer was set up. It took longer than I thought to compose myself and I swear that to this day I still think my helmet is on at the wrong angle.

18th September 1912 – St Petersburg
Father Grigory sent us a telegram today, telling us he is going back to his home village for a while. He sent us blessings. These are precious and will light us through the days without him. I wonder what has happened. His departure is rather sudden.

1st October 1912 – Spala
Alexei bumped his knee this morning, setting off a haemorrhage in the same area that he damaged a month ago in Bjeloveji. By afternoon a swelling had developed and by evening, the inevitable happened and he came down with the usual fever. His

poor body so desperately tries to heal itself that it regards the bleeding as a disease and tries to elevate his temperature in order to halt its progress. A substitute for blood-clotting. Except it doesn't work. Mama and I sat with him all night. She got not one wink of sleep, no matter how much I tried to persuade her. Dr Botkin and the others are very kind, but they are all impotent in the face of this illness and no matter how Father Grigory tries to tell her she is not to blame, she takes no notice. Papa has forbidden her to contact him. I don't know why. Olga tried to talk to him about it earlier and he said that there were some things that he would rather not be drawn on. Olga was perplexed and frustrated. Papa has never blocked a question from her like that before. My poor brother. I held his hand for hours. Sometimes his grip was so strong that my hand went to sleep. But I don't care. He knows I'm here. That's all that matters.

6th October

Alexei just the same. Swelling horrible. Fever stable, but no better. All we can do is sit and hope. I hate feeling helpless like this.

9th October

No change. This distress will kill Mama if it goes on for much longer. Olga came and sat with us. She held my hand, as I held Alexei's. Darling Olga. What would I do without her?

10th October

Mama and Papa had a horrible row this morning. Mama has resolved to contact Father Grigory with or without Papa's permission. She believes it is the only way to save Alexei. For what it is worth, I believe she is right.

10pm

Father Grigory sent a reply to Mama's telegram, assuring her

Alexei would recover and telling her not to worry. Soon after the telegram arrived, Alexei's fever broke. At long last! He is sleeping peacefully now for the first time in nearly ten days, but looks utterly drained. Mama has gone to bed, completely exhausted. Olga and I held each other and cried. She is asleep on my bed as I write this. I shall sleep next to her tonight. I need her comfort and warmth after the horror and pain of the last few days. Let me know peace. If only for an hour or two. Then maybe the world will look right again.

11ᵗʰ October 1912 – Spala
Alexei is walking this morning. His knee has no swelling. All the doctors are scratching their heads. Miracles, for I have no other word to describe it, always cause confusion it seems, by violating the laws of Nature. Or, do we violate Nature's laws daily through our lack of belief in Her omnipotence? Is it this lack of connection that is the cause, in itself, of our ills? I am beginning to wonder. Papa sat in his favourite chair for the first time in what has been a very long week and cried. Olga and I knelt by him and stroked his hands. The look he gave us said more than a million words ever could.

14ᵗʰ November 1912 – Alexander Palace – Midnight
The stillness in the palace at night is astounding. A deep, dark blue, velvety kind of silence that enfolds you in its protective arms like a caring mother, only in this case a mother that will never age. I lie awake. Eternally it seems. Unlike most people I seem to only require a scant few hours a night and often find myself walking the darkened corridors in search of a lost melody. Sometimes one of our resident ghosts can be heard playing a part of a Mozart Sonata, I think it is K332, only whoever it is always gets the phrasing of the main melody slightly wrong. Frustration, it would appear, follows one even into death. Odd. For the second time this week in my wanderings, I found a cup of hot

milk on the side table in the upstairs corridor, as if it had been specially prepared for me by an unseen hand. Evidently not by our piano playing ghost, who is too pre-occupied with trying to fix his incorrect phrasing to care about the living.

24ᵗʰ February 1913 – St Petersburg
Magnificent day. It rained, but nothing could diminish our joy. Today we celebrated our family's tercentenary. All of us went in coaches to the St Peter and Paul Fortress to take Mass. The most beautiful feelings of love and warmth surrounded us. The crowds cheered us all the way there and we had fun spotting people we knew in the throngs. The service was heavenly. The most wonderful singing by the choir, an especially composed anthem by Grechaninov, made me feel as though I was in heaven already. Overall feeling was like last year in Moscow, only less oppressive. I always feel better here somehow. Maybe the ancient nature of the old capital makes me feel sad, but everything feels much more open and light in St Petersburg and I love the water, the canals and the architecture. I've never been there, but I've seen paintings of Venice, and I imagine it feels much like this. I don't think I'll ever feel more at home than I do here, except possibly in the Crimea.

Glass of hot water at night. To bed late.

27ᵗʰ February 1913 – St Petersburg
Entry by Grand Duchess Olga
Tanya has been delirious now for two days. Fever caused by drinking the water. I warned her that she hadn't heated it enough, but she wouldn't listen to me. Typical. Frivolous and flighty and off with the fairies sometimes, it's as if she suddenly acquires an empty head. She would insist on doing the maid's job for her. With the epidemic of typhoid here in Petersburg at the moment, the doctors have instructed the staff on what to do with the water, but not us. Ridiculous state of affairs. Her fever has

been appalling. Mama and I have nursed her. Her nightmares have been terrible. Sometimes her screams have really alarmed us. Temperature went up to 105 degrees last night. I thought I was going to lose her. I don't even want to begin to think that thought. Ever. Temperature 103 this morning. Still delirious. She was convinced there were angels at the foot of the bed. Smelled Roses. She might not have been far wrong. Hopefully they will take care of her and not take her from us.

28th February 1913 – St Petersburg
Entry by Grand Duchess Olga
Tanya's fever subsided last night. Temperature now down to 100. She's taking soup and drinking tea. Her hair has been shaved off for the treatment. Such a shame, she has beautiful, soft, long hair. Now she'll have to wear a wig for all our official photos. She's already said what she thinks of that to Mama and had a good cry. But all will be well. Tanya is so pretty with or without hair. When I said that to her this afternoon she said,

"That's all very well for you to say," (rubbing her shaved head) *"You* try being bald for a day and see how you feel!"

3rd April 1913 – Tsarskoe Selo
Official photos today. I look stupid in that silly wig. I don't care what anyone says. Olga reminded me that it was all my fault for drinking part-boiled water before bed last month after the celebrations. Mama reproached me and said it was a wonder I didn't die. I can say that at one stage I thought I had. There were two angels standing, one at the bottom of my bed and one to the side. The female angel asked me if I wanted to go home yet. I said no, that I thought I still had more to do. She touched my face with her hand. I could feel the other angel praying for me and I'm sure I heard or felt music in the background somewhere. Then my fever broke and they vanished. Part of me regrets not going, though; but I would have missed everyone too much. Now is

definitely not the time.

Olga didn't sit up for our family portraits. Result, there are two pictures, one with her slouching in her chair, one with her sitting up straight. What you can't see is the look on Mama's face when she told Olga to sit up straight in-between shots. And Nastya pulling faces at the cameraman. It was all rather chaotic, Alexei doubling up with laughter at her antics. It was so funny all of us ended up laughing. Now that would have been a wonderful way to celebrate the tercentenary, a portrait of a laughing Royal family. You don't see that every day!

28th May 1913 St Petersburg

Olga is very annoyed with me at the moment. So I'm sitting under a tree in the park here to keep out of her way. We were having a "discussion" about some of Father Grigory's more unusual ideas. Olga says she knows what the group he is involved with get up to. I know myself, but, unlike her, who finds the practices of the Klysty intriguing, I simply find them outlandish. All that whirling around and hitting yourself with a stick. Seems odd to me. Olga had a far-away look when she was talking about it and, for a moment, I thought she was actually thinking of going with Father Grigory the next time he went home to experience it first-hand. She saw the look I gave her – and exploded.

"You have a lot to learn about love. It's not just a mechanical expression of desire. There's so much more than that. Love is not really physical at all. Love is all around us. Can you not feel it in the air, hear it in the song of the birds, feel it in the rain on your face?"

I must have looked blank. She shook her head in despair. "You need to experience it. To feel the completeness of it. I wish sometimes I could screw off your head and replace it with one that feels more."

Olga walked up to me and crushed me in an embrace so

powerful it frightened me. Her lips were clamped to mine and I felt myself falling into her with a speed that took my breath away. In a flash I knew that I was one with the air, the sea, sky and rocks. Somewhere over my shoulder, a little bird was singing. His voice was mine.

I pulled myself away from her. My body and soul were on fire. Olga's eyes were blazing. "Now do you see?"

I had seen all kinds of images in the moment of my embrace with her, moving so fast past my perceptive faculty - images of Nature, love, both emotional and physical, of all kinds had made themselves known to me, yet the most potent and repeated image was Olga, on her knees, rapt in prayer, a cross in her clasped hands, blood pouring from a wound in her heart, and a smile on her lips, from which a trickle of red seeped at the corner...

I burst into tears. The intensity of the emotion was too great for me. I was confused. I ran from my sister, even as she tried to stop me, ran out of the house and into the blazing sunshine of mid-morning, towards the trees and the peace of my beloved park, the animals, the flowers and the breezes, gentle zephyrs from the Grace of God.

Later that same day…
Can it really be that Father Grigory is a man of God? Why do I find myself thinking "which God?" When I'm around him, I feel the Grace of the Virgin, and yet I feel something also which is infinitely older is looking at me. The pull of those emotions, which I felt with Olga before, is so compelling. Some of the images I had seen reminded me of rites I had heard about which pre-dated Christianity by thousands of years. The images were both powerful and arousing. Yet the one image I could not erase was that of Olga with the wound in her heart and blood on her lips, her closed eyes and the smile on her face...

"A willing sacrifice only brings joy and life to the giver..." Olga was standing next to me, leaning against the tree, her face backlit by the afternoon sun and strangely in shadow.

I challenged her. "Even if that sacrifice is death?"

Olga knelt facing me and held my shoulders gently in her hands. "Darling, my dear sweet love, there is nothing to fear. Even death shall be a joy and an adventure when it comes. I know it. So do you, when you stop putting a block in the way of your own knowledge."

This was too much. My nightmares had been getting worse lately. There were things in them I didn't want to face. Images of war, guns, blood and a high pitched, inhuman scream that always woke me in a cold sweat. But, worst of all, was the image of my beloved sister dead, in her coffin, with her arms crossed on her chest, lilies covering her and a beautiful red satin ribbon adorning her neck. Seeing that, I had always to stifle the compulsion to join her in death. And yet I knew I did not have the courage to kill myself. I knew that I would fail her and be left alone in an alien world where all the beauty had died along with her. As usual, she knew my thoughts.

"So stubborn my love?" She laughed. "You could never fail me. I will always love you however far apart we may be and no matter whether we are alive or dead. Love takes no notice of such insignificant boundaries."

She kissed me on the cheek. I felt warmth and truth in her love. The continuity of life and joy, even through death. I so wanted to be one with her, to feel and know her courage. She held me close and I put my head on her chest, feeling the beat of her heart beneath me. Suddenly, as her heartbeat synchronised to my breathing, it was as if she had poured herself into me. There were no longer two people there, but one person who went by two names. Under the tree, the warmth of the afternoon sun echoed the burning fire in our joined soul.

6ᵗʰ July 1913 – St Petersburg

Marie is a beautiful sight to behold. You know, I definitely think that one day she will prove to be the most beautiful of all of us. As I came today into Mama's room, I saw her sitting on the balcony outside. It is referred to here as the covered balcony. She did not hear me enter. She was looking out at the trees and the flowers, and her expression had a serene, peaceful and far-away character to it. I knew that inwardly she was praying. All of us feel like that after a morning visit to Feodorovsky Cathedral. Somehow, Communion leaves us all feeling as if we are totally safe and protected.

Masha's expression was so beautiful that I just had to capture it. Quickly, I went for her camera, hidden in the cupboard by her bed. Lost in reverie as she was, she still hadn't noticed my presence. Quietly, I sneaked up on her and, with her face in profile, I took her portrait. Only when it was done, did she turn to me and smile.

"Tanya, do you believe in Angels?"

"Of course, Masha," I said, returning her smile. "Why do you ask?"

"Because, today, after Communion, I saw an Angel. He was so beautiful! He was standing guard over Feodorovsky Cathedral and his sword was raised. He told me that I am to heal people and that people will pray to me for help one day. I am to be with God forever."

"As we all are, my darling," I said quietly.

"I hope God will not mind my sins terribly."

"I'm sure He will forgive us. Then we can help others find Him and be forgiven too."

A small robin landed on the rail next to her. He sang to us, a lovely, quiet song, without opening his beak. I saw his chest moving as he sang. We were both entranced by this everyday miracle.

"The Scriptures say that Love is God. Love is All there ever was. Remember what Father Grigory taught us…"

"…His creatures are an expression of His Love."

As we watched, the bird flew upwards, soaring and singing as it went.

Putting the camera down, I walked to the rail, put my arm around my beautiful sister and held her close. In her breathing, I could sense the beauty and majesty of Our Eternal Father, in whose Spirit we all live, move and have our being. It was a moment that was not lost and which both of us would remember in the times of darkness soon to engulf us in fear and doubt.

Part II

Prelude To War

September 1913 - August 1914

1st September 1913 – en route to Eagle's Rest Mountain

Cousin Felix, (Count Yusupov), really does have some wonderful estates in his family. One of them backs onto ours and today, we have decided to go up Eagle's Rest Mountain. Papa is with an entourage of officers, but Olga, Nastya and I have gone on by ourselves. The scenery is breath-taking. The mountains are vast, caressing the sky with their snowy tips. But around them, the fields leading up to them are equally vast. I can't get across in words the feeling that this landscape gives to me. Every time I'm here, I feel as if I have walked into eternity for a moment. It's all so peaceful. We have taken many photographs. But they are in black and white and don't do the shimmering colours of the sea and sky the justice they deserve. We also love our new "coat-dresses", specially designed for us in Paris. They are warm, but light too, and hug our figures just enough to make us feel pretty, while also being intensely practical.

While we were walking, Olga suddenly spotted a huge eagle overhead. He was magnificent, circling round us effortlessly for nearly half an hour before he flew slowly away towards the top of the mountain. Stopped after this for a much-needed picnic. The home-made pork pies were marvellous, but I think Nastya ate one too many and felt sick later. Father Grigory says her stomach is very sensitive and she shouldn't eat meat. Her response was, "I wonder. The world's first ever vegan princess. I could set a trend."

11th November 1913 – Livadia

Played tennis today with Dmitri against Cousin Felix and Olga. Papa watched us from the sidelines. Olga and Felix won. He really is a very agile player. Papa thinks highly of his abilities. Not just a pretty face then!

17th December 1913 – Royal Yacht Standart

En route to Odessa. Then home. Yuk!

24th December 1913 – St Petersburg

Olga and I rarely go out to concerts. It's such a pity, as I love the spectacle of a big occasion. Ballets are always beautiful and I know Papa likes to see Madame Kcheshinska. Mama does not. Tonight, however, we went to the performance of a work by our teacher, Mr Rachmaninov. It was his choral symphony "The Bells", after the poem by Edgar Allan Poe. I have read his poem "The Raven". It is one of Olga's favourite poems in the English language. I love it too, but find the story very sad. I always want to re-write the poem so that the poet can find his Lenore again. When I say that, Olga just laughs and gives me that "look" of hers. "The Bells" also has a sad ending, as the Iron Bells toll mournfully at the graveside. But in Rachmaninov's music, after this, the purely orchestral ending is a surprise, telling, we think, of resurrection of the soul and ecstatic union with God after death. When we asked him about it, he smiled and winked at us. He wouldn't say, nor should he; the emotions are private, but I think we have divined his programme. Death is not the end. Beauty awaits us in the Beyond. I think this message runs all through his music. It comforts and enlivens with knowledge of the true meaning of life, a meaning that can only be felt, not found by the intellect. What a miracle his music is for the soul. It fills you with goodness and the promise of light, a promise that will never fade. Sorry to run on so, but I'm still filled with enthusiasm. This is a truly great work. There is so much in it. How I wish I could hear it over and over again, especially the magical ending…

Diary Footnote May 14th 1926

I remember this night as if it were yesterday. I can still feel the pressure of Olga's hand on my arm and how that pressure increased steadily throughout the symphony. The pain was excruciating, but we were both so excited that it didn't matter.

And to talk with him about it afterwards. I think all three of us knew how much the piece meant to him. My most precious possessions are the records he brought me for Christmas two years ago and the score of "The Bells" which he sent me for my birthday last year. He has inscribed it as follows:

"To Tanya and Olya, in memory Eternal. S."

In that final meeting, we shall know that Light that he saw then.

"...and all tears shall be wiped from their eyes..." Revelation 21.

10th February 1914 – Tsarskoe Selo

I never reach the top of the snow-mountain first. Except today...I did! I beat everyone and stood on the top yelling my head off for ages. Alexei looked jealous. We usually let him win. Mama isn't watching out here and Father Grigory has told us that he will soon be cured of his illness. We won't tell her, but Alexei had a bad fall in the snow while we were playing. That was an hour ago. He yelled at me not to fuss. The look in his eye warned me off saying anything. Normally I would have run inside and called for the doctors at once, but Olga also put her hand on my arm and stopped me. He has not so far had any swelling appear. Maybe the cold is helping, but every other time such falls have broken him for days, if not weeks. I shall pray for a miracle to Our Lady...

9.11pm

Alexei is in bed and is completely fine. Father Grigory was here earlier. He seemed to know what had happened, even though we didn't tell him. He simply took my hand after dinner and said, "There now, all is well, isn't it?"

I smiled and had to agree. We both went in to Mama and Papa, and Papa read Tolstoy to us until it came time for Father to leave. He really is a magical wizard. Maybe Alexei really will be well after all. Maybe the Age of Miracles is not over. Maybe a New Age is beginning...

10ᵗʰ May 1914 – Livadia
Lessons with Mr Gibbes. I decide to deviate today from a consideration of English and European history, and corner him on the subject of Religion.

"Do you think there really is a God, sir?"

"I don't know for certain, Your Imperial Highness, but if I were a lawyer, I would have to say that all the evidence points in favour of the proposition."

"Explain."

"Well, Your Imperial Highness well knows that, for example, before you write down words on a piece of paper, they have to first exist in your mind. So first the mind, then the form. If you apply these principles to a consideration of the existence of a God, you can use the same logic. Hence, before the universe existed, since it is form and matter, it had to exist in the mind of some vast being, which we call God."

"So what would you call religion?" asked Olga.

"Each person's own way of interpreting God," said our tutor.

"Does this mean that there is one, or many ways to approach Him?" I pressed. "Is the truth one, or many?"

"The Truth is forever One, but there are many different interpretations," said a voice from the doorway.

Olga and I got up and rushed to the door to embrace Father Grigory. Mr Gibbes rose and bowed his head respectfully. His face was serious. I picked up the feelings. Olga did too. We looked at each other in alarm. Father Grigory put his arms around us and smiled.

"There is no need for fear, dear children. I have come to tell Papa about a threat, which can be avoided if he listens to the counsel of God. Do not be afraid. Go back to your lesson. I just came for the pleasure of seeing you. We will talk later."

He turned and left us. Holding hands, Olga and I resumed our seat. It was for a moment as if the world had taken an in-breath.

"Where were we?" said Mr Gibbes.

"Many religions, one truth," I said helpfully.

"Yes, Your Imperial Highness," he said, giving me a significant look. "A subject best tackled by saints and philosophers, not mere mortals, even Royal ones. Shall we get back to European History? We were looking at the Thirty Years War, were we not? Turn in your text to page 105." Looking at Olga, he said "Read from the top of the page, Your Imperial Highness, if you please."

Olga began to read. I listened. I was hypnotised and soothed to the depths of my heart by her pure, musical voice; the heart and soul of a serene river of spirit and life. Later, we were sitting on the terrace overlooking the port and out to sea.

"Those storm clouds, remember?" said Olga.

"I know, they're coming closer."

"Rain or snowflakes?"

"Rain," I said, with all seriousness. Trying to recover my self-possession, I smiled at her, with more conviction than I felt. What was it that I kept sensing in the future? I struggled to remember what Father Grigory had said about prophecy. Olga, sensing my disquiet, moved to stand behind me and stroked my hair. Usually this was calming, as it had been ever since we were small, and she soothed my terrors at night. Today, however, the gesture was hollow, and her words did not carry their accustomed weight.

"All will be well, my love."

We both continued to search the horizon for an answer to our uncertainty. Maybe the angels were on holiday. The weather was bright and sunny, not a care in the world. And not an answer or word of divine comfort from anywhere.

6th July 1914 – On board the Royal Yacht Standart
The beginning of our cruise to the Finnish islands. I always look forward to these visits. Games on the shore. Mushroom picking

in the forests and that unique, somehow dark green feel that characterises this province of our empire. The Finns are a strange people. Hard and stubborn and not at all aesthetic. I wouldn't like to oppose them in war. I think they would fight to the last man. Papa is going to have a hard time keeping them with us. He should grant them independence as Mr Sibelius wants. Olga and I really love his music and (don't tell) we are rooting for them. Perhaps in a few years we can welcome them as neighbours rather than vassals. I think I'd like to negotiate for the retention of my favourite island though, and the "Bay of Standart", where we always drop anchor. It's so picturesque. The beaches are lovely and the forests are so deep and mysterious. Father Grigory says that in Finland itself, the forest goes on to infinity, that a man could go mad, if it weren't for Pan's friend Tapio, the Finnish God of the Forest. Now he sounds like someone I'd dearly love to meet, perhaps in a wild storm in the heart of his domain. What a sight and feeling it would be to meet one of Nature's most elemental forces face to face.

Thinking of Father Grigory reminds me of the telegram we received from him just before we left port. It was addressed to Olga and me and read as follows:

TO YOUR GRACIOUS HIGHNESSES GRAND DUCHESSES
OLGA AND TATIANA
DEAR CHILDREN
REMEMBER WHAT I HAVE TAUGHT YOU ABOUT THE
RHYTHMS AND CYCLES OF NATURE STOP
TIME HAS COME TO PRACTICE THOSE TECHNIQUES WE
DISCUSSED AT OUR LAST MEETING STOP
COME TOGETHER STOP SIT OPPOSITE ONE ANOTHER
STOP CONCENTRATE ON YOUR BREATHING UNTIL YOU
ARE SYNCHRONISED STOP
THEN ONE OF YOU CONCENTRATE ON A PICTURE
UNTIL YOU ARE SURE IT IS IN THE OTHER PERSON'S

HEAD STOP
THEN CHECK WITH THE OTHER PERSON ON THE
TRUTH OF PICTURE AND CONTINUE UNTIL YOU
SUCCEED STOP
THEN YOU ARE AT ONE STOP
IT'S THE SAME TO SEND OR RECEIVE WITH ANY
MEMBER OF THE NATURAL WORLD STOP
ONCE YOU ARE LINKED TO EACH OTHER THE LINK IS
PERMANENT STOP
EVEN AFTER DEATH SHOULD ONE OF YOU DIE FIRST
THEN YOU WOULD STILL BE ABLE TO COMMUNICATE
WITH ONE ANOTHER STOP
CHOOSE ANY TIME TO BEGIN STOP
I WILL WATCH OVER YOU STOP
GOD BE WITH YOU BOTH STOP

We read the communication with mounting excitement. Always having felt close to one another, we couldn't wait to be really linked together and read one another's thoughts. Fancy communication being in pictures rather than words. Father Grigory had told us this was so. That in Nature, communication is in pictures rather than sound and that that was how he was able to talk to animals. Plants, he said, communicated with different pictures than animals and at a different speed.

"You have to be more patient with plants. But, as with trees, they are more attuned to the eternal and know more."

"Why is that?" I had asked.

"Because plants are all one consciousness expressing in the different species. They know we never die and that all is one in the Infinite."

So now, we were to try to learn how to communicate with each other via telepathy.

Carefully, we picked an area of the yacht that was unlikely to be visited. We sat opposite one another in our comfortable cane chairs, closed our eyes and concentrated on our breathing. Slowly, it was as if the outer world vanished and we were only conscious of the sound of each other's breathing. At first, we were not breathing together, but then slowly our breathing began to synchronise until I was only conscious of the waves of our breath rising and falling like the sea around us. The sound of our breathing rose in my ears from a whisper to a roar and was gradually accompanied by a sound like a violin string being played, at a very high pitch by a bow. This sound gradually grew to an unbearable intensity until I thought I could stand it no more. Then there was a loud popping noise and silence, deeper and softer than velvet, more caressing than satin on my skin.

"Open your eyes, Princess."

I saw, or was it felt, Father Grigory. He was standing on my left, about thirty feet from me. Except instead of his black robes, he was dressed from head to toe in white. It seemed to shine like the sun, except I could not see our sun. We were just surrounded by a light that seemed to come from everywhere at once. Then I saw Olga. She was so beautiful. Also dressed entirely in white, she looked radiant and her eyes shone like intensely black stars. As our eyes met, I heard and felt her voice:

"Come with me."

Abruptly, we were standing by the shores of a lake, with a dark green pine forest behind us. A soft breeze echoed over the lake surface and brushed us gently with a light filigree touch. Olga turned to me and put her finger to her lips. I felt the touch of the finger even though I was not touching myself at all. Lightly, I caressed my cheek. Olga leaned her head to one side, mimicking me as if the hand touching her face was her own. She took my hand and led me along the lakeshore towards a distant jetty. There, we boarded a rowing boat. Always away to one side of us was Father Grigory, his white robes shining, the light from his triple cross dazzling, as if at the apex of a triangle containing the three of us. As we reached the centre of the lake we stopped to take in the breathtaking view. Blue skies. Pine forests and the softest breeze. Olga looked directly into my eyes. I felt her pierce my heart. The pain was exquisite and made me cry out.

"Coming for a swim?"

Olga was naked now, and as she had when we were children, she dived from the boat into the lake. I felt the water close around her and longed to join her. In a moment, I was submerged also. The crystal clear water teamed with life. Shoals of multicoloured fish swam past me, enthralling me with their colour and panache. For a second I panicked. Olga was nowhere to be seen. Had she drowned? Then a voice, musical as a running waterfall ran like liquid into my mind.

"I'm always here, beloved".

I turned in the water. Olga got hold of me swiftly and kissed me on the mouth before I could protest. I felt her consciousness flooding into me with such overwhelming force that I couldn't stop it. Quickly I realised I didn't want to and I for my part surrendered my consciousness to the only person to whom I ever could. As I did so, I felt a light and a beauty in my heart so incredible that I swooned in my sister's arms. As I blacked out from the ecstasy, I was aware of Father Grigory blessing us with the sign of the cross.

Coming to on the ship where we began, I noticed that we were still sat opposite one another as before, but were now holding hands. We stared into each other's eyes for a long time, unsure where one of us began and the other ended. Overhead the seagulls were singing and in the distance, the dinner gong was sounding. Without a word, we rose from our seats and rushed to lunch, hand in hand.

7ᵗʰ July 1914 – Off the Gulf of Finland

Another day at sea. Standing on the rail of the Royal Yacht I can feel the salt sea air blowing on my face and ruffling the hair peeking out from under my white woolly hat. At a noise behind me, I turn. Olga is standing there, looking at me with a deep smile. She comes to my side and takes my arm. We nestle in close.

"It doesn't get much better than this."

"No, it doesn't."

"How do you feel?"

"Exhilarated. That was the most wonderful thing. Did you feel...?"

"Yes. I felt everything."

"He told us it would be so..."

"I know. But I didn't believe him, really. Until now. What do you think...?"

"I don't know. All I do know is..."

Together:

"I never want to lose this feeling."

"We won't. Trust me. This is just the beginning."

"It's strange. You touch your face and I can feel it. Feel you."

"And I you."

"I don't know. I feel so... wonderful. I could cry for joy."

I looked at Olga. Her eyes were brimming with tears. We embraced. The moment seemed to last forever. We were rudely interrupted by a thump.

"Come on you two, smile for the birdie!"

We had yet again become victims of Anastasia's insatiable appetite for photography. It took a moment to compose ourselves.

"I know what's on your mind, Olga. And the answer is no. You can't slap me this time. It's not my fault you're always off in that dream world of yours. You too, Tatiana. You're both off with the fairies. It's so funny watching you. Drift, drift, drift. Now come on. Olga, this isn't a funeral. Lighten up or I'll get one of the officers to throw a bucket of water over you like I did last Easter."

Olga had not enjoyed our little sister's talent for disrupting her reverie. The anger came out of my mouth, however.

"Try that again and I'll have Papa hang you from the yardarm and the fishes can eat what's left of you."

My little sister looked shocked and began to cry. I knew well that she was a prankster but didn't mean anything by it. She just liked jokes, even if they were sometimes a little weird and delivered with a sharp tongue. I had never spoken to her like that before. Getting over my own sense of shock, I realised that the words had actually been Olga's. I had simply delivered them. Anastasia was crying properly now. I must truly have delivered the words with force. A force I did not mean. She was slumped on deck beside her now fallen camera. I went over to her and picked her up gently. Taking her tear-stained face in my hands, I said, "Come on now. Let's have a picture as only you can take one. You can even cut my head off like the last shot you did. Remember, I looked like the Grey Lady of Peterhof by the time you'd finished."

She laughed. Coming out of her mood, she wiped her tears quickly with her sleeve. "That was your fault. You never stay still long enough for me to capture you."

I looked into her now smiling eyes. "You know me. Never in the same place for long. Always flying off when you least expect me to."

I cuddled her and we kissed fondly.

"Now, our picture, if you please."

I turned back to look at Olga. I knew my last words had hurt her. Or was it something else? I took Olga's arm and we smiled for our little sister. When she had gone, whistling a favourite dance tune as she went, which made me laugh, I heard Olga say quietly, "You'll leave us one day. Leave me. I will never leave you. Please, don't forget me or the rest of us when you go. I'll always wait for you, wherever I am."

"Don't be silly," I said. I put my arm around her waist and we turned to look back over the rail of the yacht at the gently swelling sea and the distant coast of the island we were approaching. In our embrace was the deepest feeling of peace and, like cygnets, safe in the feathers of the mother swan, we closed our eyes and felt the rhythms of Nature flowing through us once more.

10th July 1914 – An Island off the Finnish Coast

Olga, Anastasia and I have come ashore for some mushroom picking! Bliss. Wandering around in the forest like this is the closest to Heaven I think one can get on Earth. The peace, the tranquillity. All of Nature seems hushed in expectation of some wonderful miracle. Posing for photographs, I catch myself for a moment in one of those horrible formal poses so beloved of Royal photographers. But not Papa.

"Stand like that for too long and the trees' roots will think you are in competition."

"And if the wind blows, your face will stick," said Anastasia.

Olga's hand swiped out towards her, but she was too fast and ducked away just in time.

"Come here and repeat that you little wretch!" she shouted.

I put my hand on Olga's arm.

"Hush, darling, she was only playing."

Olga glowered in her direction...

1st August 1914 – Tsarkoe Selo

"With the net result that while the rest of us are relatively smiley, you look unnaturally gloomy," I said later.

"And the mushrooms you picked were as horrible as your expression," laughed Anastasia.

I poked Olga in the ribs with my elbow. In spite of herself, she laughed.

"There, you see, that's better. Lightens the whole mood."

Masha was standing in the doorway, looking thoughtful. "I think we need that right now. Have you...?"

Olga and I nodded. None of us said it, but all of us thought it. One word. War. It had been looming on the horizon for the best part of at least a year. Now it was condensing into a certainty. Father Grigory had already tried to warn Papa in general terms about it and had prevented him from taking us to war in the Balkans in 1912. But, if there's one thing in my experience my father is naïve about, it's the motives of the rest of our family. One in particular. Remember 1909. That's all I'll say. I think I mused enough about that at the time and I've certainly had much cause since in all the silly letters I've read. Kaiser Willy is the very best advert for a constitutional monarchy I've ever seen. The sooner his people remove him as head of state the better. And no more of those infernal pompous visits and receptions. Just thinking about it makes me angry. Picking up my thoughts, Olga pulls a face in imitation. We clasp each other and fall about laughing. Suddenly, and quite out of the blue, Masha said, "If he gets his way, we'll all drown in blood..." Her voice drifted off and her expression looked far away.

Silence.

Anastasia began to cry. Olga got up and went to comfort her. I did the same for Marie. Eventually the four of us came to the floor by the fireplace and knelt in a circle, holding hands. Together, we began to silently concentrate on the Source of Love that Father Grigory told us about. We saw it as a brilliant white light above our heads that gradually at first, then suddenly, rushes down through the four of us, filling all of our beings with Love. A love so all-encompassing that we cannot find the words to describe it. After a few minutes breathing together, holding hands and feeling the blessings of this beautiful Light, we all got up together and crossed ourselves as we have been taught. Then we kissed each other tenderly. Nothing can or ever will break the bond that we four have together (five counting Alexei). As we stood still and silent, for a moment we seemed to break the bonds of time and space. A feeling of immortality descended to us from that same Source and, without knowing (yet) fully what it meant, we were given through our feelings a taste of the answer to the question that has seemed to plague us all and that has silently driven us mad.

"Why?"

Diary Footnote – January 8th 1922

Olga and I held one another close that night. A journey was about to be undertaken. We all knew it. But to where that journey would lead us and what it would do to our lives, our hopes and ultimately our family, we were, on that night of Holy Communion, blissfully, if fortunately, completely unaware.

PART III

WAR AND TERROR

SEPTEMBER 1914 - JANUARY 1917

16th September 1914 – Tsarskoe Selo

I received my Red Cross certificate today, along with Olga and Mama. Already we have had a lot of work at the new hospital here. The wounds are shocking, but they must be dealt with. The worst ones to see are the psychological ones, the wound inside caused by shell shock. A physical wound can at least be mended, if only imperfectly. How I wish we could imitate the salamander and grow back our limbs! Maybe that's to come, who knows. But the mind? Once that is damaged, only the angels and saints can cure that kind of injury. But we do what we can each day. Many times already, I have seen Olga and Mama holding the wounded and comforting them in their distress. I do that too, but I also deal with the visitors and families of the wounded. Their distress is so poignant to see. After the war, Papa must make a new law to help out all those families who will be in difficulty if their men cannot work. They have sacrificed much for us. It will be time for us to repay them as they deserve.

I also play chess with some of the wounded officers. Just like I do with Papa. I have, so far, drawn two games, lost one and won three. But my favourite time comes in the middle of the morning when, at tea break, I get to play with the hospital cat. He belongs to matron and is a favourite of all of us here including the men. I have seen him sitting on the beds of some of the wounded. They seem to become more peaceful when he is there and I have seen many an agonised face light up in his presence. Man kills. But Nature, and God through Nature, heals.

19th September 1914 – Tsarskoe Selo

Poor Olishka! Today we had to operate on a man brought to our ward whose legs had been shattered by a grenade. He had gangrene. The smell was awful. His pain and agony affected all of us. Being short of staff, the surgeon asked Olga and me to assist. I helped with the amputation, and Olga held his hand and administered the anaesthetic. The combination of the smell, the pain, the man's distress and the fact that he partially came round during the treatment was too much for her. I saw her face gradually losing its colour, but with her iron will, she held out to the end. Afterwards, she went to the toilet and was violently sick. I went to help her. She couldn't stop and all but fainted with the strain of it. She could not stop shaking. Eventually I had to take her home. Later, the surgeon came round to tell us that in spite of our efforts, the man had died early in the evening. Olga burst into tears, blaming herself for not administering the anaesthetic properly. Dr Derevenko was very kind. He held Olga gently and told her truthfully that nothing more could have been done. The man had come round during the operation because of the extreme nature of the pain he was in, not because Olga had done anything wrong. I repeated this to her later, many times, but she was inconsolable. She cried and cried. She kept saying, "His poor family, what are they going to do now? We have killed him. We have all killed him with this stupid war. And how many more? Oh, Tanya, how many more will die before we too die in payment for all this blood. Will it ever be enough to wash away the sin?"

She would not be comforted and cried herself into an uneasy sleep. Late at night, I wrote to the dead man's family. A letter, even from a Royal Grand Duchess, is a poor compensation for the loss of someone you love.

30th November 1914 – Peterhof
I have spent a lot of today in my travelling cloak walking around the grounds here. I have been alone for once, which I have found very healing. As I write this, I am looking out to sea. All I can hear is the sound of the waves crashing on the shore, while behind me the birds sing in the trees and the wind whips around me in little spiral gusts. I feel as though I am the only person on Earth at this moment and yet I do not feel lonely. My heart is full and I am happy. It is as if nothing is here and yet everything is. I

could stay here forever. Perhaps one day, I will. [1]

Tatiana's Diary - 6th February 1915 – Tsarskoe Selo
Calamity. Our forces in Galicia have been defeated and thrown back by the Germans. They also seem to be suffering from lack of uniforms and ammunition. I even heard a terrible story about men being sent to the front line without rifles and being told to wait until someone died and to pick up the dead man's rifle! If this wasn't so real and serious, I think I would have laughed. Surely such absurdities cannot be happening to us? Papa and Mama have bought several trains and rolling stock to facilitate transport of men and munitions, but it all seems to be to no avail. Transport difficulties also seem to now be causing food shortages in Petrograd. Olga and I went out into the city this morning and found the queues for bread had become terribly long. Really, the Ministry of Supply needs to be better organised. But Papa is so caught up in the war effort that I sometimes think he does not take care of problems near home as well as he could do. Perhaps Mama could help him with things, just for a while…

21st July 1915 – Oreander
A magical day. The light here in the Crimea is fantastic. Artists now and in the future are going to love this place. I stood looking out to sea from the Greek folly that overlooks the ocean here. It was mid-afternoon and Olga, Papa and the others had gone on to explore more of the ruins of this magnificent palace. In the distance, I could see the Standart at anchor in the bay. Alexander I's spirit resides here very strongly. It is just as it was that day in Moscow, only here his spiritual presence felt more immediate. It was as if he were more real or grounded in this place, what was one of his favourite homes.

Behind me and to the right, I felt a presence, strong and shimmering. I turned. There was a tall young man there, in military uniform, but he felt odd, as though he was both "here" and "not here" all at once.

"Hello."

"Hello. Who are you?"

"Don't you recognise me from my portrait, Tatiana?"

I felt very stupid and frightened all at once.

"Your Highness." I dropped to my knees. It was my ancestor. But why had I not recognised him straight away?

"Don't kneel before me, child." He raised me up with his hand, so soft and gentle. I felt awe and wonder in his presence. His touch and feel. It was real. And yet, how could it be? This man standing with me had been dead for ninety years. He seemed to pick up my thoughts.

"Death is an illusion, my child." He had come to stand next to me and was looking out to sea. His eyes had a wistful look in them. Such beautiful sky-blue eyes. He was a true grandson of Catherine the Great.

"So is power."

He turned to look straight at me. "Remember that. The only true power you have is over yourself. Beyond that, try to help others as much as you can. Or if you cannot help, at least try to understand. That's all you can do. Everything else is ego and useless posturing."

He saw the look in my eye. "Your father knows this, but we cannot make him listen."

I was about to make a remark about his war, the one in 1812. He read my thoughts.

"That was different. Napoleon would have ruled everyone like a dictator if he could. That's not the same as our autocracy. Besides, the seeds of change were already growing."

His face took on a bitter cast. "Sometimes I think I should not have left when I did. My brother made such a mess of things."

He took both my hands in his. They were warm. I could almost feel the veins in his hands and the blood flowing in them. His look was full of love.

"Tatiana, I wish I could be with you through what is about to happen, to make the monsters go away…"

He saw my look. "Yes. It was me who protected you all those years ago. Do not be afraid of your nightmares. Olga and I will watch over you. And when you run out of strength, call on me. I will always come for you."

"Who are you, sir … really?"

"To answer that, I would have to tell you a lot more than you are ready for. Suffice it to say that you and Olga are twins. At least, that is how you were created. Know also that it is very rare for the two of you to be alive at the same time. Cherish the time you have together. It may be only rarely repeated, at least on Earth. As for me, you could say that I'm an older member of your family, but that would be only to tell you that which you already know. We have all been together forever. That is how it will always be. Your mother, father and the rest of you are here for a very specific purpose, as was I when it was my time. The trouble is that the design is in danger of failure, and I think your father is unaware of it. We have tried to get through to him, but it is as if he has put up a wall in front of us. He either doesn't know or doesn't want to know. In 1905, we thought, for a moment that the light had come. Your great grandfather and I were so pleased. Everything looked possible and, for a moment, the future came into focus. Now, it may all come to nothing, at least for now."

I was stunned. His words had perplexed and frightened me. Could it be that our ancestors were in such close touch with us all the time? Again, he seemed to pick up my thoughts.

"We are closer than you think, only a thought away. Child, the veil between your world and ours is so thin that you could cross it if you wished, in both directions. All it takes is love and desire. I can come to you because of our connection. So you also can come to me if you wish. But you do not believe it, so it will take longer for you to achieve it."

He paused. "We come because we love you. We will always

come."

He looked very serious. "And when the night finally falls, we will come for you."

He looked out to sea again. "So many possibilities our family is capable of. But no-one can over-ride free will. You have to *want* it or nothing happens."

We both stood contemplating the beauty of the waves and the sunlight on the water. "Remember to call on me if you need me. We are only as far away as you want us to be."

Then, in answer to the question in my mind, he said, "Yes. That was me that day in Moscow. I realised then that you could perceive my presence. That's why I came today. All I have to do is think of you and I can come to see you. What's unusual is for you to be able to see me. Your ability, and your sister's, is rare."

Olga had come in. She saw him too. Alexander went to her and they embraced. Then he brought her to me and placed our hands together. "There is one chance left. If you put your ability as twins together then maybe things may still be right after all. Believe in your brother. He is our successor. He has so much to give. His feeling for beauty may yet save everything. Even if there is a disaster. But you must watch over him. His intellect is strong, but fragile. He does not believe in himself enough and he is discouraged easily. You must give him the strength of your vision and help him with all you can give. And believe also in his recovery. That may still come to pass. Remember, nothing is impossible with God."

"What about Papa?" Olga asked.

"Do what you can. Your Friend will also. This war, as you well know, should never have begun. But, now that it has, your father must hold out, against any external pressure, long enough for German aggression to be neutralised. All depends on this. After that he must evolve the autocracy as he started to in 1905. Then all may yet be well. If he does not, or is unable to, all will be ruined and Russia will sink into an abyss."

His look was intense. "I must go. When you need me, just send out a thought and I will come."

We embraced him. Then we watched him walk away into the distance. As he faded from sight, Marie came bouncing up to us from the opposite direction.

"Who was that? You seemed deep in conversation."

Olga and I looked at each other.

"A ghost," said Olga with a smile. "Pay no attention to it."

Masha laughed. "What is it that Dostoyevsky says? 'There is no madness, no hallucinations, it's just that in exceptional circumstances people also see the other world.'"

She had understood.

"A pity Nastya isn't here, she would have tried to photograph it."

Now there would have been a conundrum for future historians, I thought. Olga picked up my thought and laughed out loud. Together, the three of us rejoined our party arm in arm. Could we help Alexander out? How would it be? What would Papa do next?

"Have faith," said Olga.

Even given my talk with our ancestor, I could see that was going to be more easily said than done.

5th September 1915 – Tsarskoe Selo

Papa has taken over command of the army from Uncle Nicholas. This was against the advice of all his ministers and the army. I don't want to sound disloyal. I love Papa with all my heart, but, privately I will say that I think they are right. Uncle Nicholas is a far more experienced soldier than Papa and has everyone's respect. It's true that things have not gone well for us lately, but overall the war is not progressing too badly. The German lust for conquest seems to have been brought to a standstill at the very least. Now, if we can all get together and push them back, there may be an end to it all. But for this, experienced men are needed.

Papa is not experienced enough. And, if our losses continue unchecked, all the blame will fall on him. I doubt that will do any of us any good, to say nothing of my brother's future as Tsar. But we must pray to God. Perhaps a miracle or two may save us after all.

27th September 1915 – Stavka

Sometimes, in the midst of all the horrors around us, there are compensations. On our visit to HQ, Papa has allowed Olga and me to go for a trip on the Dniepr on our own. Slowly drifting in the early morning mists, the silence of communion between us reminds me of eternal things. A look on Olga's face tells me she is "on a mission".

"I knew it! You manipulated Papa into allowing us on this trip. Why?"

"Wait and see…"

Enigmatic as ever.

It took me a while to realise that we were actually going somewhere. Eventually she pulled us into the bank.

"Come on." She handed me out of the small boat and we walked hand in hand towards a small village in the mists ahead of us.

The atmosphere of the village was utterly different from those I had visited before. Looking around, there did not seem to be any indication that there was a war on at all. We could have been a million miles away, and as many centuries. I became aware that for once, Olga was blocking me. I could not read her as I was used to being able to do. She was aware that I was probing her though and squeezed my hand harder to reassure me.

Eventually, we emerged on the other side of the village in front of a small rectangular thatched hut, on whose gable ends could be seen the sculptures of horses. Olga went to open the door. I pulled her back, fearful of what we would find. Where was this place and why had Olga brought us here in the midst of war? She squeezed my hand again and gave me a look of love that was deep and gentle all at once. Beautiful, yet different from her normal look of suppressed intensity. It was as if I was seeing a different person. Different, yet the same. I couldn't put my finger on the difference or the reason for it. She led us inside.

Inside, it was dark. And very warm. Olga let down her hair and motioned for me to do the same. I let her help me. Then we undressed each other. The feelings I were getting were strange. It was as if we were physical and yet there seemed to be, now we were inside the structure, fewer boundaries between us than normal, as if she were no longer blocking me, but letting me inside her fully. Somehow in a way even more intimate than physical contact.

She led me further into the interior. It was completely dark, except for a small torchlight. I could make out people sitting around a small fire, covered in very hot rocks. Periodically, someone poured water over them and the place filled with steam. Naked as we both now were, the atmosphere felt stifling, yet exhilarating. Olga went to a stone bench and sat, motioning me to do the same. Oddly, I did not feel uncomfortable in the presence of the others. They felt familiar somehow.

After a few minutes getting accustomed to the surroundings, the heat and the feeling of quiet, almost meditative calm that surrounded us, one of the women came up to us, holding what looked like a bunch of twigs tied together, made of birch. She motioned us to stand. We did and she proceeded to strike us lightly and fast all over our bodies, front and back, from the top of our shoulders down to our feet. The feeling was not unlike the massages I've had at home, only in this case about a thousand times more tingly and intense. I kept my eyes closed throughout. Olga's grip on my hand became gradually tighter and tighter.

Eventually, it stopped and we sat again, allowing the feelings to pour through us, sitting together, holding hands and feeling the overwhelming sensation of Inner Light as it poured through us. Throughout, we both felt connected to everything around us. I was aware of the birds, the trees, plants and animals. It was as if they were all inside us and we inside them. This is what lovemaking feels like, I thought, the connection with Nature and God. Olga picked up what I was thinking and kissed me on the cheek. That was just the beginning. The strange connection I felt seemed to extend itself to everything and everyone around us. The stifling heat was womb-like, and it was impossible not to feel the love that was coming from everywhere around us.

Unbidden, a memory surfaced - a memory of passing my parents' bedroom one night when in the grip of my infernal insomnia, only to be stopped in my tracks by Mama's cries. At first, I thought she was in distress, and instinctively went to help. But then, the manner of the cries changed, and I heard her calling Papa's name. Mesmerised, I stood rooted to the spot as her cries turned into screams, finally morphing into one loud, very prolonged cry that seemed to echo down an infinite tunnel of pure light. The light engulfed me in its beauty and for a long time afterwards I slept peacefully, as if I remembered something distant, yet beautiful about her, about Papa, about all of us.

Comforted now, in this strange place, I felt sleepy, surrounded by the same feeling of love I had sensed then. Gradually, I became aware of a very pleasant feeling in my heart. Opening my eyes I realised that Olga and I were surrounded by couples, some of whom seemed to be communing silently with one another, the men and women simply looking deeply into each other's eyes, whilst others were engaged in intense and passionate sexual intercourse. Both sets of people, however, were making love, I realised, in equally deep, but different ways. Coming out of my mild reverie, I felt a gentle caress on my cheek as Olga turned my face toward her and she gazed into the depths of my soul. Again, as had happened on the yacht, I felt my spirit merge with her at that moment and we fell into each other until I was unaware of where either of us began or ended.

The effect this time was deeper than before. I swooned out of consciousness and felt a massive rush of energy through my whole being as I was overwhelmed by memories – what seemed to be our past existences together rolled through my mind like a film played backwards at very rapid speed, taking in many times and places, times of peace and times of war, as sisters, as brother and sister, as lovers, as friends, as priestesses of an ancient culture, even as enemies, until all was drowned in what I could only assume was the original Light of our creation and I sensed rather than saw the blinding fire of our twin flames resting in the heart of God.

Our oneness at that moment seemed to coincide with the orgasm of the loving couples and was sealed forever in a moment of profound, poetic extinction, united with all of creation as it sang and played around us. Nothing more needed to be said. The experience was like very intense prayer and reminded me of our experience in the schoolroom two years ago, but it was as if that experience and the one on the yacht had merely been leading here, to our union, our experience of oneness with each other and our feeling of a wider union with creation itself. For although I realised through seeing the other couples who were with us that our story was not yet complete, in those moments of spiritual and emotional union I think I understood Father Grigory more profoundly than I had ever done before. If only we could all feel this connection. Where then would be the desire for war? Perhaps our ancient culture knew this and was keeping the knowledge safe until it was needed again. It felt as though they were. Comforted, I found myself at length in a very peaceful sleep, with my head resting on Olga's shoulder, her hand cradling my head.

Afterwards, dressed and walking slowly back to the boat, Olga pressed close to me. I did not ask how she had been guided to take us to this place, but felt a certain Siberian shaman's hand in it all. Everything that was happening around us in the "real world" was suddenly so amusing that we burst out laughing and couldn't stop ourselves all the way back to Father at headquarters. We skipped together into Papa's study.

"Please, girls, share the joke!"

We just looked at each other and laughed even harder. I have never seen Papa look so bemused. The more bemused he looked, the worse the laughter got.

Two days later when we returned to St Petersburg with the family, Father Grigory came to see us. As he took our hands, he looked from one to the other of us. The look in his eye told us everything. He simply kissed our hands and smiled. It was a smile of understanding and the deepest communion of the soul with the Earth and the Universe.

28th September1915 - Stavka

Papa's efforts to salvage the dignity and prestige of the Russian army are being brought to nothing by the stupidity and tactical incompetence of the people he commands. Had his orders been properly followed, we would now have a strong tactical advantage over the Germans along our Eastern Front. Instead of which, for some reason best known to the god of Sod's Law, the army may be in the right physical place, but it doesn't have the guns, ammunition or even the boots (!) to fight with. And after all the money we have pumped into the war effort buying whole fleets of trains to send to the front. What is happening to our money and our munitions? If I didn't know better I would suspect that someone is trying to undermine all of us.

I've come to sit and write this on the banks of the River Dniepr, which flows serenely on past HQ. Funny. Even at this most horrible time, the birds still sing, the ducks play on the water and the animals shuffle past as if nothing is happening that is of any importance. I brought some bread from the mess hall to feed the ducks and they are crowded round me as I write, each of them cheekier than the last and all eager. What was it Christ said about God feeding all, regardless? He truly looks

after His creatures. I'm constantly amazed, as Pierre says in War
and Peace, by the stupidity of Man. It is not the intellectuals who
are the most important people. For they think about everything
and understand nothing. It is the simple man of the heart who
sees most truly, like Pierre's friend Platon Karataev. He knew that
life is the simple day to day living of it. That we should take
delight in the moment that is NOW and forget the rest.

"Now is all we will ever have."

Olga was standing behind me and had placed her hand
tenderly on my shoulder. She laughed.

"That's nice to see. I haven't seen you laughing in a long time."

We kissed.

"What's so funny?"

"You and your diary. Writing about philosophy while simultaneously feeding ducks. The absurd duality struck me as funny,
that's all."

"And you don't think ducks know more about life than us?"

She was serious now. "Oddly, I think they do. They just live.
We think too much and then try to live based on our mental
distortions of both truth and reality. If we were to just have as
small a faith as an animal does, I think the great Mystery would
be revealed to us too."

"Then you believe as I do..."

"Yes."

She closed her eyes, as if thinking about something inwardly.
"Remember what we felt yesterday? This war is a cruel joke
somehow. A nonsense. A distraction from reality. It will deceive
and draw everyone's attention away from the Earth, which is
where it should be focussed."

"A war is an elaborate and expensive way to distract everyone.
Why the illusion?"

"I don't know yet. I can't see past the horror and carnage
around us, especially when I'm here... That's a part of the
illusion. It keeps me from seeing who gains from all this. There

are so many behind Papa vying for power."

She saw my face and gave me an enigmatic look, as if she were reading something in me that even I was not aware of. Then, she focussed. "In order to resolve all this, a sacrifice will have to be made. But when and how I don't know."

She saw the fear in my eyes and reacted with strength. "I told you when we were children. All will be well. We just have to hold on and keep praying to the Holy Mother for light and grace."

She paused. Her look became distant again. "I believe the most glaring lie will turn out to be death itself." She looked deep into me, as if weighing up my soul.

"You speak so calmly of sacrifice."

"Yes. I resigned myself to it a long time ago. I've just always prayed for the strength to endure when the time comes."

I got up from the bank and we walked along, arm in arm, gazing at the ravishing landscape.

"Have you never thought of what could be if all this were changed," said Olga. "Earth was a paradise of love and joy once. It can be so again. Father Grigory says so and I believe him. Can't you feel it?"

I remembered our trip of yesterday, and, for a moment, my heart sang in the sunshine. Olga squeezed my arm tightly. I replied, "Yes, but when I see it I feel so sad that it overwhelms me. You've seen what happens to me."

She turned and held me close, stroking my hair. "I've always told you, when you feel like that come to me. I will give you the strength you need."

I stayed silent. She kissed my forehead and we moved on.

"Always the sceptic. If we were disciples, you would be Thomas for sure."

"And you would be the Beloved disciple."

Strange, sarcasm was one of her traits, not mine...

Olga became serious again. "You must pray more. Father

Grigory says you do not pray enough."

I stared into the gathering sunset, saying nothing.

We stopped our progress and turned to walk back to Camp. Overhead the cranes were flying. In Norse mythology they are a symbol of Death. I pressed closer to Olga and prayed I was wrong. For in the future I repeatedly saw a time when I would walk alone by the banks of an unfamiliar river and my life would be silent, lost in the desolate mists of annihilation and an endless unhealed pain in my heart.

29th September 1915 - The Royal Train Between Stavka & St Petersburg
A rainy day. Unfortunately for the weather, my spirits cannot be dampened. Since our experience two days ago, I have felt completely different inside. It is as if my spirit and my body have been healed somehow. It is as if the lesson of the experience centred on the infinite nature of love, whatever form it is expressed in. The more you give, the more there is to give away. But one other important thing needs to exist for love to triumph. There must be no judgement of any kind. The love given and received must be unconditional. I remembered the loving couples, the joy I felt with them and the ecstasy of my joining with Olga, how my inner experience of joining with her and our knowledge of our shared past had coincided with their love for each other and us in an ecstatic, loving present. I couldn't help smiling to myself as I felt the warmth spread through me once again.

Olga came to sit beside me. We looked out of the window together. In the silence I could feel her joining with my soul again. Closing my eyes, I embraced her within me once more and we communed.

Coming out of our reverie, through the rain on the window I caught a glimpse of an animal form. Standing just on the tree line, staring intently at the train, was a wolf. I turned to Olga to tell her, but she had hold of my arm and had already spotted it. We looked at each other.

I spoke for both of us. "Father Grigory is watching over us."

Olga nodded. She paused. It was difficult to articulate with words the completeness of what we had both now come to understand. Father Grigory's opposition to the war we now fully understood in our hearts. It was an opposition which, I am sure, would be felt in the hearts of all loving people. But other forces were driving the conflict, forces which were threatening. Our storm clouds. Olga had become very serious. When I tried to access her thoughts, she shut me out. This was painful.

She squeezed my arm and kissed me tenderly on the mouth. "Not yet, my love."

She saw the question in my eyes.

"I will show you, but you are not yet ready for it."

I went to protest, but she said, "How many times do I have to ask you to trust me?"

I sank my head into her shoulder and we slept.

1st October 1915 – Tsarskoe Selo

Enjoying the canals in the park. I love the symmetry of all the designs here. The gardens and park are so beautifully controlled. Ortino is running his poor little legs off trying to keep up with me.

"You shouldn't feed him so many chocolate treats, Tatiana."

I could see Olga's face wreathed in smiles at the breakfast table this morning, Papa laughing, Ortino nuzzling his head into my hand looking for more.

"I want you to live a long, happy life my little one," I said, bending down to him and stroking his head.

He stroked my hand with his head, a gesture of real trust and affection, making small, almost purring noises. At that moment, Pascha, Lilly Dehn's cat, came out from behind a tree. Ortino was off, barking in high-pitched squeaks. I doubled up laughing. He'll never catch her.

On an impulse, I took off my shoes and stockings. Walking barefoot on the earth brings me close again to my experience in the hut. It is still raw. I find the wonder and beauty of it overwhelming. But it is the feeling of being united with God in those moments that I cannot escape from. The earth, the dear earth, the plants, trees, birds, even the insects all seemed to be singing a hymn of praise. I have heard Father Grigory talk many times about Russia's Old Believers. These people hold to beliefs that, behind the Orthodox rituals, were current in this land long before Christianity came. Somehow, although I can't think how, today when I looked at the Icons, it seemed as if I were able to see past them to a more emotional reality that lies behind them. That of our forebears, just wearing new clothes. Sitting cross-legged on the ground, I closed my eyes and tried to imagine a world without war. A world finally at peace with itself.

"It will not be a reality for many centuries."

I opened my eyes. Father Grigory was sitting with me, although how he came to be there was a mystery to me. I never heard him approach and I thought he had gone home hours ago. The warm feeling from his greeting of us earlier was oddly changed and I sensed a warning in my head.

"What do you mean?"

"I mean, dear child, that Russia has lost its opportunity. If Papa had not declared for war last year, all would have been well. The world would not have fought without her. Now, blind greed, lust for money, exploitation of the earth and her wealth; all will come and overwhelm us. Papa's throne will come to be known as the throne of blood."

I must have looked shocked.

"You are surprised at my fatalism? Every action has its consequences. We are merely playing out this drama to its end now. There is one question yet unanswered, but I predict that within eighteen months, the answer to this will be known, too."

There was a strange look in his eye, which I could not read. He continued, saying, "Every few centuries, there are openings which allow for an accelerated evolutionary pace. The last two years were one such opportunity. Russia had the key when war was possible and could have led the world into the next few hundred years as a beacon of light and peace. Your father has squandered the chance. Now the time of the monsters is upon us. Demons will be unleashed and it will take a great effort to reconnect to the soul of creation."

He took my arm.

"Four days ago, you and your sister experienced such a reconnection. Treasure the feeling. It will be a while before you experience it again, but remember it, for you went to a time when the earth and its people were and are in a much more balanced state than that which currently exists."

"Went to a time…? Were and are…?"

"Yes, did you not know? The place you went to has no existence on the earth as it is now. You were able to get there because of your connection to each other. The two of you already have an existence that is not quite here. A part of you both already exists beyond this earth."

I must have already begun to look ill.

"My Princess, don't fight what you know to be true."

My head was reeling. I could feel my mind rejecting his words. Already, some nagging doubts and feelings of personal discomfort were coming to the surface. What had been beautiful and life enhancing was swiftly turning ugly and demonic. Suddenly, all I saw before me was a smelly, unkempt man with lewd and lecherous feelings and desires. My memory of what had happened and what I had seen turned to ashes of disbelief. Olga was walking up to us, smiling, and blissfully unaware of what was about to explode around her.

"How *dare* you refer to Papa's glorious reign as a throne of blood," I screamed at him.

Olga looked shocked. I was fighting feelings of extreme

nausea and panic.

"What's the matter, my love?"

Olga tried to touch me. I felt suddenly very sick at the thought of the intimacy of our connection and wanted to be as far away from her as possible. What had we both been turned into? I slapped her with all the force I could muster. She fell awkwardly on the turf and her hat flew into the canal. Crying uncontrollably, I ran from them, forgetting completely about Ortino. I ran into our house, up the long flight of stairs to the second floor and our bedroom. I was sick into the toilet. Violently. Again and again, for what seemed like hours. When it was over I plunged myself into a cold bath, then dressed simply and went to our little cathedral. I stayed in there for the whole night kneeling in prayer before the icon of St Michael, praying for God to forgive my sins and trying to forget the little voice at the back of my mind telling me that all was not as it seemed.

1st/2nd October 1915 – Alexander Palace

My night in the Feodorovsky Cathedral brought me no peace, only sore knees and the beginnings of a cold. I have spent the day avoiding Olga, who appears now to have the beginnings of a bruise on her jaw even through the concealing make-up. I really must have hit her hard. Mama cancelled my official duties. I even missed my weekly committee for the children and felt terribly guilty. But my mind was racing and I would not have been able to concentrate, so I was glad for the quiet time. In the evening, I saw Father Grigory as I walked in the park. He did not approach me, but simply bowed low and moved on to the house. At night I found it difficult to sleep; even Ortino's presence was not enough to calm my nerves. Eventually, I did fall into a fitful slumber.

"There will have to be a sacrifice..." Olga's voice to me repeats over and over again, fading into green, images...

...whirling images of dancing ... dancing. The noise of drums

around me is deafening. Loud drums, insistent, interlocking rhythms repeating. My feelings are ecstatic, almost orgasmic in their intensity. Dancing, dancing, but I am barefoot and dressed simply but elaborately in a white dress, with red flashes on my shoulders and chest. This is not ballet. The grass is wet under my feet and the smell is distinct, sharp and alive, as of dawn and a new day, the day of the Dark Moon. In the semi-distance, I can see a forest, as if we are in a clearing on the edge. There are many people gathered, watching me dance.

I have chosen to be here, in this place, and I know that I shall die at the end of this ceremony. It is an elaborate ritual of death and rebirth, one in which, by ancient tradition, many girls in the Royal family, my family, have been involved before me. Today, it is my turn. I am alone in the centre of a large circle. The drummers are at the edge.

Gradually, my dancing becomes more and more ecstatic, the rhythms more and more intense, my feeling of joy so overwhelming that I feel I am going to explode. The rhythms of the drums come together inexorably in a giant interlocking fugue which settles on one loud, insistent heartbeat. I whirl on the spot, over and over, then, at a signal from one of the priestesses on the outer circle, I drop to my knees and close my eyes. From a point on the outer edge of the circle, I sense an opening in the ether, created by the percussive drumming. Through its spiralling form, a figure emerges, a feminine being of great beauty and compelling power. Her grace and physical allure is so strong that I feel my breath taken away. It is she that I have been taught I will meet, the great Goddess. This is my reward and the goal of my journey of life.

Instinctively, I know that this means death.

Her smile reaches out to me with so much love. She holds out her hand to me and I feel intense pain tearing at my body as the light around her overwhelms me, a physical force, setting my soul alight with an exquisite agony. Her hand takes mine. Her caress is so gentle, yet strong. I do not resist, feeling almost uninterested now in what is being done to my body, of which I am only dimly conscious. Strange; I am aware of being able to see the ground, and for a moment, my senses focus. Quite how I got here I do not know, but I have been suspended by my neck from a tree on the edge of the forest. The pain I felt when I sensed the Goddess appear was evidently the pain of my suspension. The people are gathered around the tree, watching me.

For a moment, I panic, realising the crushing reality of my impending death and I dance frantically, trying to free my hands, but they have been bound behind me too securely and my fingers simply open and close impotently. There is nothing I can do. I feel like crying out, but can no longer get any air. Is this really the end? Has it all been darkness and lies? My struggles slow down.

But then, just as all feels hopeless, I sense the Goddess again. She comes silently through the throng of people, unnoticed, to stand next to the presiding priestess, who is watching me with a powerful intensity. As her eyes look deep into mine, my feelings begin to transform, the pain I felt slowly becomes a feeling of euphoria and the Goddess smiles at me as I dance now for a second time, for her. This dance is slow and intense. My legs and body move in perfect harmony, tracing natural rhythms and arabesques in the now deafening silence, as if I am drawing sacred symbols in the air around us with my feet. There is no longer any feeling of struggle. I do not want to. I realise I never did. In the background I can feel the rhythms of the dance being played slowly, as by celestial musicians.

Gradually I become completely dissociated from the Earth. Above the tree where I have been hanged, a portal of light opens up. I feel warm now, and strangely protected, and, as my feet gently caress each other one last time, I feel every cell alive with life as the light shoots downwards through my crown and into my body, setting all my centres ablaze at once. The Goddess comes close to me, embracing me, kissing me deeply and releasing my spirit. She is so soft and loving, just as the elder priestesses foretold, and I can feel them gathered around me in a protective circle, each of them placing flowers beneath my feet. Somehow, I know that they are aware of exactly what is happening to me, and that they are smiling. As they do, I love the Goddess and trust her, even and especially now in this hour of death. The fragrance of roses permeates the air around us, saturating everything in its beauty. The smile of the Goddess finally becomes mine as I feel us merge and the darkness of oblivion becomes the light of noonday. Her loving hands, having gently held my hips, steadying me in my dance, almost a partner in a pas de deux, now propel me upwards into the light as I feel my lungs and heart burst and I scream as my freed spirit drowns in an orgasm of infinity.

Later, regaining consciousness, I wake to find myself standing in a field surrounded by flowers. The fragrance and beauty of this place is overwhelming. In the unearthly light which seems to be coming from everywhere, the elaborate tattoo of a firebird on my arm glows with a mysterious Inner Light of its own, echoing the design on the front of my dress. There is a deep smile on my face. Liberated from fear through my willingness, like my sisters before me, to die in the ceremony, I know now the peace of liberation from death as well. In death I have become the landscape. All around me teems with life and growth in all its abundance. I can hear the voices of my people inside my mind. Their world and the one I am now in have become one through my dance of death. I shall be their bridge, their link with the abundant beauty that lies waiting in the beyond. My sacrifice, my willing ecstatic sacrifice has once more healed and protected the land, affirming the cycle of life, making possible a wider rebirth of both body and spirit. Those people who came to watch my death know that it is a birth into life, in joyful surrender to the Goddess, my eternal Mother.

In the distance I hear a woman crying out in the pain of child-birth... a little girl is placed into her loving arms. The Shaman is there with her. I must go to him. I feel irresistibly drawn to the sound of the baby's cries ... I cannot wait to begin ... suddenly I feel dizzy ... sleep is coming ... and awakening. I feel warm, peaceful, relaxed and safe as I drift back into unconsciousness... My experience has filled me with a knowing that goes beyond all my self-imposed boundaries – beyond any boundaries. I know what was, what is, what is to be ... and it is love, only love ... and we are all forever a part of it... I drift... I must rest. Olga's voice sings to me on the wind, in the fragrance of the flowers, and I see her on the horizon, a figure of dancing light in a world that

89

stretches to eternity...

I wake in St Petersburg once more, Ortino curled up in the crook of my arm, snoring, as usual. The morning sun filters through the curtains of our room, casting beautiful dancing shadows on the walls ...dancing ... *dancing ...dancing ... I drift away and dream again... of a ballerina at the Maryinsky ... flowing movements to a waltz... waltzing ... waltzing into a light that has no beginning or end.*

Everything I have experienced has led me to this. The sacrifice has been made. **My** sacrifice. **My** choice. **My** death. **My** rebirth. All done in a strange mixture of joy, pain and love for my people. I understand Olga's meaning now, and that of Our Saviour's sacrifice on the cross, in the depths of my soul. For a long moment, but only a moment, my world is at peace.

"He who wishes to find his life shall lose it..."

"Greater love hath no man than this, that he giveth his life for his friends..."

14th October 1915 – Tsarskoe Selo
Incongruities. I am sitting under my favourite tree in the park. Ortino is playing happily near me, catching his ball, while, in front of me, I am reading a newspaper, and the description of conditions at the Western Front in France is matching, rather too closely for comfort, an awful vision I had last month when we all visited Papa at HQ. I feel sick. The sight of Ortino playing in the sunshine is oddly out of place, as if I am living on the wrong planet. Perhaps I am. Who knows..?

12th November 1915 – Alexander Palace
Night. The lights are low in Papa's study. It still smells sweet from the tobacco he usually smokes. I like to come in here sometimes after dinner to soak up the atmosphere, so tangible, you can feel it seep into your very pores. I sit at his desk. All Papa's papers are neatly filed and indexed. So meticulous. He has always been an

inspiration to me. Efficiency comes so easily to him; I wish it were so for me. One of the papers catches my eye. The name on it – Rasputin. I cannot resist a look and, in the low light of Papa's desk lamp, I read the report from the Okhrana.

Report on the activities of Grigory Efimovitch – known as Rasputin
November 5th

1.25am – Rasputin enters his apartment with the prostitute Lena Petrovna Katina. Spends two hours with her. They are drinking and having sex throughout the time.

1.35am – Rasputin's housekeeper, Dunia, takes a phone call. Duration 5 minutes. She does not disturb him.

3.30am – Lena Petrovna Katina leaves the apartment. Rasputin has given her money and a note. When questioned, she replied that the note was to be passed to the Prefect of St Petersburg on behalf of her brother, sentenced to transportation to Siberia for multiple acts of theft and sedition.

3.50am – Rasputin, still heavily drunk, leaves his apartment to go to Elizavetskaya Street. There he attends a party given by the Gypsy Petrovitch. He is seen there drinking and consorting with gypsy dancers.

5.50am – Rasputin leaves the party to go back to his flat. When questioned some of the partygoers revealed that he boasted of his relations with the Tsaritsa. One of the girls even stated that he said he had had her with her head in his lap and that the Grand Duchesses were his playthings.

6.35am – Rasputin enters his apartment building and attempts to wake up Madam Grevetskaya. He shouts through her door that her husband does not love her and that she should come and have union with God to experience His love. When she shouts at him through the door to go away, he climbs the stairs to his apartment, where he is let in by Dunia. He falls onto his bed in a stupor.

8.45am – Rasputin receives a call from the Alexander Palace. He answers it and speaks with the caller in a voice that is clear and sober. His language is pious and fawning. At the end of the call, he collapses on his bed in a stupor once more.

9.30am - Rasputin receives a visit from Countess Drubetskoi. Dunia tells him that it was she who called in the night while he was with Lena Petrovna Katina. She is evidently in some distress over her marriage. Rasputin persuades her to come away with him to Siberia. He promises to teach her the mysteries of life and healing. After some moments of seduction, she is observed having sexual intercourse with him. He is heard shouting "God is Love". The countess's words were inaudible.

10.50am – Countess Drubetskoi leaves the apartment. Dunia, who evidently has heard and watched some of his activities, is heard remonstrating with him about his drinking and his women. He is heard to shout, "I can have anyone I want. I can even have the Grand Duchesses. I'll have them all at the same time kneeling at my feet and worshipping God from the palm of my hand. Don't you tell me what to do. I carry Russia's pain and I'm her only saviour. If I die, so does she. So do they."

A crash is heard, as of breaking crockery, and Dunia is seen leaving the apartment in tears. He shouts after her. "Run, you frigid little sow. You won't escape. You'll all suffer the same fate. Do you hear? All of you!"

I had been aware for some time of conflicting feelings regarding Father Grigory. But this was a terrible shock. I knew Papa had been hiding certain aspects of his character and other events that the Okhrana were obviously telling him about. But to hide this behaviour, this language, these words about us. Boasting of his relationship with Mama openly, at a party with gypsies, while drunk. Calling us his playthings. Saying he would "have" us. I was stunned, not knowing in that moment how to react. Suddenly all was confusion and instead of the kindly Nature Mystic, a shadowy monster revealed itself. My heart was beating wildly. I was sweating and developing a headache. Think of the

Devil they say, and he will appear. What do you think happened now?

"You appear distressed, Princess. Can I help?"

It was him. He had appeared suddenly right in front of me, looming over me like a dark spectre from a Mary Shelley novel. I was so startled that I nearly fell over backwards in the chair. Not even the friendly scent of Papa's tobacco smoke could calm me down. I couldn't contain my rage.

"Help? You? I think, sir, you are far more of a hindrance. You are a nobody with ideas a long way ahead of your worth. And, I am beginning to suspect, a lot of it is lies."

He was oddly peaceful in the face of my verbal assault and his reply was compassionate. "You are fearful, princess. That is not the natural state of Man, as I have told you many times."

I erupted. His serenity was irritating me. "Fearful! I have every right to be fearful. To say nothing of disgusted! Have you seen this?"

I thrust the offending report under his nose. "What else have you been shouting about our family from the rooftops? Tell me! What other lies have you told about us?"

I was crying now. Father Grigory approached me and tried to touch my arm. I flinched away in disgust.

His voice was calm. "My dear child, I ask only that you read the report again, and look with the eyes of love. As Papa does. As Mama does. As Alexei does. As Olga does. Yes, I drink, Princess. Yes, I go to parties. But God is present in our Joy. He loves to laugh and he comes through us when we move our flesh out of the way or elevate it to His heights of Bliss. In your heart, you know this, but you are afraid of your own passion. If you continue to repress yourself and deny yourself Joy, your body will wither."

I was turned away to the study wall, and hidden in shadow.

"I would rather wither than be a drunken dirty fool like you. I feel ashamed that I ever knew you. Perhaps the doctors are right. You are a trickster. A con-man."

"Listen to your heart, Princess. It and it alone will guide you to the Truth. Above all, remember the Firebird Girl."

What did that mean? How had he known about the Firebird Girl? A most personal experience of mine that I hadn't let on to a living soul, not even Olga. If he knew about that, what else did he know? Who was this man? Looking into his eyes, I saw only an enigmatic gleam of a smile, giving nothing away.

Grigory Rasputin bowed, turned and left me, stunned and sobbing with unexpressed fear in the semi-twilight of a place no longer warm and friendly, but alien and cold.

4th January 1916 – Tsarskoe Selo
Walking in the snow with Olga after breakfast. In the distance, I see our snow mountain, and I stop in contemplation. Olga is silent, feeling the emotions. I feel less like our usual games now, and more like going to our cathedral and kneeling in prayer. She squeezes my arm and we move on, walking through the lines of trees and into a desolate and cold landscape.

Behind us, laughter approaches, at first dimly, later more closely. Nastya and Masha have decided to throw snowballs. Masha also has her skates with her and later I watch her skating on the frozen lake. She cuts a beautiful figure on the ice. Makes me long to see her doing ballet, but since the early days, she has never carried on her lessons as Olga and I have, nor shown such a cultural level of interest, in spite of being a very good pianist.

"Shall we?"

Olga interrupts my reverie, and we leave my sister to her skating and contemplation. In the background, I am aware of Alexei and Derevenko throwing snowballs at Nastya. She squeaks, "I'll tell Her Majesty on you both."

A perfect imitation of Anya. In spite of our seriousness, we laugh out loud. On impulse, I throw a snowball at Nastya. Olga and I are pelted in return. In the general melee that followed, I think it was a draw. All of us laughed until we were sick.

Tea with Mama and Anya mid-afternoon. More hilarity. Anya's clueless expression made our laughter worse.

6th January 1916 – Tsarskoe Selo
Breakfast without Papa. Again. Must he be away so much? Olga is very close to him and this morning cried because he is away. She doesn't talk much to Mama and only reveals herself to me or to him. Sometimes I know there are things she wants to talk to Papa about without Mama hearing her. I saw her writing him a long letter this morning. I squeezed her shoulder and she squeezed my hand back, but did not break her concentration for a minute. That was when she cried. I know that sometimes she feels so frustrated she could burst. Then we can console one another usually, or play piano together. If it was summer I would challenge her to a game of tennis, but it is winter and intensely cold outside.

Later, we go skating together and afterwards cuddle up in the pavilion and watch the snowfall. Words are pointless in this beautiful place. For a moment, the tensions ease.

7th January 1916 – Tsarskoe Selo
"Yes, Your Majesty. No, Your Majesty. What can I get you, Your Majesty? Moo Moo, Your Majesty."

If Nastya was here, she could show you a perfect imitation of the eyes at such a moment. Anya has been with us these past ten years, but sometimes she grates on my nerves. I do wish she wouldn't fawn so much. I sometimes think she is not as dense and naïve as she seems. The feeling I get is that it is a mask.

Even Father Grigory once said, "Watch that one. She'll have all your heads if she could."

I laughed.

This was summer last year and we were sitting under a tree in the park.

Father Grigory did not laugh. "All that fat is protection. For herself. She doesn't want to be seen. Especially by you."

He went very quiet. He was sad. I had rarely seen him in this mood, so I took his arm and put my head on his shoulder.

"You are very kind. But remember that Anya keeps herself hidden. Remember the iceberg; only a small amount can be seen above the water. If you want to know what it really looks like, you must go into the ocean depths."

He had said no more. But this morning, when I saw Anya fussing around Mama, I caught a look in her eye for a fleeting second that frightened me. Then it was gone again. I wonder if I was really seeing things, or if we are seeing things for the rest of the time. Why am I uncomfortably reminded of the spider and the fly? Surely, I must be wrong. But what if I'm not?

26th July 1916 – Tsarskoe Selo
Riding soothes my soul. Somehow, being one with a horse is like being in prayer, yet riding through countryside such as that on our estate is like being a part of some unimaginably vast cathedral. My brother will be twelve years old in a few days' time. Seeing him suffer from his injuries as he does tears me apart every time I see it. It's not the same as tending to the wounded at home. I hope they will not mind me saying that there is a sense of distance there that I can "tap into" as it were. He is close to me, closer almost than my own soul. I feel for him in a way I cannot describe. The feeling is beyond pity. Olga is always going on about Fate. But somehow it feels as if he is fated to suffer as he does. Father Grigory has promised a cure will come for him and on a sunny day like today, I can believe it, if only for a moment. But another part of me wonders whether he is destined to suffer like this all his life.

I recall a passage in Scripture that has always intrigued me. Jesus and His disciples come across a man who has been born blind and they ask, "Master, who has sinned, this man or his parents, that he was born blind?"

If the man has sinned, he has to have lived before and to be paying off an old debt. This means disabilities are no accident, but Fate, as Olga says, forcing payment for old unpunished misdeeds. If this is the case, and my logic tells me it is likely, then the Universe really is intelligent after all and Mama really is not to blame. What a gift for her that would be. My hope is that Grace, as the Saints say, can go beyond this and cause a Miracle. I look out at the beautiful Black Sea shimmering in the morning sunlight and I can really believe such things are possible. Whoever my brother was, whoever we all were, we are different now. May our lives be reparation for our past sins.

"Our Father, who Art in Heaven, Hallowed be Thy Name...

...and lead us not into temptation, but deliver us from evil..."

22ⁿᵈ October 1916 – St Petersburg

I'm not quite sure where to begin this entry. What started out as a very ordinary afternoon has turned into one of the most peculiar, exhilarating and finally disturbing evenings I can ever remember.

Olga and I had decided, as we often have during this dark time, to leave Tsarskoe Selo and go into the city to visit the families of the men in our hospital and take them food and personal letters. We had dressed simply, so as not to alert our ever-present security guards and had gone out through an old passageway put in when our home was first built. No-one was the wiser. Not even when we took one of the smaller cars, a tiny Renault that I have christened Ortino. Olga drove.

All was going well. We had visited Vera Lebyadkin and Maria Kondryachev and were on our way to see Captain Kuryakov's sister in the Old Quarter when suddenly, turning a corner, we ran straight into Father Grigory. He had his long travelling coat on and his rather odd looking bowler hat, but he was very obviously drunk and didn't recognise us at first. Olga and I looked at each other quickly and were going to pass by, hoping he hadn't noticed when suddenly he shouted out.

"Children! Children! The Holy Mother told me I would see you tonight. But I didn't believe her. And here you both are."

He clapped us both around our shoulders, a little too familiarly I thought. Oddly, although he was intoxicated, his grip was very strong. I got the feeling that the drunken state was, at least partially, a blind. He wasn't nearly as drunk as he seemed. Or else he was, but only part of him, while the other part was wary and watchful, and in control. The Angel and the Demon all at once. I got no time to further my musing.

"Come, come. This is a good meeting. It is time for you girls to come out. I have taught you about Nature and the animals. Now it is time for you to learn about the joys of Man."

His grip was inexorable. He guided us, talking to us the while about his most recent journey home to Pokrovskoe, round several corners and down an alley. I should have felt scared, but strangely, I just felt curious and maybe even a little excited. Finally, we reached a small house on the right hand side of the road, illuminated from within by candlelight, flickering yellow through its small ground floor window. From inside, I could hear the most beautiful music playing. But it was like nothing I had heard or played before. This music was intoxicating in itself. Its rhythms invited dancing, but not the ballet. It was familiar to me, but in a distant and rather frightening way, it felt dangerous.

Before I knew what was happening, the three of us were sitting at a small table, watching the performers, a small gypsy band and their dancer, a beautiful woman with black hair and eyes whose form and movements held me in a vice. As she danced, the singer intoned an ancient gypsy ballad of love and death. The girl's movements invaded my mind. As time went by, I began to lose consciousness of myself and seemed to go back to an earlier age. I do not know how, but I found myself dancing with the gypsy girl. Eventually, the music and the atmosphere took me over to such an extent that I became completely wild. I remembered my horses, the feeling I had in the forest with the animals, the song of the birds. I was lost in the feeling, utterly lost. My movements became frenzied, but in control. I saw Olga smiling at me deeply. She and Father Grigory joined me, and together we sang and danced with the gypsies until we were hoarse. I promise you, at no time did any of us drink a drop. We were made drunk on the atmosphere, the company and the dancing most of all. I realised then that that had been the state Father Grigory had been in when we met him. The Okhrana are wrong! He is not drunk on wine, but on life!

Afterwards, he took us back to where he had met us and told us to go home as it was not safe for young ladies, even two such beautiful girls as us, to be alone on the streets of St Petersburg at night. As we said goodnight and walked away, I turned and looked back. During the evening, I had been dimly aware of the form of another aristocratic young woman in the house with us. She did not take part in the revelry. She just sat watching, it crossed my mind, in an oddly dispassionate way. Now, as I looked back, I realised that the same young woman had been shadowing the three of us as we left and while we had been walking. Now, I saw Father Grigory engage her in conversation. But his attitude was not conversational as it had been with us. He seemed to be remonstrating with her. And there was something in her stance that struck me as odd.

As I was trying to figure out what it was, Olga stopped my thoughts dead, saying "Didn't you realise cousin Felix was watching us tonight?"

Stupidly, I replied, "You don't think he'll tell Mama and Papa where we've been, do you?"

Olga gave me the look she gives me when I'm being either immensely vacuous or immensely slow. I think this was a bit of both.

"What's Father Grigory doing talking to him like that?" I

wondered, even more stupidly.

"Best not to ask, or even think about it," said Olga curtly. "Dmitri was there as well. Didn't you see him sat with Felix?"

"No," I said rather vaguely, now really sounding as though I had lost the thread.

All I could think of was how Mama would react to us going to a party with gypsies.

Olga was on a completely different page of the novel.

"They're up to something. I'm sure of it. So is Father Grigory."

She shook her head. Tiredness was creeping up on her. She took my arm. "We'll figure it out together in the morning. Come on, let's get home."

We began to run. Getting home took longer than we expected, as we had to avoid the guards keeping watch on the gates of the park and take the long way round. Our heads hit the pillow at about 2.30am. I couldn't sleep and am writing this now at 3.40am, but I have ballet practice tomorrow with a new teacher, so I must try to put all this to one side for now and get some rest. Felix and Dmitri. I wonder what Olga meant and why seeing Felix like that has triggered an odd memory from my past. If only I could put my finger on what it was, but it's elusive, I can't see it…

23rd October 1916 – Tsarskoe Selo
Walking along the ground floor corridor on my way to my meeting with the Committee for Lost Children, I saw Dmitri walking towards me. I was uncertain what to do at first. I wanted to walk in the opposite direction, but instantly realised that would look far too obvious. I decided to act as if nothing was amiss. Dmitri had other ideas. He made straight for me, grabbed my arm and pushed me into a doorway. His scent was nause-ating. He was too close. I felt claustrophobia and nausea overwhelm me. It was as if he had me immobilised.

"You looked beautiful last night, dancing with those whores," he whispered in my ear. "Imagine what your father would do to you, and that slut of a sister of yours, if he found out his precious, oh so sensible daughter had been in the low quarter. And that con man too. Thinks he rules Russia? Well, that's coming to an end. If you're too stupid to do something about it, then we will."

He pressed himself in so close I thought I would pass out. The sun was coming in through one of the windows opposite and it was blinding me. His hand was on my breast. I had never felt so sick.

"I'll destroy him and then I'll have you. Mark my words. When this dynasty falls, there'll be a new family ruling Russia. With me at the head."

He looked at me contemptuously. "But I need a good brood mare. I think you'll do."

The light was blinding.

Suddenly, Dmitri yelled out and bent over backwards, falling away from me. I had been holding my breath and had begun to feel very dizzy. My vision was going red. I just retained consciousness long enough to see Olga smash Dmitri over the head with her walking stick. She continued to attack him. Hitting him over and over again, so fast that he had no time to react. Olga was yelling for help. Yelling at the top of her voice. The last thing I remember is her loving arms around me and my hysterical screams, fading into black. Olga told me later that Dmitri had run from the guards and out of the palace. I never saw him again, at least, not to speak to.

Diary Footnote – 31st January 1922
Afterwards. Olga told Mama and Papa about our night with the gypsies and what we had seen. She also told them other things that she knew about Dmitri. I knew that he had seen himself as a prospective suitor of mine. But Papa angrily put an end to that forever. His chances of "ruling Russia" had come to an abrupt and sordid end. I have always believed that what happened

hastened the events that followed. Night was about to fall on us, and fall it did. With frightening suddenness.

30th October 1916 – Tsarskoe Selo

Committee for Lost Children. The situation is getting worse by the day. There are so many children and parents separated by this dammed war that our resources have been stretched beyond their limits. The home we have for them is now overflowing with refugees and we don't have enough people to assist in the searches. They are becoming so numerous that we can't cope. This conflict will have to end soon, or I don't know what we will all do. Food is becoming more and more scarce. A trip this morning into Petrograd revealed bread queues so long they were almost out of sight. People are getting tired and dissension is threatening to cause riots. You can feel it. The mood of the country is changing. Why did we ever think fighting a war was a good thing to do? It is utter madness. I feel numb. The situation is beyond us now. Maybe Olga is right about fate after all...

29th December 1916 – Tsarskoe Selo

An icy night. Light snow after dinner. The four of us girls sat together. Unusual. It was as if we were all waiting for something. All I kept hearing in my head was a silly little song that had recurred in nightmares since I was a child. The only difference is that on this night, the song was both loud and insistent. The words "Yankee Doodle Dandy" kept repeating over and over. The images always the same. Ending in fire and blood. I rose from the couch. Olga tried to hold me back, but I needed to walk. I began pacing the room. Finally I sat at the piano and began playing a Chopin etude, hoping that the complex music would take my mind off the sounds in my head. Time passed. Eventually, Olga joined me and we began playing four-hand waltzes. Little by little, we all seemed to feel more cheery. Unfortunately though, the insistent sound of "Yankee Doodle" was always there, to the extent that, without realising it, I began to play variations on the theme.

"What's that melody?" Olga asked. "I know I've heard it before, but you've never told me what it represents."

I was about to explain about my nightmares when Anya came into the room, very obviously agitated.

"Can I talk to you, Your Highness, alone?"

"Of course," I said gently, trying to hide a rising feeling of fear. But was it mine or had I picked it up from her? As soon as we got into the small anteroom, she let it all out in a rush.

"Something's wrong. I phoned him earlier this evening, asking him if he would accept a call from Prince Yusupov. I've been acting as a go between for them. They had a falling out. Oh, he was very nice. Said he wanted him to meet Princess Irina, but I didn't know it would be tonight. Masha rang to tell me Prince Yusupov's arrived with his car and she's worried. Why tonight? It was supposed to be another time. It's too early, too early..." she tailed off.

I instantly realised she was talking about Father Grigory. At the mention of Felix, my stomach turned over. That song in my head. Felix adored vaudeville. It and the nightmare had to be to do with him somehow. And what precisely did Anya mean with *"It was supposed to be another time. It's too early...?"*

All my alarm bells were going off at once. I had to warn Father Grigory.

"Telephone him. Try to stop him," I barked at Anya.

She was in tears now. "I tried. I telephoned him, but Dunia said he had already gone. And then I got another phone call from Masha. She was crying..."

I stopped Anya. "Don't worry. I'll deal with it." I tried to put a nasty suspicion out of my mind. What she had said sounded wrong and I got the uncomfortable feeling that she and Felix were up to something. But I had to get to Felix's place as fast as possible. I would try and figure out what Anya's involvement was later.

I went straight to our room, found my coat and hat and went out, using our usual route to avoid people. Ortino took me swiftly into town. I parked in our usual secluded spot and headed for Felix's place. Something was wrong. As my feet guided me there, the images and feelings became stronger and the song in my head got louder.

Eventually I arrived to find the gate open. A car was in the driveway that I recognised as Dmitri's. I could even see his chauffeur lounging around smoking a cigarette. The lights were on. I could see them blazing through the ground floor windows. Quickly, I made my way across the courtyard and through the open front door without the chauffeur seeing me. This was most odd. Where were the staff? There did not seem to be anyone there. In the distance, I could hear that song playing, but it was obviously on a gramophone, as the needle had got stuck and the phrase "Yankee Doodle Dandy" was repeating over and over. I froze. This was just like my dream, the recurring one from my childhood. From upstairs, I could hear muffled shouts. I hid in the shadow of a doorway as I heard footsteps rushing down the stairs. It was Felix. He looked like himself, but his face was a mask. He was sweating profusely and he looked very scared. He was also carrying a pistol. By this point I was terrified. What had I walked into? On and on the song droned, repeating and repeating until I thought I would explode. Otherwise, silence.

Suddenly two shots rang out. Simultaneously the song stopped. Then, nothing. There was silence for a long moment. Then without warning there was a loud, elemental roar, of a kind I had never heard before and never wish to hear again. There was the sound of a very heavy gait coming up stairs and, out of the door opposite me burst Father Grigory. He was dressed in his best white peasant shirt with cornflowers on that Mama had made for him with her own hands, and the trousers that we girls had bought him for his birthday earlier in the year. But his shirt was stained red where he had obviously been shot. Instinctively,

I rushed out to help him. His voice sounded loudly in my inner ear…

"No…o…o…o!"

He saw me. His look was angry and terrified. He gestured me urgently back to where I had been and his look told me in no uncertain terms to stay put. Then he paused, turned and roared at the top of his voice back down the stairs. I realised later, with the most immense sorrow, that pause had saved my life and very probably cost him his own.

"I'll tell Mama and Papa what you are, who you are, all of you pigs!"

Footsteps were coming from beneath and above. As Felix attained the ground level, Father Grigory distracted him so that he didn't see me at all and just followed him outside. From above came Dmitri, and a third man I didn't recognise. They were also wielding revolvers. They followed him outside, never seeing me in my hiding place. I felt an agony so intense I almost passed out from the pain. So this was what Dmitri had meant in his words to me in October. I heard Father Grigory shouting and the sound of the men's boots in the snow as they ran after him into the courtyard.

Suddenly there was a shot, a loud thud, and a pause. I was in agony. The waiting seemed to last an eternity. Finally there was another shot… and a long silence. At that moment, I felt a long and intense shout in my mind that seemed close and then seemed to go at high speed down an echoing tunnel until it disappeared into nothing. I felt an intense flash of light in my mind and beside me, for a split second, I saw Father Grigory standing next to me, dressed in white, as I had seen him that day on the Royal Yacht with Olga a few years earlier.

"Go, Child. Before they find you. Tell your sister, but be gentle with my little sailor. He won't understand."

He got fainter very rapidly.

"I shall always watch over you."

The last thing I saw was him giving me a blessing. Then he faded away...

Quick as a flash, I saw all the images of him over the years. Our Friend. He had been close to God the whole time. I saw myself kneeling with him, smelling a flower, stroking the head of a bird. I saw us taking tea and heard his Christmas stories again. Watched as he played with Alexei and saw the look of deep love that passed between them. No. Alexei would not understand. He wouldn't hear those stories any more and that comforting voice would no longer lull him to sleep when he was in pain. I would no longer feel his strong hand giving me faith when I felt all was useless. Somehow, that hand had carried more than simple human warmth. It was truly the hand of a wizard. Not a man with a long, white beard and stars and moons on his pointy hat, but he might as well have been. That joy in life and love of it and us was all there. I remembered the night with the gypsies. It was all magic and pain combined. With his death, we were on a road with no turns. All this happened in a split second. I was frozen and too scared to cry or to move.

"GO!" I heard yelled in my ear. It shocked me out of my inertia.

I ran as he had told me, across the courtyard. Dmitri and Felix were standing over the body. They sickened me. They were kicking him, while the third man stood at a distance, revolver in hand, simply looking on. In an oddly detached way, I realised what they were doing was futile. It no longer mattered. Nothing did any more. It was over. In my mind's eye I saw a castle tower falling in the distance, along with the flag of the double headed eagle.

30th December 1916 – Tsarskoe Selo
I returned home finally in the early hours. I had been walking and walking in the city, round and round in circles, not caring where I ended up. I could not get the images I had seen out of my

mind. In my aimless wanderings I felt I wanted to be anywhere but Russia, any time but now. Why did Papa always have to be absent just when I needed him? His empire was crumbling. We had just lost (I was sure) our best friend and, what was even worse (if that were possible), it was members of his own family who were raising their hands against him and us. My mind was in a complete whirl. I found it difficult to make sense of things. But going home was impossible. Eventually, I sat on a bench by the canal and cried and cried. At length I began walking towards the car and finally reached my room shortly after 2.30am. I should have known Olga would be awake.

"He's dead isn't he?"

"I don't know, Olga. I didn't see him die."

"But you felt it. I felt it too, saw him as well, in my mind, just as you did. He gave me his blessing."

I had been standing looking out of our window. Olga came up behind me and put her arms around me. I began to cry again and turned myself to her for comfort. We fell onto my bed and both of us cried our hearts out.

"It was Dmitri and Felix, wasn't it?"

I nodded.

"And some other man I didn't recognise…"

"Any idea who he was?"

"No, but I heard him speaking in English with Dmitri…"

Olga looked away for a moment, thinking, then I sensed her dismiss her thought and she returned to practical matters.

"I told Mama he is missing. Told her about his daughter's call to Anya. Anya came with me. But Mama refuses to believe anything is wrong. She says he's always going off. She'll call a search if he isn't back in a few days.

"Should I tell Mama…?"

"Absolutely not! We don't want her to know you were there. There would be too many questions to answer. Did anyone see you?"

I told her everything else. All I had seen and heard and about Father Grigory and what he said to me. We were satisfied I hadn't been seen. We were wrong.

30th December 1916 – Tsarskoe Selo
At breakfast, I was called in to see Mama. This was odd. She never summoned me. When I came into Papa's study, I could already see from the balcony that she was seated at his desk and looking deadly serious, almost furious. With her was a man I didn't recognise. He looked official, and uncomfortable.

"Tatiana, this is Inspector Grushchenko. He is investigating a report of shots fired at Prince Yusupov's Palace last night. His men were greeted by Felix, who was drunk and lied to them – some silly story about a dog. They have so far been able to confirm that shots were fired, that Dmitri was there, and his chauffeur has said you were there as well. He has said you were Dmitri and Felix's 'guest'. Do you have anything to say?"

I must have blanched. I tried desperately to maintain control. This was Dmitri's revenge for Olga's attack and my rejection of him. The implications of the word 'guest' were obvious. A deliberate attempt to ruin my reputation. I denied being there or being the guest of anyone, especially Dmitri. I cited the recent incident without revealing what it was but made my dislike of the man very obvious. I think that partially convinced the policeman that the report was a fabrication, especially after Olga was called in to say I had been in bed all night in our room with her. His eyes still looked suspicious when he left.

Mama was furious. She demanded that I explain myself. So I told her everything. This coincided with Olga's report of the night before, Anya's phone calls, and that of Father Grigory's daughter who was concerned about her father leaving with Felix at dead of night, supposedly to see Princess Irina. Mama looked alarmed, as if she had suddenly remembered something.

"He can't have wanted Father Grigory to see Irina."

"Why not, Mama?" asked Olga.

"Irina isn't in Petrograd now; she's in the Crimea."

Mama called in the Okhrana immediately and initiated a discreet search for Father Grigory, asking that they begin with Felix's house and suggesting that they arrest and interrogate Dmitri as well.

Later that evening, word came back that a body had been found in the Neva. Father Grigory's boot had been discovered on a bridge over the Neva not far from the Yusupov palace. It had been identified by Maria as one belonging to her father. Investigators discovered that the body had been pushed through a hole in the ice.

So it is true. He has really gone. What to tell Alexei? And worse still was to come within the day.

31ˢᵗ December 1916 – Tsarskoe Selo

Found in our Friend's apartment:

"To Papa and Mama and the Children.

I know now that I will die. But know this. If I am killed by my brothers, the Russian people, then you will be safe, you have nothing to fear and your throne will survive for many years. But if you hear the bell telling you that Grigory has been killed and that it was done by members of your family, then none of you, not one member of your immediate family, will survive for more than two years. Pray for me. I am no longer among the living.

Grigory"

31ˢᵗ December 1916 – Tsarskoe Selo

"Be gentle with my little sailor. He won't understand."

His last words to me. Olga wanted to come with me, but I took on the responsibility as it was given to me. It was my duty to our Friend and to the love I have for my brother.

I went into him. I had taken the morning tray with me off the servant, thinking to take him tea and pancakes in bed, as I had done when I looked after him when he was younger. Pancakes with Siberian Honey. His favourite. Alexei was sitting up in bed reading. It was a book of inspirational poems collected from Russian sources over the last 300 years and had been published to honour our tercentenary as a family.

"Hi, Tanya."

I put the tea and pancakes on the bed near him. He spotted them and his eyes lit up. As his hand reached out he saw my face. Even trying to remain impassive, I had not been as successful as I had hoped.

His hand stopped in mid-air. "What is it? Something's wrong, Tanya. Tell me. You haven't given me these for years, and then only when I was ill. What's wrong?" His tone was now alarmed. "Come on, Tanya, I demand to know."

There was a long pause. I had not thought this out as well as I'd hoped. "Father Grigory won't be coming to see you anymore."

I suppose I thought that at this stage I could possibly make him think Father Grigory had simply forgotten him. Nice idea. Trouble was, Alexei was not going to accept that for a minute.

"Has father sent him away again? I'll just ask Mama and she'll get him back for me."

He looked at me brightly, then examined my face, as if he suddenly saw in it the horrible truth. Very, very quietly, he said, "He's not been sent away. He's dead, isn't he?"

I didn't know how to react. I was frozen. I wanted desperately to deny this. For his sake. Freezing was the very worst thing I could have done.

"Isn't he?"

I felt as though I had been hit over the head by a cricket bat with the force of his outburst. I looked at him, and for a split second I saw my brother as he was meant to be. Strong, powerful, in total command of himself and his abilities. As Father Grigory had seen him. As Alexander I had seen him. Then, just as suddenly, he diminished right in front of me into the small, fragile twelve-year-old who had just lost his best friend in all the world. There was nothing I could do. I burst into tears.

"Get out! I never want to see you again!"

In slow motion I saw Alexei overturn the tea tray and send its contents flying across the room. The teapot broke in pieces and I was covered in hot tea and pancakes. I didn't care. My poor brother. I could feel it. All his hope was gone. I went towards him, to try to console him. He wrenched himself out of my grip.

"Go away. Get out!"

His voice was small and weak now. His tears were unstoppable. I had to leave. As I closed the door, I heard my brother scream. It was a scream of hopelessness. Then the tears. Loud and long. He locked the door and wouldn't let anyone in. When I went up to his door to try to talk to him during the rest of the morning, all I could hear were his strangled sobs. He wouldn't even talk to Mama.

At lunchtime, I saw him out through the window of Mama's balcony. He was dressed in his uniform and had Joy with him. Ignoring Olga's restraining hand, I rushed out to him, but as he saw me approaching he simply ran away into the park. It was as if he had imploded. I could feel him retreating inside himself. My last sight of him was of his eyes, terrible, sunken and dark. He appeared suddenly, shockingly and prematurely old. His wizard had gone. So had his world. And there was nothing any of us could do or say to help. All is now over. All that is left to us is to play out the last few pages of this play and let the cards of Fate fall where they may.

2nd January 1917 – Tsarskoe Selo
We buried poor Father Grigory this morning. Mama, Olga, myself, Marie, Anastasia and Alexei were there. We buried him in a corner of our park, surrounded by trees and flowers. Eventually, Mama intends to build a church on the spot. I found it so hard, looking at his body, knowing what I had seen,

wondering if there was anything I could have done to save him. As the birds sang in the trees around us, I was reminded so much of my beloved St Seraphim and his animals, and I prayed that he take care of Father Grigory and show him the way into the light. As for us, the light has dimmed now. All of us were in floods of tears. I cannot describe to you just what he meant to us. It goes so far beyond friendship that it is something else altogether deeper. For myself, I feel that I have lost my wisest counsellor. The things he knew, not just about our world, but many others too, are beyond imagining. The lies and slander being spread about his gentle soul are already shocking to me. It seems that it is always the good and the peaceful who suffer the worst. But in the end, it is that suffering that brings the beautiful and the brave to the throne of God Himself. In Eternity, I shall find him there once again, and we will sit and talk of the bounty of Nature, as we always used to. Rest in Peace, my beloved Friend.

3rd January 1917 – Tsarskoe Selo
The first snowfall of the year. Heavy, as it often is here. Normally, we would have gone and built a snow mountain. But this time, all we could do was look out of the window at the falling flakes. Marie began to cry. Anastasia joined her and they put their arms around each other. Olga and I held hands. I put my head on her shoulder. No words were necessary. At tea later with Mama we were all unnaturally quiet. Bed at 10.30.

4th January 1917 – Tsarskoe Selo
Loneliness. Walking in the park this morning, it is as if Nature herself has taken on the garb of mourning. I tried to remember the happy times, the sunlit games we all used to play here, but it all seems so faded now, like a damaged sepia photograph. I can't even hear the voices of my family. It is as if I am enclosed in my own world, a lost world. All I can do is walk on into the cold air and try to forget where I am. Curious. At this moment I wouldn't

mind forgetting who I am as well. We read that after death, we pass through the river of forgetfulness. Bliss. To remember nothing, to be nothing. A consummation devoutly to be wished...

6th January 1917 – Tsarskoe Selo

Christmas. Passed with all the usual ceremonial. The candles, incense and light as usual, but it is all hollow. It remains unsaid between us all, but I know that we are all just marking time now. Waiting for something to happen. I remember the conversation with Alexander I. It all seems so remote now and I wonder if I dreamed it all. Talking with a ghost. It seems so implausible. At all events, whatever was supposed to happen, has not. It has failed. Whatever "plan" there was has not worked. Papa will go back to the front tomorrow. But I know in my heart it is all useless. He too is now just playing out this game of Fate. And I know where that ends...

PART IV

DISINTEGRATION

JANUARY 1917-JULY 1918

7th January 1917 – Tsarskoe Selo
I am dreaming. I am on a battlefield. This has happened before. All around me is fire, blood and smoke. Men are falling on all sides. My men. I am shouting orders frantically. My sword arm works ceaselessly, killing the enemy, for whom I feel a strange pity. The odds are hopeless. We are losing. But I have never lost a battle. I feel my legs cut from under me and a sharp pain in my back, but, as I go down, and I feel blows rain on my head, my last sight is of my beloved Eagle standard and the thought that, even through death, I will win. I will win … I WILL WIN.

9th January 1917 – Tsarskoe Selo
Nursing duties at the infirmary take my mind off things, at least, for a while. I assist in operations, helping to sever and bind shattered limbs, tending to head injuries and those with damaged hands. I sat for a long while with a young private, Yuri. We talk about our families. We are not so different. Masha is always going on about being able to marry one of Papa's officers. What would be so weird about falling in love with a "commoner"? After all, we are all human. I hold his hand and watch him for a long while as he falls asleep. To bridge the gap. To finally know that there is no gap. Eventually, I blow out the candle beside his bed and make my way home.

Later, in Papa's study, I write to Yuri's mother and sister. They haven't seen him for over two years. I make sure they have money for the return trip. It's the least I can do, for a fellow being…

16th January 1917 – St.Petersburg
At 9.16 this morning a flight of cranes flew over the Winter Palace. The birds, sixteen in all, circled above the Imperial flag four times before flying away in a ribbon towards the North. I have only seen such a flight once before, around the time of my visions at Stavka in 1915. In Norse mythology, cranes represent

Death… and Eternal Life. I have a horrible feeling that events are about to be wrenched finally from our grasp. *Into thy hands O merciful Mother of God do I commend my Spirit, and those whom I love most dearly.* Kyrie Elaison…

9ᵗʰ March 1917 – Tsarskoe Selo
Committee for Lost Children. My last meeting. Felt feverish and dizzy the whole time, but stuck it through till the end. The conditions of the war and especially those in Petrograd have finally made it impossible for us to do our work. All those poor children! Undaunted, I have instructed a skeleton staff to remain in our HQ and carry on the work as best they can. Even if one lost child is reunited with their family it is worth it. In the worsening political climate, it is thought unwise for me to carry on as head of the organisation. The wife of a prominent Duma member is chosen to succeed me. May she have better fortune than I. As they are leaving, and we shake hands, I wonder, when shall we all meet again…?

11ᵗʰ March 1917 – Tsarskoe Selo
Helping Mama with "the invalids". Everyone else but Masha and I have gone down with measles. In the darkness at night, I seemed to hear a string quartet playing in one of the downstairs rooms. The slow movement from Borodin's Second String Quartet in D. The sound was so hopeless and lost. I sat on one of our sofas in the dark and cried my eyes out for what seemed like hours…

15ᵗʰ March 1917 – Tsarskoe Selo
Ill with measles myself now. Confined to bed with a temperature and bald (again! – remember 1913?) having had my head shaved. The frustration is unbearable. I just want to run away. From everything!

22ⁿᵈ March 1917 – Tsarskoe Selo

Papa is home. He came to see us this morning. Olga is delirious and didn't know he was there. I seem to be fighting it better, although why I can't imagine, and if Olga dies, I have definitely decided to die too, even if I have to slash my wrists to do it. I hope it won't come to that. Papa seemed sombre. Mama had been crying and there was a strange atmosphere around them. Something has happened.

27ᵗʰ March 1917 – Tsarskoe Selo

Such a small word. Abdicate. Such a small word. So full of meaning. This is the end of our world - at least the world as we have known it. And, do you know something strange? I feel fine. But why? I am sitting outside and it is sunny. In front of me are two guards. Here for our "protection". Olga is sat with me, her arm linked through mine and she's resting. I feel her breathing against me. Such a blessing and a comfort. She almost died at the end of last week. I was with her, holding her in my arms, crying, begging her not to leave me. I swear she heard me through the illness. I saw her smile. After that her fever broke at long last. She has been very slow to recover. This morning, seeing the sunshine, I carried her out here in my arms and we are now sitting together and I write while she sleeps. God, it seems, is merciful. At least for now.

Papa seems to be taking it all very well.

"At least I didn't get the measles too. Think how I would look bald. Not a pretty sight!"

I had to laugh in spite of myself.

Not a word about the "A" word. He seems to be in very good spirits. He even jokes with the guards and, in spite of their every effort to humiliate him, they seem to be coming to respect both him and us. Yesterday, a soldier even offered me a cigarette. Had I been Nastya I would probably have accepted, and then been spanked afterwards. But at least the offer, the human gesture was there. That was enough. Maybe there is something beyond this after all. Olga is smiling now. I'm sure she picked up my thought. Maybe… Maybe…

30th March 1917 – Tsarskoe Selo
Already feeling infuriated by the conditions of our "house arrest". Prince L'vov came to see us yesterday, accompanied by his "Justice Minister", a Mr Kerensky. I sat in on the meeting at Papa's request. The prince was trying to puff himself up and act self-important. Kerensky, on the other hand, simply sat and observed his boss's bluster. I like his eyes. Twice during the meeting, he looked straight at me, and although his mouth didn't smile, his eyes did. Whatever the prince is like, I feel we can trust Mr Kerensky. I told Papa so afterwards. He nodded thoughtfully and squeezed my arm. I think he feels as I do. We may have discovered an ally.

31st March 1917 – Tsarskoe Selo
My infuriation, which I alluded to yesterday, grew enormously during a very sleepless night. I found myself confined to our room. Couldn't even go for my night-walk, as I tumbled over a guard in the corridor outside. This is all getting ridiculous. I feel really annoyed watching the men come and go over the little bridge that marks our "boundary". This is our domain, not theirs. So, this morning, on impulse, I commandeered M.Gilliard and his camera and asked him to follow me, but at a distance. I had Ortino with me and we made as if we were going for our normal walk.

Five minutes in, I diverted away towards the bridge. I had observed that the guard had become lazy and was talking to one of our servants, so he was away from the bridge and not looking at me. Glancing over my shoulder, I spotted M.Gilliard. He looked concerned. I think at that stage he had already realised what I had in mind and was trying to encourage me to stop. But

I will not be confined. By anyone. The guard still hadn't noticed me. There was a large gap between him and the bridge. I could just make it.

Once onto the bridge, I planned to scoop Ortino into my arms and run for it. They wouldn't dare shoot me. I'm too valuable to them alive. The bridge was so tantalisingly close that I ignored the sick feeling in the pit of my stomach until it was almost too late. Eventually, and with the bridge mere feet away, the feeling made me turn. What I saw made me stop dead. About a hundred yards away, I could see Olga in the throes of digging. What she could not see was the semicircle of guards who had materialised behind her, all with their rifles pointed at her head. Behind M.Gilliard, their CO was grinning at me. He had evidently been watching me without my knowledge. Given that I could see that the grin did not extend as far as his eyes, I knew. One foot on the bridge, and they would shoot. So much for "humanity". I had to act quickly. I shouted to M.Gilliard. "Monsieur. I think here would be good. You, " to the bridge guard who had been talking to the servant, "would you like to pose on the bridge with me? I think I'll sit here."

Fortunately M.Gilliard read my intentions perfectly, and set down his camera as I sat opposite him on the pillar of the bridge. The guard posed on the bridge above me with a huge silly grin on his face. The semi-circle of soldiers around Olga dissolved as I sat down. She never knew they were there, or their foul intent. The failsafe plan to make it look like a set-up for a photo had worked. But what no-one realised was that, technically, as I sat on the pillar of the bridge, I had made it to a place beyond their boundary, as the pillar is ahead of the foot of the bridge. This is just the beginning. I'll think of a way to escape for good eventually. Not just for myself either, but for everyone. [2]

6th *April 1917 – Tsarskoe Selo*
Out in the garden. Mama supervising from her wheelchair, in

which she seems to be spending more and more time. The situation has affected her much worse than the rest of us, especially Papa who seems on the whole to be quite sanguine. We are all, including M.Gilliard and Mr Gibbes, planting vegetables. It's quite exciting really. The whole park is being turned into a vegetable garden. It will fill all of our needs for the rest of the war and, maybe fill some for Petrograd more widely too. I must say, I'm quite looking forward to seeing the results. And what a miracle that everyone passes by every day, that one can plant a seed in the ground and get from it something that you can eat that sustains you and makes you well. People don't realise. So much is taken for granted.

8th April 1917 – Tsarskoe Selo
Horrible dream last night.

Sat looking out to sea. Beautiful coastline. Time was late afternoon or early evening. The sea was coming in. I tried to get up to walk to safety and found I couldn't move. The sea came in very slowly. All my calls for help went unheeded. I drowned, but not all at once. My body gradually became numb all over, and cold. In the end, all I could move was my eyes, then, not even them. Final sensation of falling down into a deep, black well of utter loneliness.

Woke up screaming. A horrible ringing noise filling my head. Not even Olga could comfort me.

1st May 1917 – Tsarskoe Selo
"Papa, what do you think will happen to us? I heard a rumour spoken among the guards that we are to go to England. Is that true?"

"I think it may be. I'm sure Cousin George won't let us down. After all, we have always been the very best of friends. Maybe we can all go and live in a small country house. I can retire there and your mother can knit and boss the gardeners about, just like she's doing now."

In the distance, we could see my mother talking to one of the servants who was planting some cabbages. She was sitting in her wheelchair and waving her stick in his general direction, obviously making a forceful point. Papa sighed. "I don't think your Mama will last through this. The strain is telling on her heart."

"I think her soul is weary, Papa. She is always so tired."

"Angry too. With me."

"Never with you, Papa, she loves you too much for that."

"Ah yes, but I don't think she will forgive me soon for giving up the throne. She was devoted to the Divine Right of Kings. I think she learned that from Granny in England. You don't remember her, do you?"

"You mean Queen Victoria? Yes, I remember her vaguely. She always seemed so serious and sad."

"That's right. She lost her husband, Prince Albert, when still young. I think she never got over that. But more than this, she ruled England quietly but firmly from behind a constitutional mask for nearly sixty-five years. Your mother was virtually brought up by her and got from her this powerful view of a strong monarchy. That's what she wanted for us."

Papa paused and drew thoughtfully on his pipe.

I thought for a moment before carefully adding, "But you didn't want it, did you, Papa?"

"Initially, I thought I did. But I hadn't learned how to govern. Your grandfather always ruled and did everything by himself. He didn't trust anyone with the affairs of state. He had to be in control all the time. But Russia is a big country. Too big to be controlled by just one man. My father kept on citing the example of Peter I. But Tsar Peter had almost superhuman strength and a ruthlessness even my father couldn't match. I began by thinking I could follow my father. But even lesser ruthlessness such as his doesn't come easily to me. After a while I saw that Russia needed something new. The miracle of Father Grigory suggested to me that some kind of constitutional monarchy was the answer. That's why the Dumas were created. I realise that now. Your mother always thought to reinforce the old order through the obedience of the peasants. But she is wrong. She misread our Friend. You and Olga know what he wanted for us and for Russia. Harmony with Nature. Which means rule of Parliament, with the free will consent of all classes working together, and a constitutional monarchy at its head showing everyone what all can aspire to - if the cycles of life permit it. I'm sure your great-grandfather would approve."

"I believe that is what Mr Kerensky wants," I said quietly.

"So do I. That is one of the reasons why I abdicated. I remember him from before the War. He is the most intelligent man in the new government. I believe that events will draw to a swifter conclusion and a better one once he is in charge. Sources loyal to us have told me that Prince L'vov will not last and that Kerensky will soon replace him. L'vov has neither the spine nor the depth of knowledge needed for high office. But I fear the Bolsheviks. Did I ever show you any of the reports about Lenin and his men? They just want power for themselves. They'll try to fool the people into thinking that they want power in order to give it back to them, but they'll only keep it for themselves. I foresee a time ahead where they will rule with even more ruthlessness than old Peter did. Their logic, if you can call it that, says that Russia needs an iron fist in order to control the numbers of people who live here. The tragedy of that view is it is behind the times. Your great-grandfather knew that the only way to rule was by common consent. Those like Lenin who saw their chance for power being taken away by this view destroyed him and plunged us all into fear and doubt. I realise now, I hope not too late, that there are other, darker powers at work, that we don't always see, until they surface and make themselves known indirectly through other agencies. Always they want to rule by fear and hate instead of tolerance and love. If these people ever get into power, my child, I don't know what will become of us. I leave all to the Lord. I trust Him to watch over us."

"And for insurance, shall I speak to Mr Kerensky?"

"Yes. He is due here tomorrow. I shall make my excuses and say I am too unwell to receive him. Use your charm and diplomacy. Find out what he wants for us. Try, if you can, to persuade him of the benefits of the constitutional approach. This will save much more than just our lives. If you can succeed then I shall talk to him myself next week and we will see if a deal can be worked out. Maybe we can then all go to the Crimea after all."

We had stopped walking and were standing by a tree overlooking our home. The Alexander Palace looked beautiful in the afternoon sun. Even more so surrounded on three sides by vegetables. I knelt down and stroked Ortino's fur. Taking his little face in my hands, I said, "You'd like to stay at Livadia, wouldn't you?"

"Woof," he barked, in answer to my question, licking my face.

"See, Tatiana," said Papa, "Father Grigory always said he understood what we were saying."

"*As do all God's creatures,*" said a familiar voice in my head.

2nd May 1917 – Tsarskoe Selo

Kerensky's visit. He began in his usual roundabout way to be full of praise and diplomatic. I always feel like shouting at him to get to the point, but I sense that to do that I would knock him off his stride and he would only start again, from the beginning. He started by showing concern about Papa's health, as I informed him of the Tsar's indisposition. As the conversational small-talk continued, he gradually got to the point. Our allowances were to be cut – again! All necessary cash was being diverted to the continued efforts against Germany. All unnecessary expenditure was being diverted to that cause too. This meant a further cut in our maintenance allowance. I said that I was sure that His Majesty would not mind, as the issue that was uppermost in his mind was prosecution of the war to a successful conclusion. We could adjust. I thanked him for his concern for us. Then I came to the point. Swiftly.

"Mr Kerensky, it is my belief that you wish for Russia to have a constitutional monarchy, as Great Britain does, is that not so?"

He hesitated. In the act of lifting his teacup, he paused. Then he drank slowly before putting it down on the saucer ever so carefully. I sensed he was having to couch his reply in such a way that he could not later be reproached for it.

"I have always admired Britain's style of government, Your Imperial Highness, that is so."

"But you would like that for our country also?" I pressed him.

Quietly, he said, "If that is the will of the people."

I sensed fear in him. I wanted to know what he was afraid of, though in my heart I knew what the answer would be. So I changed tack.

"In an ideal world, how would you like to see the future for us? Let us assume the war is won. What do you foresee?"

"I am no mystic, madam, just a humble lawyer," *(note the mild sarcasm in his tone),* "but," *(I went to speak again and he overrode me),* "if you press me, I would say that I would wish with all my heart to see your family survive…" He paused. "Possibly in retirement, in your father's case. A new monarch would ascend a constitutional throne and all power would be in the hands of elected representatives of the people. As to who the new monarch would be," *(he gave me a suddenly searching, yet unreadable, look),* "I cannot even begin to speculate at this stage."

Kerensky seemed flustered now. My questions had evidently touched a nerve. I sensed our position was not as secure as I had hoped. I dreaded the answer to my next query.

"Are we to be sent to England, sir?"

"Representations have been made to King George's government. I gather your father's cousin would like you to go, but it is in the hands of his ministers that the final decision rests.

Beyond that, if they do send a ship for you, I fear for the problems we might have getting you all across Petrograd unnoticed."

"Then what is to be done?"

He was testy now and rose to his feet abruptly. "I will let you, or rather, His Majesty your father know - when I know what is to be done myself."

Suddenly, he softened. His hard look vanished and was replaced by one of kindness and concern. He approached me, took my hand and kissed it gently.

"Your Imperial Highness, I am sorry if I was brusque, please forgive me. Things are now approaching a critical stage. The next few weeks will tell if we survive or if others take our place. I will do all that I can to protect you. I hope and believe that you will be a part of all our futures. Let us pray God make it so."

And with that Alexander Kerensky, would-be head of state and very troubled man, clicked his heels, bowed to me, turned and walked briskly from the audience room. It was only later that I noticed that in conversation with me, he had emphasised the word *you* in his last two sentences. The emphasis had been subtle, but quite direct. He had evidently been referring to me specifically, rather than the family in general. What I couldn't work out, was why. As soon as he had left, having taken a little time to recompose myself, I reported back to Papa. He was disappointed, but not surprised.

"It is as we thought. He obviously wants constitutional government, but the wreckers within this revolution are gaining ground and becoming more threatening. Truly, the only way for us to survive is if the war is won quickly."

"What of the Bolsheviks, Papa?"

"Aye, what of them. They have no love for us, that is certain. And people are getting tired. I don't blame them for wanting the war to be over. Too many people have been lost. If something isn't done soon, the pressure to sue for terms will become too great. And we will be blamed for the disaster. I will never put my name to any document handing the victory to Germany. Do what they will to me, I will not see Russia humiliated like that."

I had never seen Papa so intense. I felt he would give his life to protect the country we all loved. Maybe we all would be called on to make the sacrifice. And yet, I found myself feeling rebellious. My acceptance of the idea had always been tenuous and questioning, aside from that one night when the feeling of a willing sacrifice had been made clear to me by the Firebird Girl. After our recent experiences, that feeling of beauty and acceptance was long dead. I was angry.

"It isn't fair, Papa. We have done nothing wrong. All we have ever tried to do was help."

"Yes, my child. Sometimes the helper is killed by the one he is trying to help."

Gloomily, Papa walked past me and went from the study, down the corridor and down the stairs into the gardens beyond. I went to the window and looked out. In the early afternoon sun, I could see him walking past the rows of planted vegetables towards the park, shadowed, as ever by a guard. He was so deep in thought that he didn't even stop to say good afternoon to M.Gilliard, who was busy digging, and for whom he always had a kind word.

It was a beautiful day outside, but my father's inner landscape was cloudy and it was beginning to rain. A rustling noise behind me made me turn. Olga was standing in the doorway.

"He fears for our lives, doesn't he?"

"Kerensky, yes. He doesn't think we will live much longer. He fears Lenin and his Red thugs."

"So he should. I read one of his speeches once."

I gasped.

"Papa never knew. In it the most significant thing he said was that the only way to maintain a revolution was through terror. These people will do anything for power and that is all they want. They will replace Papa with something infinitely worse. We will die. It is only a matter of when, not if, now."

I saw red. "So, you've given up. How spineless of you."

Olga smiled and said, "Sarcasm is one of my character traits. I didn't realise you had it too."

Her expression was mocking me. I couldn't help but laugh. It broke the mood. "I'm sorry. I think I just picked up Papa's gloom."

"Yes, he seems to be getting worse lately."

"As if he has the weight of the world on his shoulders."

"Like Mama."

We embraced and, as always, I gained comfort from the nearness of Olga's body and her presence.

She kissed me. "I'm always here, you know. Never doubt or forget. Nothing you ever say or do to me will hurt or anger me. I love you."

"I love you too."

We turned back to the window and looked out, arm in arm.

"Up for a spot of digging?"

She saw my face.

"Aw, come on. Bet you I can plant more carrots than you today."

"You couldn't plant a straight furrow if you tried. Some peasant you'd make."

"There you are, then. The revolution is called off because Grand Duchess Olga plants lousy carrots!"

We held each other and laughed.

David Lloyd George - 15th May 1917 – 10 Downing Street London

Lloyd George looked at Stamfordham fiercely. The King's private secretary stood his ground.

"His Majesty has made his decision. The offer is to be withdrawn. That is final."

"I must say, I find this very perplexing. He is family, and I gather His Majesty is supposed to have very strong feelings for the emperor. I know that there are strong feelings in some sections of the media that are against the move, but, since when does Royalty allow itself to be influenced by the press? And there is also the human angle. Does he care nothing for the children? At least they should come, if nothing else."

Stamfordham was immovable. "His Majesty has made his decision, sir. Let that be an end of it."

Lloyd George played his card. He had been waiting for this.

"It is not the end of it. We have been having negotiations with Prince L'vov and Mr Kerensky. You should know that in the event of the Provisional Government retaining its hold, it is their intention to restore the Monarchy as a constitutional force. There will be a Parliament and Prime Minister as here. The chosen regent and future sovereign is the Emperor's daughter, the Grand Duchess Tatiana. Accordingly, we are presently choosing a team of people to get her out of Russia in the event it becomes necessary and the family's position becomes dire. She must be protected at all costs."

Stamfordham sat down. Very slowly. Lloyd George chose his next words carefully. "She will be taken to safety, looked after by His Majesty at our expense, and kept out of sight until the Provisional Government achieves victory. As soon as the newly elected Prime Minister is firmly installed in the Kremlin, the Monarchy will be restored and the Grand Duchess crowned Empress of a new, democratic, Russia. One which accords more closely with our interests than the old regime did. You will inform His Majesty that I wish to see him regarding this urgent matter at his earliest convenience."

The interview was over. All Stamfordham could do was bow and leave. Had he bothered to look back, he would have seen a smile of deep satisfaction cross the face of David Lloyd George.

Tatiana's Diary - 26th May 1917 – Alexander Palace

Night. Everyone else was asleep, or so I thought. Our guards are much more relaxed about us now and only seek to confine us on the outside. Within the palace we are now mostly left to ourselves. Wandering the corridors as usual, I came to Papa's study. The light was on! At 3am? Cautiously I pushed the door open, and descended the stairs to find Papa sitting at his desk, shuffling papers as he used to before the Revolution.

"I find it hard to break old habits, as do you, I see," he said with a wry smile. I must have looked shocked.

"Don't you think I notice anything? You're an incurable insomniac. You've been wandering the corridors at night these past few years. With amazing regularity. That cup of hot milk you found in the corridor on the side table last month? That was me! I thought you'd need it … to give you strength for your journeys."

I laughed out loud and embraced him as he sat there. He put his head against my shoulder. It was comforting.

"Do you want to know what I was looking at?"

I sat beside him. It was an old letter, dated August 24th 1911, from Pyotr Stolypin. In it, he describes with obvious satisfaction the state of the economy and the predicted good harvest for that year.

I must have looked sad. Papa took my hand. "I know. I remember, too."

There were tears in my eyes. "You do realise, don't you? This was the beginning of the end."

"So much was lost with his death. I didn't realise myself at the time. Pyotr really was my best man. It was he who took your great-grandpapa's manifesto and made it real. Think about it. Universal land ownership. Small farms governed by those who live on them producing all their own food, enough for themselves, and the surplus for the rest of us. That's what poor Grigory always said would save Russia. And he was right. Universal Suffrage too. I never saw it, until it was far too late. The keys were in my hands and I lost them, Tatiana."

His eyes filled with tears. I embraced him, trying to comfort him as best I could.

"What we have lost, and the magnitude of what will happen now, are overwhelming me."

I thought about what he had said, and something dawned on me. "Papa, think about it. There have been those who wanted to stop this all the time, ever since 1881. Those terrorists, or more likely those controlling them, who killed great-grandpapa, must have known there would be a backlash. More repression. It's a typical human response. Grandpapa reacted predictably. That fuels more terrorism, more repression. Like follows like until you get a breakdown. What they didn't count on was your granting of the Constitution in 1905."

"Of course. I know there were difficulties with the Dumas at first, but when Pyotr took over and took up your great-grandpapa's reins, things started to go right. Here, Tatiana, look at this letter from Trotsky to Lenin, intercepted by the Okhrana."

The gist of the letter, written shortly before Stolypin's assassination, was to tell him not to bother coming back to Russia, as there was not going to be a revolution. Everyone was too well off, and democracy was gaining a hold, defying extremism.

"The key," Papa continued, "would have been, at every violent action of the terrorists, to have done exactly what they were trying to stop. For every action against freedom, you increase it. For every action of war, you bring more peace. You don't react to individual or group terrorism by increasing the terrorism of the state. That only delivers everyone into the hands of the Devil."

"As Father Grigory always tried to say," I commented.

"You are right. Father Grigory never wanted us to enter the war. I've often wondered what would have happened if he hadn't been wounded just at the time all that trouble in the Balkans was breaking out. I really think he might have persuaded me to keep us out of the war, just as he had once before, in 1912."

"And what then?" we both wondered. No revolution in Russia. And the war might have been shorter and far less damaging altogether. Papa gave me a very deep look.

"Those are all might-have-beens now. All we can do is deal with the consequences of what is. And, if necessary, give our lives for our home."

In my head I heard again, *"There will have to be a sacrifice."*

The summer night was warm and dry. But the clouds were over us all now. And it was definitely raining. Hard.

King George V - 4th June 1917 – Buckingham Palace

"How long will she need to be kept here? I don't seriously think I can keep her confined against her will for too long. She will have to know the purpose, surely."

Lloyd George puffed on his pipe and looked thoughtfully at a rather flustered King George V.

"I think, sir, that rather depends on the success or otherwise of the Provisional Government. If things proceed as they are at present, Grand Duchess Tatiana could well be crowned within twelve months. Indeed, Mr Kerensky has already set the date of June 10th next year for the purpose. This assumes that the war can be brought to its conclusion by then. If not, there will have to be a postponement. He is proposing the 20th August this year for her to be transferred to our jurisdiction. Her family will remain behind. It will be impossible to transfer all of them to us without some general outcry. Kerensky thinks to please everybody by doing this, as the Tsar must still stand trial for the crimes of his reign, so his family must stay."

King George gave him a look. "Who was it who said, you can please some of the people some of the time, but you cannot please all of the people all of the time? In trying to please everyone, he may end up pleasing no-one."

"Quite. Also, if things get dicey with the Reds, he may have to send them all out eastwards. A second plan must be in place, depending on where the family is taken."

"It's a colossal risk, Prime Minister."

"Yes. But to safeguard Democracy, Monarchy, and our wider interests, I think the price worth paying. After all, we are fighting the war against Germany for no lesser stakes. Her Imperial Highness could be the fresh beginning Russia needs. I'm told she has a good head on her shoulders, and is quite a diplomat."

"I think she will need to be."

The two men looked into the fire. The visions they saw are a matter for conjecture.

Tatiana's Diary - 28ᵗʰ June 1917 – Alexander Palace

A feeling of utter exhaustion. I'm slumped against the hut in the garden. It seems as if I've been digging and hoeing, fetching and carrying water, harvesting fruit and vegetables since before the beginning of time. I really can do no more. It's so bad that my lungs hurt with the effort. Somewhere beside me, I can hear Marie and Alexei joking around, pushing each other and shouting and screaming. The guards, who watch over us "for our own protection" (Kerensky) have become so much a part of our existence that they no longer feel like the alien intruders they once were. We are on first name terms with them. I have been working closely with Pyotr. He was once an infantryman on the front line in Austria. He has seen horrors in the war, which I don't want to think about, and returned suffering from mild shell shock. All he wants is peace and a chance to start a family and settle down. As we have spent time together, the barriers of social class have dropped – from his side. They never existed for me.

Yesterday afternoon I was wheeling the large water container from the canal towards our garden. Anastasia was helping me. Marie stopped us in mid-wheel to take a picture. I'm sure I'll look terribly glum as the effort was hurting my back, but it seemed to satisfy her. She laughed.

"All right Masha. If it's that funny, you come and wheel this thing."

"Oh no," she said, gesturing to the rake on the ground. "I'll stick to this, thanks." And ran off giggling. In spite of myself, I laughed too.

Pyotr was approaching us. We began to push the barrel again. It was then that it happened. There was a huge cracking noise. The heavily laden barrel broke its connection to its left wheel and it broke and turned over. I kept hold of it. It happened so fast that it had turned and fallen, twisting and felling me in the process. Anastasia jumped clear with a squeak, but I hit the ground awkwardly on my side. I could feel the muscles in my back pull violently. I screamed in pain and was covered in the water.

I was aware of Pyotr. He lifted the barrel off me and gently helped me to sit up. He asked me where it hurt. As I told him, and evidently without thinking, he had pulled up my blouse at the back. He loosened my corset stays and slipped his hand inside, placing it on my flesh. Instantly, I felt his warmth. There was utter stillness. I felt a powerful tingling sensation which seemed to go from the strained area into my lower parts and then rush from there through my stomach and heart and throat and rush out of the top of my head. I let out a deep moan, completely involuntarily. When he removed his hand, all the pain had gone. I felt fresh and alert.

He gave me his hand and helped me to my feet. "I used to do that in the war all the time. There were few nurses in the front line, fewer doctors and no medicine. I learned it from my grandmother." He smiled. Then he took his shirt off and offered it to me to replace my soaked blouse.

"It's clean, I assure you," he said with a smile.

I demurred politely. I would go inside to dry and change. He looked disappointed. I could tell that he wanted me to stay with him. I would have enjoyed that too. In fact, I must admit to feeling really quite attracted to him. I suddenly felt warm and aroused. Quite unbidden, a picture came into my head of Pyotr and myself making love under the trees in the sunshine... Reality crowded in on me unexpectedly...

"Tanya, you're blushing. I'll tell Papa you fancy Pyotr."

I went to cuff Anastasia. I had completely forgotten her. She must have seen everything. Blushing furiously, I ran from the scene, feeling suddenly ashamed of myself, with Pyotr's bemused look following me and Anastasia's girlish laughter ringing in my ears like an accusation. I wish, oh how I wish I could cut the part of myself away that has these forbidden feelings. What Father Grigory unleashed in me all those years ago now seems alien and twisted. I am fighting an ungovernable force. In the end, either it will kill me, or I it. But I would, I confess, have loved to have given in to that inner impulse with Pyotr just now, even with Anastasia watching us. It felt – there is no other word for it – natural and – right. Why can we not just love? Why must we be followed through life with these stupid, negative voices that prevent our natural instincts from flowing? Entering our room, the strain finally overwhelmed me and I collapsed on my bed crying, the fantasy image of myself loving my young friend taunting me, driving my hand to give me relief from the unbearable pain in the only way I knew. [3]

Alexander Kerensky's Office - 13th August 1917 – Moscow

"When was this?" Kerensky looked at his secretary with some astonishment.

"Last night, sir. The message was received just before 5pm."

"Why wasn't I told at once? This is too important to ignore. We must move the family immediately. Despatch them to Tobolsk. I have had the governor's house prepared. And they are to take nothing but the barest essentials for now. Tell them nothing, I don't want them alarmed. And, Glebov..."

"Yes, sir?"

"Despatch a coded message to London. They must know of this change of plan at once. Tell them the cruiser must turn back. Say, the package will have to be delivered later."

"Is that all?"

"Yes, dammit, now get on with it!"

Glebov left hastily, forgetting to shut the door on his way out.

What am I to do? Kerensky thought. Everything had seemed ready. The cruiser HMS Calypso had been heading to Kronstadt as planned. He only had to give the word and Tatiana would have been rushed across the city and away to safety. Lenin's men must have infiltrated Tsarskoe Selo. That his death squad were planning to murder the family had come as a shock, but not a surprise. His sympathisers were everywhere. And with Trotsky whipping up the masses with his anti-democratic garbage, they were primed for anything. If only he had been better at propaganda. But these days, spin was everything. Politicians were becoming frighteningly adept at convincing a gullible population that lies were truth and that truth was a lie. In a democracy, that was all right. If you were adept, you could easily expose such pathetic manipulations. But the people were war-weary. A few cheap slogans, which were actually meaningless, were coming to mean more than love of your fellow man, or love of your country. Quietly, he said a prayer. Not for himself. But for a family whom he had come to love as dearly as his own, and also, for Russia Herself.[4]

Tatiana's Diary - Tobolsk - 14th January 1918 – 1.00am
Night-time. Never a comforting sensation. Always pregnant with unexpressed feelings and longings. Now even worse, the only feeling was that of frost cracking the windowpane outside. Stifling, almost hot silence. The sound of distant breathing, slow and uneven as someone moves through an alien landscape. I stand at the window of our room unable any longer to see even

the semblance of the winter garden in the deepening gloom. Even the street lights have ceased to work outside so the only shadows cast on our wall are those cast by the deepening shadow of my soul as it diminishes and sinks further from the light of its own transformation in bitter silence. Standing still in the calm of the arctic night I turn without thinking into a statue as millennia pass beneath my unsleeping gaze. When I awake from my trance, the house and my family are gone and I find myself, yet not myself staring in raptures of joy at a sparkling lake on the edge of infinite pine forests bathed in a cool blue sunshine. Night-time, still cold, razor sharp silence and the hollow ringing of a dark moon in shadow. Sleep. Oblivion without light. *Ingenting.*

C – Head of British Intelligence - 20th February 1918 – London
Memo from C, Head of British Intelligence:
"All efforts to recruit people in Tobolsk area re-former Tsar have failed. Evident imminent move planned. Intelligence suggests Ekaterinburg. Ural Soviet anxious to take control. Rescue attempt for family planned from within Moscow. No evidence as to who has planned it. Can only hope it is not bungled. Attempt will be made to get daughter of former Tsar out with respect to plans of Government in Exile. All efforts must centre on Preston, in Ekaterinburg. Meinertzagen to head Operation Eagle."

Tatiana's Diary - 26th February 1918 – Tobolsk
Snow mountains. Not as high as the ones we used to build back home, but still good fun. All of us got to have a go, even Alexei, who slid down most comically on his rear end. What most fired his imagination was the archery, though. I wonder if he is at last beginning to get past childish games. One of the guards showed him how to make a primitive bow and arrow. He then taught him how to use it. He got the hang of it very quickly. So much so that the captain of the guard became alarmed and ordered it to be

taken away from him. As if Alexei would use it as a weapon. I'm sure it didn't even cross his mind. As for the rest of us, we were quite looking forward to having a go and were quite miffed when the new toy was taken away.

Still no word on what is to happen to us. Rations have been cut again, but people in the city have been very kind and we still get letters and occasional gifts from home, although how many of these represent the total sent to us I cannot be sure. Our watchers are generally all right with us, but I have lately sensed a growing mood of menace, mostly from outside the walls. Inside the house, things are becoming strained. The atmosphere between the four of us girls has darkened lately. I know Olga finds the idiosyncrasies of Marie and particularly Anastasia very irritating. She has slapped her several times; on a couple of occasions hard enough to make her cry. She received a lecture from Papa who rightly pointed out that things are bad enough for us at the hands of our captors without us falling out with each other. I think the captivity is getting to her. Papa suggested that she join him in the usual sawing and chopping of wood. Happily, it seems to have relieved some of her tension. But I think that also has other causes. The other day I went outside and found her at the chopping block. But the axe was on the floor and she was holding her hands to her face and crying.

"What is it?"

"It's too much. I can't face it. I just can't!"

"It's only a small block of wood."

She cuffed me in frustration. "You mean your head, I suppose? No, I mean the situation. It will all be over soon. Just as Father Grigory said. We will die. It will be horrible and painful. I can't face it."

She broke down in uncontrollable sobs. I had never seen my beautiful sister in this much pain. She was usually the strong one. I held her. She pushed me away. "No! You'll leave me."

"Nonsense."

"You will," she said fiercely. "I must get used to it. But I can't. Don't you see, Tatiana, without you I may as well be dead. My heart won't survive without you. The loneliness. It will kill me, even with the others to comfort me."

I tried to approach her, but she backed away. For a moment, her eyes had an insane look that was positively scary.

"Help me… I feel like I'm dying inside."

She fell to her knees, clutching herself, her eyes closed tightly and her mouth open in a silent scream as she rocked herself back and forth like a sickly pendulum. This was now truly scaring me. I was always the one to lose control. To see her in this much distress was worse than awful.

I knelt beside her. "Darling, you always told me that, if the time came and a sacrifice was needed, we would die together. Or not at all. I am with you in that. All the way."

She looked at me with a strange, faraway look. "But you see, you aren't. Even if you don't yet know it, I do. When the moment comes, you won't choose me. You'll choose yourself. I have seen the future. You aren't there with us."

"But you were always so strong in your acceptance. Even at Stavka that time. You told me you were resigned and prepared."

"I still feel that way. But I hadn't really thought I would lose you. The reality of your leaving had never really struck me until now. When the time comes, my love," she said, stroking my face, "you will not be there. I know you have sensed it, even if you haven't told me directly, there have been times when I have seen your own vision. You, alone, walking by a river in sunshine, walking slowly with a stick." She saw my look. "Yes, Tanya. I have seen it, too."

For a moment, fear overwhelmed us both and we clung tightly to each other, realising the implications of what we had both seen.

I tried in vain to be cheerful. "You also know what Father Grigory told us about prophecy. Remember, a vision only holds true if the people within it don't change their minds about the outcome."

"But I fear the current situation may have gone beyond our small ability to influence things. I shall pray hard to commit my body, my soul and my destiny into God's hands."

The look of resignation on her face was depressing. I reacted with too much air. "Destiny in God's hands? Try taking it out of His hands and putting it into your own. Cheer up. There may be much we can do yet."

Olga gave me a look. "If I didn't know you better I'd say that was a stupid and superficial remark and totally unrealistic."

I made it worse. "Well, I don't like reality. I prefer fairy tales."

Recovering her self-possession at last, Olga picked up the axe and carefully selected a small log to chop.

Not looking at me, Olga said, "Not all fairy tales have happy endings."

And then recited two lines from an English nursery rhyme Mama had once taught us. Observe her timing:

"Here comes a candle to light you to bed…"

Swinging the axe.

"Here comes a chopper to chop off your head." (BANG-CHOP).

I had no way of countering her pessimistic sarcasm and I had the feeling that anything I said to cheer her up would simply make matters worse. I went indoors, feeling for the first time since our house arrest that perhaps all would not end well after all. [5]

Tatiana's Diary - 17th May 1918 – Ekaterinburg
It may be spring outside, but we cannot see any evidence of it in this bleak and desolate house where we are now prisoners. Ever since we arrived we have been treated with nothing but harshness and cruelty, trying our collective patience to near breaking point. I'm sure Mama's health will not stand this kind of

humiliation for much longer in spite of the stoic front she puts on to hide her feelings. For myself, I am continually surprised and appalled by the crudity and lasciviousness of the people around us. We have a guard on the outer gate, who drinks so much I'm sure his breath will stink across the city, and a guard on the inner gate who is so tense that you feel a light breath of wind will snap him in half. I'm sure he lives completely on his nerves, which, by now, seem to be nearly shot. In the house, we have guards on every floor. We are not allowed to close our doors for privacy. Olga is getting near to boiling point. I know this, but we haven't spoken in a while, for reasons I'm about to relate.

Last week, one of the guards, a nice young man called Ivan, was abruptly replaced by the taut, nervous young man I mentioned. Ivan had been paying a lot of attention to Marie. We all thought it was just amusing fun, but after a while, Olga and I and Papa realised he was serious. What was even more alarming was that she was allowing the attentions and even appeared to be encouraging them. I had a word with Papa about it.

"I wouldn't be that concerned, my child, and, even if there is a mild flirtation, it might do us all some good to have one of the people guarding us on our side should anything be necessary."

"What do you mean?"

"Let me just say that he has brought word that there are some of our friends who do not want to see us imprisoned here for much longer. I believe an attempt will soon be made to rescue us."

He put his arm around me to stifle my expression of shock and to ensure no-one paid attention to us.

"Ivan is a member of the old Imperial Regiment the 8th Ulans. You were Colonel in Chief, remember. Well, it looks as though one of them has contacted British agents and has learned that Cousin George is sending a rescue party after all. Your mother and the rest of us are going to begin to make preparations from tonight."

Fancy my old regiment coming through for us like that, I thought. It brought a glow to my heart that I hadn't expected.

"Marie has always wanted an ordinary life. If we get out of this, and she wants to marry one of my officers, I shan't stand in her way. You girls have been denied that happiness your mother and I have shared for too long."

He gave me a significant look. "Anything that helps our cause at the moment and buys us a little time will be helpful, so let her continue with the flirtation, if she chooses."

At night, and to my shock, the situation changed radically and in a way I never expected. Ivan came to our room while we were all undressing. Instinctively, we all covered ourselves up, except for Masha, who proceeded to slowly open her gown and reveal herself to him in all her beauty. We could not move. She walked over to him, rose slightly on her toes and kissed him fully on his mouth. He in turn picked her up and carried her across the hall to the unoccupied room opposite. It was obvious that he intended to make love to her; equally obvious that she was going to let him. I moved to stop her.

Olga crossed my path. "Let her go, Tanya. It is the only happiness she will know. Let her join with God this once in her life. There is only the tomb facing her now. Let her know joy. Then death will be easier to bear for her."

I could feel her own frustration welling up powerfully inside her. Dare I tell her about the imminent rescue attempt? Would it ease her feelings or make them worse? I, too, felt frustrated, and vented my anger on her.

"I don't believe that. How can you be so stupid, so pessimistic, so accepting! Have you no spine? Do you want to just roll over and die? I hate this fate rubbish we are always being fed and I hate your acceptance of it. You are weak! Feeble minded! Use your brain Olga, if you have one! There might be a way out of this for all of us. Try thinking about that instead of succumbing to this idiocy about Job that Papa keeps spouting. In fact, I wouldn't be surprised if that thought is drawing death closer to us! I wish I could escape. I've been a victim of all this clairvoyant nonsense ever since we got involved with that stupid shaman who claimed he could cure Alexei. Well, he couldn't. He was a con-man. Alexei's disease was an accident. Mama wasn't responsible, no-one was. And you all fell for it. Well I refuse to be anyone's clockwork doll. I'm going to survive, even if you've given up. Why don't you all just go and lie down and die, then you'll be very happy, you sad, brainless fools. And you, Olga, are the worst and stupidest of all. How could I ever have thought I loved you? I must have been barking mad!"

This speech came out much more vehemently than I ever intended. I knew the pain it would cause and yet I still went ahead and did it deliberately, mortally wounding the person I loved most in the whole world. I realised much later that this confrontation only increased Olga's gloom and feelings of fatalism. She finally felt that she had lost my love and me. While that would never be true, I had done a frightening amount of damage with my words and, where we would in the past have comforted each other in the circumstances and given each other mutual consolation, now, she simply gave me the coldest look I have ever seen. It chilled me. The last thing I remember about it was Olga slowly walking through the open door and the supreme irony of the sounds of our sister's lovemaking very audible through the closed door opposite. I sat down on one of the small wooden beds in the room and cried my heart out with only a shocked Anastasia and my faithful Ortino for company.

18th May 1918 – Ekaterinburg
Masha came in from a walk round the garden in floods of tears. The guards have been taunting her. It seems that young Ivan, who was abruptly replaced last week, has been tried and shot for "getting too close to the family of the crowned executioner Nicholas". All I could do was to put my arms around her as she

sobbed. Papa was wonderful and sympathetic. He came and knelt next to us and held her hand tenderly. It was obvious that she had loved Ivan. And now the man she willingly gave all of herself to is dead. What to do? Or say? Eventually we laid Masha down on her bed and covered her over. She was inconsolable and eventually cried herself to sleep. Olga had retreated inside herself and was unreachable. She never even raised her head or offered one word of comfort. Anastasia was down the hallway with Mama. Papa and I went for a walk.

"I wonder if they know?" he said.

"Apart from that one change of guard last week, there have been no indications of anything, so, I don't think so. Unless I see something else more serious, I shall assume that whatever young Ivan knew he took with him to his grave."

"I pray God you are right," said Papa, "but I fear the worst."

I said nothing this time.

"Poor Marie. I feel for her. But she is young. Maybe..."

He drifted into silence. I didn't know why until I looked in the direction he was looking. It illuminated further the reason why Masha had been crying. On the whitewashed wall of the guard hut in the garden were two pictures, one of Masha, the other of Ivan. They were horribly explicit, and contained a fantasy of what some people would have liked to do to them, Ivan dead on the ground, with his genitals cut off, and, next to him, Masha hanging from an improvised gallows. Poor Ivan, of course, was already dead. The words on the wall were horrible and sinister. They were written in colloquial Russian, but the meaning was unmistakable:

"First the traitor. Then the whore."

This was too much. Papa was usually such a gentleman. I had only ever seen him really angry once before.

"What is the meaning of this? Get out here now and face me, you drunken cowards!"

Evidently shocked at my father's outburst, the gate guard

stumbled out of the hut. He was so shocked that he even saluted. I hadn't seen a soldier do that in months. We both stood our ground.

"This is a grotesque and disgusting insult to my daughter! I want whoever is responsible court-martialled and replaced!"

"I... I..." stuttered the guard.

"And what is more," continued Papa, "If I catch the man responsible for this, I don't care much what you do to me after-wards but I will personally kill him with my bare hands if it is the last thing I do. And you may quote me. Verbatim!"

Entry added 11th February 1919

With that, Papa turned on his heels and walked briskly, but in control, back to the house. Somehow, in that confrontation he got the better of the guard and reasserted his dignity and that of the rest of us. From that day until the day they were replaced by Yurovsky's group, they treated us with a respect that bordered on deference. I did not realise how serious this would later prove to be for us all until it was far too late and by then, any control of the situation was way beyond my or even God's control.

13th June 1918 – 3.00pm

Our guards, with whom we have become fairly well acquainted, were replaced today by a new group. Accompanying them was a horrible man named Yurovsky. He is apparently a doctor, but he has a very creepy feeling about him. It is exacting, fussy and brutal. I can tell he is utterly without feeling. In that vein, the new men, who are a mixture of Caucasians and Letts, are just the same. You cannot talk to them. All you get is swearing or monosyllabic replies. There are apparently some more senior officers to come in the next few days. Hopefully they will control this mob a little better. At the moment I have a nasty feeling that these men will try and have their way with us if they are not soon under some sort of disciplined control.

3.50pm

All doors have now been removed, even the toilet doors. Now we are not to be allowed any privacy, even to relieve ourselves, which we must do with the guards watching. The humiliations just keep on getting worse!

15th June 1918 - 10.35pm

Entry by Grand Duchess Olga

We have enough crosses to bear in our lives and I pray that the Holy Mother will give us the strength to endure to the end, but I am writing this in my beloved Tanya's diary because the event that has just happened must be recorded. Tanya is too distraught. She is curled up on the bed near this desk, sobbing her heart out. If I did not have the mental ability I do to cut off, albeit briefly, I would join her in her sorrow. Soon, I shall go and comfort her, but you must know this.

Perhaps the greatest sorrow that a person can endure is the death of a beloved companion. When it is a natural death the sorrow is great enough. But when that death is a senseless murder, inflicted out of callousness and without feeling, the pain is infinite, the horror everlasting. Ortino, my sister's lovely, if somewhat eccentric French bulldog, was killed earlier this evening. To be blunt, he was kicked to death by one of our guards, a boorish, slovenly drunk called Boris. He did not die at once. It took time. The incident blew up out of nowhere, as these things often do. My sister and I had been walking in the back yard. Ortino accompanied us, but I thought he was having trouble keeping up.

"He's getting fat you know. You feed him too much."

"How can I? We are all but starving now."

"Yes, but you are going thin because you feed him your own food. So he gets fat and you lose weight. You're much too slim now."

"But he loves his food. I can't refuse that sweet little face, can I?"

Tatiana got down to stroke Ortino's head. He responded, jumping up on his little paws and licking her face. We had not noticed Boris behind us.

"Move along *'ladies'*." He swiped towards us with his rifle butt. Being drunk his aim was off and he hit Tanya on her leg by accident. She yelped in surprise. Ortino thought his mistress was being attacked and bit Boris on the ankle. He responded with a kicking attack of such fury that I swear it was inspired by demons. Tanya and I tried and tried to stop him, but his strength was almost superhuman.

Eventually the rage subsided and he walked off, muttering obscenities under his breath. Tanya and I were covered in mud. Father, Masha and Nastya had come running out to see what the commotion was. Behind them stood a few of the guards. Nonplussed. Not knowing what to do. They knew very well that they were witnessing a tragedy. Ortino was lying very still in the churned mud. He moved his front paw very feebly. Tanya picked him up and cradled him in her arms. She began singing an old Russian lullaby to him. It was slow and soothing. Tears were streaming down her face, making track marks in the mud stains. The little bundle whimpered. As Tanya carried on singing, I saw the light go out of him. Kneeling with her, I took her face in my hands and told her as gently as I could that he had died. At that moment she let out a scream of pain that was so loud and inhuman in its ferocity that I think it frightened everyone present, even us. Ortino has left us. And I think Tanya's light has gone out too. The end is coming. I pray for death now. Only its sweet embrace and the bliss of oblivion will be sufficient to soothe the agony that is tearing apart our Souls...

19th June 1918 – 1.40am
Sitting by the fire in our sitting room. The guards are snoring, or out cold drunk, so they have not seen me. In the grate burns the

last remnant of Father Grigory that I have left. The diary of his letters and sayings that I've kept ever since I first knew him. It all seems so useless now. The final straw came this afternoon. I went to Ortino's little grave to put on a small memorial, only to find one of the louts kicking over the cross I'd placed there and trying to obliterate the traces. I felt like killing him, except I no longer have the strength. Olga took me back inside and I was sick. Afterwards sat alone, trying to find any crumb of comfort in my little memoir of Father Grigory. All the letters and telegrams that I faithfully copied seemed like so much worthless and dead air. I am no longer living on the green earth he so loved, but a sickening parody, ruled by hideous demons masquerading as people. If this is the new world, then I pray I shall die before I live to see them destroy it and everybody unfortunate enough to share what will be left of the world with them. [6]

30th June 1918 – 2.45am

I'm going to have to be quick about this. Either today (June 30th) or tomorrow (July 1st), there is scheduled to be a rescue attempt made for us on behalf of Papa's cousin, King George V. Funny, I thought originally in 1917 that I would be going to live in England. Now I see that that was true after all. One of our new officers is in fact a British agent, based at the Consulate here. He "replaced" the original officer. I didn't ask how. The rescue is posing some very difficult decisions however. The White Russian army is approaching Ekaterinburg. We are told that one of the regiments is under the command of Uncle Mischa. *(Grand Duke Michael, the Tsar's brother - Author.)* Papa's thought has been to get the four of us girls out and then for Mama, Papa and Alexei to await rescue by the White Army, who are only a few days away at most. This is very risky. I am worried that they may kill the others if we leave. Papa, however, made the point that if we stay together and things go wrong, then we will all certainly die. At least this way, there is a chance that some of us may live. The plan is for the agent, Michael, to get Olga and I out and then for a colleague to get Marie and Anastasia out. It will not be very difficult to convince the others that we are being taken off for "sexual" reasons. After all, look what happened to Marie with Ivan. The men will mutter about officers' "privileges", but it should not go much further than that if we're lucky. Papa and I are going to tell the others discreetly and then await further instructions. I will write more when I can.

2nd July 1918 2.00pm (entry written in on 12th January 1924)
I don't know what to write here or how. My soul still feels numb. There was almost a blanket refusal by the whole family to participate in the rescue. Alexei was to stay with Mama and Papa anyway. Marie also opted to do that. Their reasoning was the presence nearby of the White Army and Uncle Mischa. I felt that was too risky. Papa backed me up and urged Masha to reconsider. She did not and stayed with them. The biggest disappointment was Olga. She flatly refused to even consider going without everyone else. Later, I engaged her on her decision. She wouldn't even talk to me about it and said that the matter was closed. I pressed her, perhaps unwisely.

"You don't believe you will get out alive. You are just waiting for death, aren't you?"

There was a stony silence. Eventually her expression softened and she looked into my eyes kindly. "Do you remember a conversation we had, years ago on the Standart? Anastasia had just taken our picture and there was some irritation at the manner of it?"

I laughed, recalling the incident. The first laugh for a while, and almost the last...

"I told you then that you would leave me. That time has come. Tanya, we are one, remember. You know my heart, as I know yours. Fate has cast its hand. You must leave. I must stay."

The pressure had been building up in my head all through

her talking. I could stand it no more. I got hold of Olga by her shoulders and shook her. I was crying almost uncontrollably. "Please, please come. I'll die without you. You know this. I'll die... I'll die..."

She smiled at me compassionately. At that moment, I saw the same look that had been in her eyes at Krasnoe Selo in 1912 when we were about to go on parade. She was seeing something that I either could not see, or, I have to admit, more likely would not see. To this day (1924) I still wonder what it was she saw with her vision.

Her reply destroyed me. "Tanya, you won't die. Even if I do. Even if the others all do. You will survive. It's what you do. What you've always done. You always want to win. Even if the cost is appallingly high. You have to learn that sometimes what appears as loss is actually a victory. There is much more at stake here than just our lives or the throne of Russia. Our ancestor was right. What happens here will affect the world for decades to come, possibly centuries. We are no longer alive, my love. I can feel it already. When I sleep, I know I have already gone from the Earth. So my physical death no longer matters. But I promise you this. Wherever you go, I will always be with you. I shall never leave you as long as my soul exists. I shall wait for you wherever I am and when you are finished with your path, you will come to me and all shall be as it was. Now go. You must. And do not mourn for me. This is God's will."

Through floods of tears, I said, "Then I *hate* God. I *curse* the god you worship that would do this to us. God's will is *stupid*."

She was so gentle. She held me to her one long last time and I was reminded of the times when we were young and all of this was a universe away.

"One day, when you return to me, you will understand what is to happen here and you will understand that God's will is right and beautiful. But you are so afraid."

She fixed me with the most intense stare I would ever see – in any lifetime. *"Always remember that I love you."*

I pulled away from her embrace and walked away, convulsed with sobs. That was the last time we ever touched one another.

2nd July 1918 - 4.15pm (entry completed 13th January 1924)
In the bleakness of my despair, suddenly a light shone.

"Can I come, Tanya?"

Anastasia was stood in the doorway to our room, a quizzical look on her face, as if she was afraid to approach me.

"What does Papa say?"

"He said it was up to you. He wants me to go if I can. I'm sure they'll all be rescued too by Uncle Mischa, but it'll be an adventure, won't it?"

She was bouncing up and down on the balls of her feet. Darkly, I remembered our lessons with Ceccetti, and, for a fleeting moment, remembered my surprise on witnessing my apparently awkward younger sister doing the most beautiful bouree en Pointe, bending low to the floor, brushing it with the tips of her lovely fingers as she did so. Our eyes had locked then, in an eternal moment, as they were doing now. I saw the woman she was becoming, and fell in love with her. Then, without warning, the spell broke, and there she was, gawky and awkward, fidgety and with feet that were somehow not quite right. With difficulty, I focussed.

"An adventure? Maybe. But it'll also be very dangerous. If they work out what's happened, all our lives will probably be in danger. If we make it, then this group will probably cut their losses and ransom Papa and everyone else to the Whites. But while we are escaping, we will all be in danger. Are you prepared for that?"

Anastasia paused. I saw the indecision flash across her face like a cloud passing over the sun. For myself, I no longer cared either way if I lived or died. A dark stubbornness was beginning to take hold of me. It was a spiritual virus that has gradually taken me over until now, in spite of the affable surface, there is not much left other than that. That and fear. And scepticism. And a complete unwillingness to engage with life. It all seems so hollow and useless. She replied, a little too airily, "I'll take the risk if you will..."

Followed by that silly, impish smile of hers. In spite of myself, I found myself smiling back at her.

"Then be ready. The agent could come at any time. We'll go together, as if he's taking us back to his billet." I saw her face. She was about to make a joke. I cut her off, brutally, saying, "Don't bother with jokes. This is neither the time nor the place. Just be ready. When I come, there won't be any time for sentimental goodbyes, so get them said now and then be ready. I'll come for you when it's time. Now get out of my sight."

In retrospect, my ill-tempered and over-aggressive response to her attempt at humour was very poorly judged and, in light of what happened later was both sad and tragic. It was no way to end our relationship, which had been filled with joy, humour and gentleness. It left a scar on my soul that was my own fault and one that has not yet healed. When you read what happened below, I think you will see why I feel it never will.

3rd July 1918 - 6.15pm (entry completed 25th May 1925)
Poor Anastasia! I warned her of the dangers, but she still came, thinking it was some silly adventure. That it was not play became rapidly obvious. Michael, the British agent, came for us at change of shift. I wrapped myself up in my travelling coat and went to get Nastya, who was playing with Masha and Alexei. I had coached her in what to do. As the guard watched, Michael kissed first Nastya then I on our lips and felt my breasts quite obviously. Then, taking our arms, and amidst muttered remarks about "damned officers" having all the luck and hearing one say, "Give 'em one for me, eh?" we strolled quite easily out of the gate and turned right towards the outskirts of the town. As we turned out

of the gate, an aircraft flew low over our house, and suddenly dipped, coming to land somewhere ahead. We had been going for no more than a minute or two, trying to look as nonchalant as possible, when there was a shout behind us to stop and a bullet was fired that whizzed over our heads and struck a telegraph pole, sending splinters in all directions. Nastya, who had been enjoying the fun, pulled Michael violently to the left in her fright and one of the splinters struck her in the calf.

"Run!" yelled Michael. "The plane's waiting about five hundred yards in that direction." He pointed up the road directly ahead. I hadn't realised the aircraft I had heard was our rescue craft until now. It galvanised us into action.

We began to run. The shouts behind us were getting more numerous by the second. Suddenly, shots were ringing out all around us. The noise was deafening. Michael was trying to defend us but he only had one pistol and he quickly ran out of ammunition. Eventually, ahead, I saw the plane. Its engines were on and it was beginning to move. A grenade must have been thrown, for there was a huge explosion behind us. I was unhurt, but I heard Nastya scream and she fell. Michael was running ahead. I turned back. I was going to pick her up and carry her.

"Don't be a fool! There's no time. If we don't keep going, none of us will get out of here alive! The rest of you'll be next. Leave her. They'll take her back to the house. She's worth more alive than dead, especially if you get out."

I hesitated.

"Leave her, or everyone dies!"

Nastya was in agony on the floor from the shrapnel wounds to her legs. In that moment, I would have gladly traded places with her. I took her hand, and for a moment, we were a world away. She pressed something into my hand. I kissed her and then Michael pulled me away and we ran for the plane as fast as we could. I did not realise at the time, but the explosion had also injured me. I had a shrapnel wound to my hip. But the real

153

disaster came when a second grenade exploded right next to me. In the moment of the explosion, I half turned my back. The shrapnel tore into me. I screamed in pain and the world went a funny colour of red as I hit the ground. The last thing I remember is a feeling of flying through the air and hitting something metallic very hard, while bullets whizzed over me, it seemed, in every direction. Then the world went black and, for a while everything became hallucinatory and confusing. I never saw Anastasia alive again. And when I had sufficiently recovered to be shown what she had pressed into my hand, I burst into tears and didn't stop crying for almost half a day. She had given me her small teddy, Oscar, which she had been given as a present when she was born and had been carrying with her for luck. The gift was symbolic. I felt it. In the moment she gave it to me, she must have known that she would die...

Leon Trotsky - 3rd July 1918 - 10.00pm – Moscow

Leon Trotsky - 3rd July 1918 - 10.00pm – Moscow
Consternation reigned at Checka Headquarters.

"*Two* of the Imperial daughters escaped! How? With whom?"

"I don't know, sir. All I can tell you is that one of them has been recaptured. We think, the youngest one, Anastasia."

"But not by us?"

"No, sir. There are a lot of renegade groups around the Ekaterinburg area. We think it's possibly an anarchist group, who intend to hold her for ransom from the Whites, who may have her."

"They'll be waiting a long time, then. The Whites want a return to the Romanovs as little as we do. And besides, how will they know whether they really have a Romanov? Put out some more stories about the family. Let people think as many different versions of the truth as they want. What happened to the other daughter? Does anyone know?"

"As far as we can tell she was badly injured. Our units saw her being thrown into an aircraft, which took off from Ekaterinburg and headed east. They came under heavy fire. It's not known if they have crashed or not. Our people are searching the area now. No sign yet."

"Do we know who?"

"We think British Intelligence, but sources within MI2(c) are denying any knowledge of it. This could be an unsanctioned operation..."

"Or one sanctioned so high up it's out of sight of the usual people. Have our forces keep watch on every exit from this country. It will be difficult to hide her in the state she is in now. I want her alive. The other one too. Have Ekaterinburg searched. House by house if necessary. The whole family must be saved for a trial. Then we'll publicly hang the lot of them in Palace Square. The world must see the line we draw, and their bodies, or we'll never be legitimate. Understand, I want *both* girls recovered."

"Yes sir, but, with all due respect, about Ekaterinburg. It's a mess. They may not listen to us...follow their own agenda...especially with the White Army closing in..."

Trotsky sighed, and put his hand gently on his subordinate's shoulder. "Send the message to our forces. Then we've done what we can. The rest is for the Fates to decide."

Leon Trotsky left Checka HQ and headed for the Kremlin. He was a very troubled man. Without a public display, the world would never recognise the new regime. Damn Kerensky and his high-mindedness. A simple trial and execution would have done the job months ago. But keeping the family out of reach had almost cheated him of his prize. He had so looked forward to the oratory. The shocked face of the Emperor. The weeping daughters. The pathetic pleas for life. He felt irritated. Now it was all slipping away from him. Things had been going so well. Now what? He felt sure that Vladimir Ilyitch would want rid of the problem. But how to do it? The lines of communication were shaky. It was difficult to be sure if your orders were being carried out. He grimaced to himself. When you began a regime with lies, you must expect the same from others around you. How was anyone to know now what was the truth and what was not? And then there was the White Army, moving closer to Ekaterinburg with each passing day. They would use Nicholas and his family as pawns in their own jaded games, too.

Suddenly and, quite against his own better judgement, he felt sorry for the Tsar. There really was no way out for any of them. As for the girl who got away, perhaps, he thought, it would be better for her if her plane did crash. She would have to be considered dead anyway. Being seen in public again would certainly result in death. He caught himself as the full panorama began to unfold in front of him and he saw Russia from above as if it was being eaten alive by angels. But these were no heavenly creatures with wings, but horrible, twisted dark creatures with piercing yellow eyes. Their course was relentless. Their intent obvious.

"What have we done?" he thought.

In the distance he saw a small light, as if it were a candle light in the darkness and for half a second he swore he could see a small boy in a military uniform, and a spaniel. The boy was laughing and the spaniel's name was Joy, though how he suddenly knew this he was unsure. Equally strange was the sight of the figure with them, a tall, impressive looking man with a long beard dressed in the black of a priest and carrying a triple cross on a long pole. He saw them both laughing for a moment in the dim light of the late evening and then they were gone, leaving him feeling very uncomfortable. This meeting would be the most difficult of his life and, although he did not yet know it, his one chance for power, as leader of the world's largest country had slipped away as completely as had Tatiana into the mists of lie, counter lie and utter conjecture.

Grand Duchess Olga – Ekaterinburg - 4th July 1918 – 1.15am
It was a rare moment. Olga was alone and the house was quiet,

save for the distant snoring of some of the house guards. Quietly, she began to play a passage from Rachmaninov's Etude Tableau op.33 No.3 in C minor. It had been a favourite of hers and Tatiana's. It made such a change from the crude revolutionary songs the guards had made her play earlier in the day. As she played, the darkened colours of the walls were replaced by the richer hues of their room back in St Petersburg. As if by magic, there by her side was her love and best friend, looking fondly on and awaiting a signal to turn a page. Although there was no-one to see, a single tear began to fall slowly from Olga's left eye. As the main theme appeared, in spite of herself and all her efforts, her body began to erupt with sobs. A sorrow only ever briefly given full reign slowly rose from within the depths of her heart until she could bear the pain no more. Along with the pain came rage. A rage she had tried, all her life it seemed, and with very few lapses, to contain. All her restrictions and the demands of duty came flooding in on her with the force of a tidal wave along with the fear and doubt of the last few weeks. She had had many experiences in her life, some of them intensely mystical, but the months of captivity had taken their toll on even her profound faith. Tatiana was now no more to her than a ghost and yet, in that moment of her greatest sorrow, Olga became aware that that fact no longer mattered. Her tears were washing away from the bleak shoreline of her mind all the debris accumulated during their prolonged imprisonment. And along with the sludge, the fog that had lately invaded her brain also began to clear. Peace overwhelmed her, covering her body and soul with a comforting protective blanket...

Out of the corner of her eye, she caught sight of little Ortino. He looked as alive and friendly as ever. Abruptly she ceased playing and swivelled around in her seat. In the doorway of the room stood Boris, the slovenly lout. She would never forget what he had done. She could still feel Tatiana's tears wet through her dress and see and feel to the depths of her broken heart. Boris was drunk. He lolled in the doorway and made a lewd remark about Olga's breasts.

"Do you want to see?" Olga let her hands slip casually over her form, caressing herself, showing her shape and smiling gently at the young man. As he looked on, seemingly almost hypnotised by her beauty, she began to unbutton her dress, slowly revealing her firm, uplifted young flesh. She leaned forward seductively, her cleavage inviting a touch...

The heat in the darkened room was almost unbearable. Olga rose slowly from her seat and walked towards Boris. When she was close, she knelt in front of him and looked straight into his eyes.

"Kill me."

"What?"

Olga's voice seemed to stroke him like cool satin against his skin. "Take out your revolver, put it to my head, and pull the trigger."

Stupified, Boris reached for his pistol. He pulled it from its holster and pointed it at Olga. Looking up at him and keeping her eyes locked on his, she took hold of his hand gently with both of hers and directed the weapon to her left temple, then dropped her hands, and placed them on her knees. She closed her eyes and waited. Boris could see the line of Olga's neck as it swept down from her upturned chin in an elegant curve to her shoulders and on to her breasts. He so wanted just to touch her...but to *kill* her, as she had *asked* him to...? In the heat and semi-darkness of the room, neither realised that they were holding their breath.

An eternity passed.

Silence.

A few moments later, Olga opened her eyes to see Boris slumped in the corner of the room, his unused pistol on the floor. His body was shaking and he was silently crying. Olga gave him an unreadable look, slowly buttoned the front of her dress, rose from her knees and walked quietly to the room she had shared with her sisters.

2.35 am

Olga felt a hand shake her awake. She stretched and looked to her right, sleepily opening her eyes. Marie was kneeling by the side of Olga's bed, looking at her as she lay there, a smile on her face.

"Is it time?"

"Yes."

There were tears in her eyes. Olga leaned forward and kissed each one away for her sister, finally, tenderly kissing her on her lips. Behind Marie, a guard had taken hold of her arms and was tying the girl's hands behind her back. Boris was standing behind him, waiting, a tense expression on his face.

Olga got quickly out of bed and stood in front of him. Her expression was one he would remember for the rest of his life. Complete and total serenity. She put her hands behind her and allowed him to turn her around and tie her wrists together.

Around them chaos reigned. Soldiers were clearing all their possessions away, throwing things into boxes at random, while below, she could hear the commander shouting orders frantically. Olga watched calmly. The threads of their lives were finally snapping. What she had never told her beloved Tanya was that this was how her childhood vision had ended. Her leaving would be the direct cause of the family's death. Distantly, she was aware of three shots ringing out into the darkness. Papa, Mama and Alexei. She smiled. They had found peace. Soon, she and Masha would find theirs. One final sacrifice and it would all be over.

Masha had been pulled up off her knees and the two girls stood together, still visions of beauty in their now rough, worn, nightdresses. Olga smiled at her younger sister. She was just nineteen, Olga twenty-three. Time enough. One guard took each girl and they were led through the melee down the dark back staircase, round a corner and out into the garden. Their bare feet felt the earth, hardened by summer heat, the ground still warm, vibrant with life. They reached the large triangular pergola. The guards detached from them, each one throwing a long rope they had been carrying over the cross beams. One rope for each girl. Two soldiers stood on each rope, while a third noosed them. A small crowd of soldiers had gathered to watch the final act of the House of Romanov. Out of them came their commander, flustered, angry. Walking up to Olga, he looked her straight in her eyes.

"Do you have anything to say?"

Olga stood quietly, the noose around her neck, looking back at him. He remembered later how kind her eyes were in that moment. Unknown to him, she had caught sight of a priest, standing in the shadows of the doorway to the house they had just left. Their eyes met. For a moment he looked shamefaced, but then recovered his poise and stepped forward to give the girls his blessing. Suddenly, almost in unison, Olga and Marie began to sing. An Orthodox Kontakion to the Mother of God. Their voices rose in harmony, like nightingales soaring into the clear summer night. There was a pause as the girls continued to sing, as if their passion was bringing peace to the war-torn earth. Silence reigned around them.

Abruptly, breaking the strange spell the music was weaving, the commander turned away from Olga and gave a sharp signal to the two guards on her rope. They pulled her quickly and efficiently into the air. Marie's two soldiers hanged her simultaneously and the two girls' voices were reduced to a horrible gagging rasp. Then the men tied the ropes off and stepped back to watch.

Through the intense pressure pushing behind her cheeks and eyes, as she turned on her rope, Olga was inwardly aware of the quiet sound of drums, and of a distant, but tangible feeling of beauty that began deep within her and spread rapidly throughout her body. Her last sight as her vision faded to black was that of the Commander of the execution squad, talking earnestly and urgently to the priest who had blessed them. She was not surprised, but felt comfort, peace and not a little euphoria.

As the assembled company watched, the two beautiful female firebirds accomplished their slow, coordinated and elegant dance of death. Some twenty minutes later, as the shuddering of their bodies ceased and as the firebirds were finally annihilated, their souls let forth a cry that echoes down to the present day...and onward into eternity...*the sacrifice has been made...*[7]

Dr Nicholas Clarke – A Revised History of the Russian Revolution – pages 445-446

...following the few shots heard on that night and with the apparent murder of the Tsar and his entire family the new regime's attempts at grandiose self-justification through propaganda really began. The self-important rhetorical ideological posturing that was typical of the Communist Party machine began here in vain attempts to legitimise itself and build up a picture of the planned execution of a cowardly Royal family by heroic red guard units. However, the stories filtering out of Ekaterinburg became ever more lurid and shocking in their content. One interesting story involves the apparent showing of five Royal bodies to a startled British Consul in Ekaterinburg, called Thomas Preston on the night of July 17th, but no corroborating evidence to prove that two of the daughters had escaped execution was later forthcoming. Deliberately misleading accounts were being circulated as to the family's fate and whereabouts. It was later agreed at the highest political level that to avoid difficulties with the new government, as well as potential embarrassment to the British Royal Family, it would be made official that all the family had died on that night. Politically, it was expedient to say that there had been no escape. The quasi-

French Revolutionary stance however fooled no-one for long. Every sensible thinking Russian eventually came to see their new masters, once the excitement of a new beginning had worn off, as no better than thugs and mass murderers masquerading as liberators and philosophers.

The die had been irrevocably cast. Communism was declared necessary as an experiment in Human Engineering. This experiment was to cost the lives of tens of millions, oppress an entire race for nearly three quarters of a century and be an indirect cause of the Second World War. Thus began the looking-glass world of the 20th century, as Russia's Silver Age passed into memory and one of Mankind's greatest chances to accelerate its evolution and turn the Silver Age to Gold was lost.

Grand Duchess Tatiana – Eastern Siberia – nearing Vladivostok -6[tth] July 1918 -9.00pm?
I can't think why, but whenever I've been in the worst trouble, I always find myself sitting by a lake looking at blue skies and surrounded by pine forests. A silly recurring theme. What I want to know is, what is Olga doing here? This place is my personal refuge from strife and the "horrors of war". What's even weirder is, she's swimming in my lake. As I look on, oddly tranquil in all this strangeness, she rises out of the lake and walks towards me. The sun glistens and shatters into rainbows refracted through the water droplets on her body. As she touches her skin, I feel the coolness and the sharp liquid sensations as if the water were on my skin and not hers. She smiles. A sunburst of joy and I'm jolted by a burst of electric shocks like multi-coloured flowers bursting in my head. Level with where I sit now, she kneels at my feet and leans forward to kiss me.

With her lips brushing mine, I hear her voice like a silver bell in my head. *"I have come home, my love. Now I can be here forever. Remember this, and my presence in the lakes, forests and mountains, even when you cannot see me. Above all, recall my Soul. Remember, I told you... I shall NEVER leave you."*

Her kiss, like liquid fire, ravages my whole being and I'm jolted awake to flames, smoke and the feel of dried blood caking my mouth. Screams of pain appear not to be coming from me, but from some place in a weird echo chamber far away. There is an acrid smell of burning oil and a man in military uniform, whom I do not recognise, leans over me, his face streaked with mixture of oil, dirt and blood. He is worried, I can tell, but is it about me, or something else? Intolerable loud noises in my head and ringing through me like an earthquake. Wistful, why can't I feel my back any more? Feelings of pointlessness. Sleep. Drowning in smoke and confusion. Curious, I can't even remember who I am... black...

Suddenly...

Tatiana's Diary – Tsarskoe Selo -25th *June 1916 -2.35pm*
Sitting beneath a tree in the Imperial Park, I am visited by a small robin that lands on my discarded shoe and chirps at me. Absurd, this notion of being able to talk to Nature.

"Everything speaks with but one voice."

So much for yet another of Father Grigory's ramblings. I laugh to myself. The robin puts his head on one side and hops neatly onto Ortino's head. He opens one sleepy eye and closes it again. I doze in the mid-afternoon heat haze. When I awake, Olga is lying in my arms. How did she get there, I wonder. I kiss her head and, wondering more, there is the robin, still on Ortino's head, looking at me with one open eye. What is he trying to tell me?

"That all things are together in the Light of God," says a voice in my left ear.

Father Grigory kisses my ear – what impertinence! - and walks past me on his way up to the palace to see Mama and Papa. I hear a soft chuckle. How did he know what I was thinking? Still less what the robin was doing on Ortino's head.

"He must be psychic," said Olga, answering my thoughts and, as usual, mildly sending up my scepticism.

"Stop it you two!"

"This is getting scary."

In the distance now, Father Grigory turned round and said – in my mind's ear and clearly as if he were sat next to me, *"Truth is always scary to those unprepared for its painful surprises."*

Slowly he turned to face the palace, walked towards the small white panelled side entrance he always used when attending Wednesday audiences, and disappeared.

Grand Duchess Tatiana – Imperial Japanese Battlecruiser Kirishima – The Pacific Ocean - 20th July 1918 – 4.30pm

Semi-conscious. Lying on my side. The pain in my back is unbearable. The feeling in my legs seems to come and go at unpredictable intervals. Strange. I don't seem to be here. Most of the time, I find myself sitting on the shoreline of my beloved lake. It is sunny. Overhead, I see sixteen black swans flying into the sun. There is a beautiful melody accompanying this that I can't quite catch... The light from the sun draws me into death along with the swans... but I must go back... a caressing, familiar hand touches my cheek and for a moment I'm home again...

"The fever's still high."

"She's been fighting it for nearly ten days now."

"Remarkable she's still alive."

"If I was her, I'd want to die. She'll have nothing left if she ever recovers..."

"She'll never walk again. Such a shame. She's such a beauty..."

"Who was that nurse with her before?"

"Nurse? Why that would be Lieutenant Ayumi."

"No, this was a woman."

"There are no female nurses on board. We were ordered out here on short notice. Lieutenant Ayumi is temporarily assigned to her until someone from London joins the ship. They're coming on board when we reach Canada."

"This was a young woman. Russian appearance. About her age. She had a Red Cross uniform on, but had an aristocratic manner and spoke perfect English. When I asked where her Doctor was, she told me he had stepped outside. I went after him and when I got back, the woman had gone. I assumed she was with His Highness Prince Arthur's party. Are you sure there are no Red Cross nurses here?"

"None."

Lieutenant Commander Shimoda went to the com link.

"Intruder alert. All personnel, be on the lookout for a possible enemy agent. Young woman. About twenty five years old. Russian appearance, in Red Cross uniform. Apprehend, but do not harm. I want her brought to the Brig and held for questioning."

As the commander left Tatiana's room, he caught the distinct smell of roses; English Tea Roses. It was there for a moment and then vanished as completely as a morning mist in the rays of the rising sun.

A Monastery outside Ekaterinburg, Siberia – 24th July 1918

Sunset. As the monks intoned the Funeral Ikos, five bodies lay, wrapped in simple white sheets, before the altar. The Father Deacon conducting the solemn service kept looking anxiously towards the West Door, as if he were waiting for something, or someone, to interrupt him. Eventually, as he was anointing the bodies with incense, the door opened with a bang and a man in a worn military uniform walked briskly into the church, carrying another body, wrapped in a white shroud.

One of the monks detached himself and went towards him. "Are you sure this is her?"

He grunted. "See for yourself."

The man pulled back the top of the shroud to reveal the face of a young woman. She was no more than 18 years old. Her face was distorted, puffy and blotchy and there was a deep groove around her neck where she had obviously been hanged, but the monk recognised the body immediately as that of Anastasia, Nicholas II's youngest daughter. She had evidently died the same way as her sisters. He felt profoundly that it all had a kind of divine symmetry. He nodded briefly, and the man took her body to lie beside her two older sisters and with those of the rest of her family. The service continued without interruption and the six bodies were buried, quietly, but with dignity as the music they so loved was intoned around them. There they would stay, where prayers would be constantly chanted over their bodies. For as long as the secrecy, demanded of the Church as the price for their continuance, was necessary, and until the soul of Russia was ready to emerge from the long night of suffering into which this act of mass murder had plunged her.

Investigator Ivan Sokolov – Report to the Central Committee of the Communist Party on the captivity of Nicholas II and his family – Page 189, footnote 3

Found written on the back of an orthodox prayer card – written by Grand Duchess Olga during the family's captivity in Tobolsk:

"Papa asks us to remember that the evil which is now in the world will only increase. And that it is not evil that destroys evil, but only love."

INTERLUDE

JULY 25TH & 26TH 1918

Grand Duchess Tatiana – Victoria Island off Vancouver
25th July 1918

The crutches were just too tempting. Swinging her legs off the bed, and with some considerable difficulty, she exerted all of her strength and heaved herself onto them. Her unsteadiness made her wobble precariously, but with the total of her will she righted her posture and stood up straight for almost the first time in a month. With her eyesight beginning to clear, she made her way to the window and looked out on the bleak landscape before her. From her window, there was a view straight down into the bay and the ship at anchor there, flying the Japanese flag proudly from the stern. Tatiana shook her head. Most of the last month had been a terrible blur. People's faces coming and going constantly, looks of concern, interspersed with odd memories of Olga being with her, especially when the pain got so great that she felt she could bear it no longer. She shook her head again. That was impossible. Although there was no one to tell her so, she was convinced Olga and the others were dead. Tears began to flow slowly down her face, but with a mighty effort, she controlled them. What was it Olga had said to her that last time in Ekaterinburg?

"Tanya, you won't die. Even if I do. Even if all the rest of us do. You'll survive. It's what you do. What you've always done..."

Well, she had survived. But at what cost? And for what purpose?

At that moment, there was a knock at the door.

"Come in."

A tall, distinguished gentleman Tatiana hadn't seen before came into her room and stood looking at her intently, smiling. His eyes were kind and gentle. Tatiana took an instant liking to him.

"I'm Arthur Connaught. Cousin to His Majesty King George. We haven't met before. I'm glad to see you up and about. We were very worried about you for a while."

"As you can see, I'm rather hard to kill..." Tatiana smiled. But the smile was weak and the Prince noticed that it did not carry as far as her eyes. He was under strict orders to reveal nothing to Tatiana about her family, and was glad of it. He knew how close they had been. That job was one best left for a later time.

The Prince tried to lighten the mood. "Do you want a walk out? I can accompany you. There's no one around at the moment except my ADC and the Japanese nurse from the Kirishima." He noticed Tatiana looking at the ship. "Magnificent, isn't she?"

Tatiana nodded absently, then turned back to look at the Prince. Her eyes frightened him at that moment. They had oddly changed colour and were of the deepest black. He had the feeling he wasn't looking at Tatiana any more, but someone else, a different person altogether, one much more focussed and powerful. In an instant, she blinked, and her eyes were normal again, that lovely colour of unfocussed light grey.

"Why not? I'd love to feel the air on my face."

Prince Arthur held the door open while the Grand Duchess moved past him. He could feel her determination. He also felt her desire to be alone. So he let her move away down the slope towards the edge of the cliff, keeping his eye on her all the while. He didn't think she would do anything stupid. But it was best to be certain.

His ADC coughed discreetly behind him. "Your Highness, communication from London. The party from Intelligence is due here tomorrow morning. We're to expect a Mrs Amorel Meinertzhagen and a Miss Henrietta Crawford, a Matron from the War Office. They will take Her Imperial Highness across Canada and then on back to England."

The Prince was still watching Tatiana intently. "Very well."

The ADC bowed and left Prince Arthur to his contemplation. On a hunch, he walked over to where Tatiana was sitting, the crutches by her side. He sat beside her. They said nothing. The mid-morning sun warmed them both as they stared out over the bay.

At length, Tatiana turned to him and looked at him, with her head on one side. "Did you know?"

"Know what?"

"That you were coming for me?"

The Prince considered lying, but only for a split second. This girl would see through it at once. He relaxed. Somehow her presence was soothing. He smiled again. Tatiana smiled back.

"Yes. I knew. His Imperial Majesty the Emperor of Japan knew too. Your cousin, His Majesty, and a unit of British Intelligence set up your rescue. You'll meet the wife of one of their senior operatives tomorrow, in fact, a Mrs Meinertzhagen. She and a War Office matron are coming to escort you home."

"Why can't I continue with you?"

"You can't be seen in public yet, I'm afraid." The Prince's countenance turned serious. As Tatiana went to protest, he said, "That comes direct from His Majesty. I suggest you ask him why when you see him. I'm sorry. I really am, but I can't tell you any more."

His expression was pained. Tatiana realised he was restricted, and that he hated it. Gently, he put his hand on hers. The softness of his touch broke Tatiana's resolve. She broke down and buried her head in her hands, sobbing. Ever so gently, the Prince put his arm around Tatiana and cradled her against his shoulder, allowing her, after weeks of semi-consciousness, to finally begin to grieve, releasing her emotions as the Prince stared out to sea, beyond the horizon, and into an unknown future.

Amorel Meinertzhagen and Prince Arthur of Connaught – Victoria Island off Vancouver - 26th July 1918

The Prince shook his head sadly.

"The poor girl is absolutely distraught. I've spent as much time with her as I can, but, even allowing for the time she's spent outside, her spirits are still very low. I don't even want to think about what she'd do if she knew…"

Amorel Meinertzhagen squeezed his arm. "Such a tragedy. It seems certain now that all the rest of them are gone. The last hope was the youngest girl, Anastasia. As you know she was apparently lost during the escape operation, but we've discovered from unimpeachable sources in the last few days that she was recaptured by a separate group in the Ekaterinburg area. It would appear that once they realised the rest of her family was dead and she was no longer of any use, they hanged her along with a local engineer's daughter they were holding for ransom. We've heard rumours that the two girls were cut down by some local villagers after several days and given a Christian burial in the forest outside the city, but of course there's no way to find out for sure, about any of it, at the moment. The area's in complete chaos."

Amorel paused, noticed the look of deep sympathy on Prince Arthur's face, then straightened her back, and adopted a look of steely resolve.

"Don't you worry about Tatiana, Prince. However upset she is, she's a survivor. I could tell that as soon as we met. And she's young, with all her life ahead of her. There's much to fight for yet."

They both looked at Tatiana, who was sitting on the grass overlooking the bay, sketching the ships as they came in and out.

"It was a good idea of yours to get her sketching. Occupy her mind with something else to help get her over the shock. It'll be very therapeutic. I've brought my husband's notes about Canadian birds with me. They should keep her mind focussed. And she can draw any we see on the way."

"The colonel is a bird fancier?"

"Yes, he's forever going off with his binoculars and sketchpad when he's not working. I think he loves the birds more than me."

They laughed.

"How is she. Really?"

"The Japanese doctor who examined her really doesn't think she'll ever walk again. The damage to her back seems too severe. But just look how determined she is. I wouldn't put anything past that young lady. I wish she were mine. I'd happily give her my home in an instant if she needs somewhere to live."

Amorel Meinertzhagen gave him a look.

"You know what His Majesty will say about that. She needs to be somewhere away from the public. At least for now."

"Is everything set for your journey home?"

"Yes. All the cover is in place. We should be in England by the 8th of August. From there, it's up to my husband and his men, and then His Majesty. But I'll look after her the best I can."

Tatiana looked over her shoulder at Amorel, and they smiled at each other. Strange, she thought, it was almost the smile of a ghost.

Prince Arthur of Connaught and Amorel Meinertzhagen went indoors to formally complete Tatiana's handover as the matron passed them by, on her way to collect Tatiana and take her to the waiting car. From there, they would together transfer to Vancouver, and then would come the long train and sea voyage to England, and exile. [8]

Book II

The Isle of the Dead

PART I

RECOVERY AND EXILE

SEPTEMBER 1918 – JUNE 1920

Tatiana's Diary –1st September 1918 – Harrogate Spa

Cousin George's doctors have insisted I come here for treatment. All the shrapnel from the wounds in my back has now been removed (finally – I've had three operations and had to endure much shaking of heads from the assembled surgeons. At one stage last month they didn't think I would walk again, but, ha ha! I have proved them wrong) and here I am, on my feet, or rather, in the water next to "Auntie George". She is my great aunt and also a great eccentric, member of an extended Russian Royal family currently living here. Hiding me with them while I convalesce at her house in Park Place has been one of my cousin's best ideas. The house is lovely, set grandly in its own park and away from prying eyes. Her doctor has been wonderful. Harrogate is a very beautiful town and I'm enjoying being among ordinary people, even if it is painful emotionally.

The new sights are distracting, at least to some extent, but I have a nasty feeling that the family has other plans for me. I do hope this freedom I have here will not be taken away. "Auntie George" is such a wonderful person. She reminds me a little of Mama, but much louder and more flamboyant. I can relax and fade into the background when I'm with her.

This afternoon she buttonholed King Manoel of Portugal. Poor man, I don't think he knew what had hit him. There were journalists around from a local paper and they took the party's photograph. I was warned to stay in the background, out of sight of the photographer, but I just couldn't resist peeping out from behind Lady Radcliffe. I saw the picture later. The caption mentions everyone but me, of course. My face is half concealed and my hat hides the rest, but it's still me, although, I'm definitely thinner than I was in my last official photograph. Maybe I wasn't exaggerating the fading away after all. Perhaps I should. They're all gone, I know they are, in spite of there being, as yet, no confirmed news, at least not that I have been told… what am I to do without them…?

21ˢᵗ September 1918 – Harrogate Spa

Grand Duchess George has founded hospitals here for the war-wounded. I'm only sorry I can't use my skills as a nurse to help, but at the moment I'm supposed to be keeping a low profile. Today, however, I succumbed to temptation, donning the uniform of a "flag-girl" and going out with her daughters Nina and Xenia to raise money for the hospitals. It's the least I can do for all the help I've received. Was only able to do a couple of hours as my back began to ache. When I got home again, Auntie George was furious, as I'd gone out without asking her first. But when she saw me in the flag-girl outfit she creased up with laughter. I have to say it was very funny, and I felt the others would have laughed too. It reminded me of our times collecting money at Livadia in the White Flower Festivals for TB sufferers each spring. My laughter was mixed with tears at the thought. Auntie George and her daughters are so kind though, and I feel for them. Her husband, Grand Duke George, is trapped in Russia too, just like we were and there's been no news of him for a while. They must be awfully worried, but Auntie George never lets on. I admire her stoicism and inner strength very much. It makes me feel secure. After dinner they got out the photo albums and we all talked together long into the night.

King George V - 24ᵗʰ September 1918 – Windsor Castle

"You do realize the seriousness of this, sir?"

King George V looked at Lloyd George, his expression unreadable. "I do. We need to stress that everyone died in that house in Ekaterinburg. This report can't go unanswered. How is the investigation going?"

"The Whites have found a lot of circumstantial evidence, but nothing to suggest that there were any survivors."

"And Preston?"

"Paid off. Besides, I think there will soon be so many rumours floating around that it will rapidly become impossible to tell truth from lies."

The King smiled. "Like looking for a needle in a very large haystack."

"Precisely. And a Russian one, which is worse. Have you seen their fields? There are always so many of them, all identical."

George V laughed. He seemed to relax for the first time in the meeting. Lloyd George became serious. "How is Her Imperial Highness?"

"Recovering. Very well by all accounts. Her back is considerably better and she is walking without crutches. But she needs to be back here soon. Harrogate is far too public. If the plan as we originally conceived it still has any relevance at all, she will need to be hidden away. How long do you think will we need now?"

"Lenin and the Bolsheviks are very unstable. Our people tell me that support is wavering. There's a lot of anger about the treaty they signed last year, and it's growing. I don't think the Russian people will take kindly to so much of their land being just given away, no matter how war weary they were. This will help us. The propaganda is already having an effect. A year. Two if we're unlucky. Can you do it, sir? She will need to be told."

The King gave him a look. It told Lloyd George to keep out of business that was not his own.

"Now that she is in my care, *I* will decide where and when my cousin should be told, first about her family, and secondly, about what we plan for her. That choice and the telling will rest with my wife and myself. Alone. Is that quite understood?"

"Yes, Your Majesty."

"Your job is to make sure that the shattering of her life and that of my cousins was not in vain. Their deaths must have meaning… " He became very quiet and turned away. "Or we are all lost…"

There was a long silence. Lloyd George got up, bowed, and left King George V staring into his fire, alone.

Tatiana's Diary - 16th October 1918 – Balmoral

Early morning. Meeting with King George and Queen Mary. They told me about Mama, Papa and the others. Thomas Preston's report from Ekaterinburg seems irrefutable. I felt too numb to cry. Even knowing what I know inside, the report was still a dreadful shock. They also pointed out that I would not be safe for a while. The new regime is saying we have all been killed and it is apparently politically necessary that we co-operate with these "things" called Bolsheviks, although why that is I can't imagine. The snivelling cowards surrendered half of Russia to Germany in that damned treaty over a year ago! So I have been told I have to stay out of sight until the smoke clears from the war and then I can come out and be seen in public again.

I am to be sent to live on a farm on the estate at Sandringham with Prince John and his governess. I shall be allowed to write my letters to Grandmama. I shall enjoy being in Nature again and away from responsibility. I have begun writing poetry and when I do so I feel closer to Olga and the others. It soothes some of my pain and reminds me that I shall see them again one day. And Prince John is lovely. I remember him from our time here in 1907, so I'm looking forward to meeting him again. Let's see what this future holds.[9]

Tatiana's Diary - 15th November 1918 – Sandringham

Olga's twenty-third birthday. Cried all day. Ran away from everyone into the fields. Lay in the pouring rain and screamed my heart out until I fell asleep. Woke this evening with Lalla by my bedside. Johnny had apparently come out after me on his own. Picked me up and carried me back to the house. Lalla had undressed me and put me to bed. Strange, as I awoke, I swear I saw Masha and Olga behind Lalla in the faded candlelight in the room. They were smiling and holding hands. When I came to properly, they were gone. Illusions created by a desperate mind. I felt no comfort, only more pain and sorrow... Dreamless sleep...

31st December 1918 – Sandringham
New Year's Eve. Shut away here on the farm, I could not even bring myself to celebrate with Johnny, Lalla and the others. Tears at midnight... Dreams of my lake and the trees... Olga's voice in the distance. Unbearable pain and the feel of a hollow joke being perpetrated and the joke being on me. Where is there a revolver when you want one? Oblivion calls like a sunset in my soul... but I will not give up yet. I remember Rome. The battle rages, yet I will win... I will win...

18th January 1919 – Sandringham
Another loss. I'm beginning to get used to this (grimly). Today Johnny died suddenly. None of us expected it. He had been growing so strong and healthy and hadn't had a fit in months. He was out walking in the fields on the estate with Georgie when he suddenly collapsed. In spite of everything we did, saving him was impossible. The fit was just too overwhelming. Afterwards Lalla and I made him comfortable in his bed. He had a smile on his face that looked positively angelic. I will say privately to you that that is what I think he was. I remember getting occasional letters from him when I was still in Russia. While the language was obviously retarded, the "feel" was not. I showed Father Grigory a page once.

He could not read the English, but he said, "That one is closer to God than all of you. Knowledge is not contained in book learning or university, but in the essence of things. Behind that writing, you will find the essence. It is the simple mind that most easily comprehends the Nature of God."

Lalla understood that, as did our friends the farming people who helped out. And the animals all loved him too.

King George and Queen Mary just seemed embarrassed by him. They may be German, but they act so English. So closed-minded. I find it infuriating. Their attitude to their own son is disgusting. Papa and Mama would have been furious. They should have sent him to live with us. Father Grigory would have taken him to Pokrovskoe and his life would have been happy. No wonder he died. The restrictions on him were intolerable. I am beginning to feel it myself. I must have some freedom or get away somewhere. This Royal life is beginning to get on my nerves and the loneliness is crushing. I shall ask to move back up to the main house. Cousin George can stick me in one of the wings on my own. I shall disturb no one and maybe I can work on finding some tranquillity. Alas, that is more than Johnny ever had…

21ˢᵗ January 1919 – Sandringham
Sorrow and rage. Johnny's funeral this morning at Sandringham Church. Lalla, Georgie and I were present along with all our friends. I was in black and had to hide my face behind a black lace veil attached to my hat. I stood at the back of the church, away from everyone, accompanied by an intelligence minder, posing, I suppose, as my husband so as not to attract attention. The service and burial are not like our beautiful Orthodox ceremonies. I would so love to have been able to give him one of those to say goodbye. The English service is simple and direct. A shade too direct actually, not acknowledging the emotions as it should. I said an Orthodox prayer for him in my heart and I believe I felt him near, a sunburst of simple joy in spite of the unseasonable rain. Not a sign of love was visible from his parents. They can't even acknowledge him properly in death. I'm beginning to think the English cannot be trusted, especially not these "English". Part of me wishes the "rescue" had never happened. But maybe I need to be here for some reason. I pray God show me before I lose all the patience and faith I have left.

Left leg painful today. No apparent reason. Went riding in the afternoon to try and forget the suffocating feelings I had at the church and managed to escape my minder for a while. Cousin George was furious. So was Queen Mary. But after their lack of any display of emotion with Johnny I am never taking any notice of them again. They are contemptible people. The lowest peasant back home had more of God in him than they do…

"Vengeance is mine sayeth the Lord… Dies Irae…"

23rd August 1919 – Sandringham
I have my own rooms and staff at last. Cousin George and Queen Mary have granted me this on condition that I do not venture outside the estate without first asking permission, and then I have to go with a minder, selected for me by Intelligence, as happened at Johnny's funeral. I've been reassured that this is only a temporary measure and that things will be back to normal in a few months. In the afternoon, sat under a tree in the park and dozed in the sunshine. First time in many months I have felt a modicum of peacefulness. But my dreams were fitful and haunted. I have become used to it now, but wish I could forget more. Woke with a start. A tall young man was leaning against the tree, holding the most beautiful hunter. He laughed.

"No need to be alarmed. I'm not a ghost."

He extended his hand. "I'm sorry, we haven't been introduced. Owen Tudor, Lieutenant, 20th Hussars. My uncle is visiting His Majesty. Something to do with Intelligence, I think. I've taken the opportunity to ride while I'm here. You are?"

I got up slowly. My leg hurt suddenly. I nearly collapsed. Lieutenant Tudor caught me. In the pause, a look passed between us. I felt as if I knew him somehow. The feeling was comfortable, and maybe something more too.

I straightened up and extended my hand. "Tatiana Romanov." I smiled. Strange. The smile wasn't forced, and I had told him my real name. It didn't feel dangerous.

"Are you all right?" His concern seemed genuine.

"I think so. I'm staying here with my cousin until I get better and things calm down."

I saw the look on his face, felt his unspoken question, and nodded.

"So you *are* Nicholas II's daughter? I read about your family last year. I'm so sorry. Our people got you out? But we were told you had all died."

I gave him a wry smile. "We all did. Haven't you realised? It's me who should be alarming you. After all, I'm the ghost. I'm not really here."

The memories were coming back. I felt the tears near the surface, but didn't want to break down in front of a stranger, no matter how handsome.

He seemed to realise, and extended his hand. "Can I take you back to the house? You can ride, and I will lead, how's that?"

His smile was a sunburst.

"How can I refuse?"

He helped me to mount. The first time I had ridden like this, straddled, in a number of years. The pain I felt mounting the horse was worth it. He picked up my stick from against the tree and began leading us back to the main house.

"Is the walking stick a permanent fixture?"

"I hope not."

He smiled again. I felt warm and safe with this man. For a moment, we seemed a world away, not on the estate at all, and I wished we were at Tsarskoe Selo, heading back to my stables.

"I was colonel in chief of a lancer regiment once."

"Perhaps you would like me to call you "Sir", Your Highness?"

I laughed. For once, the laughter seemed to come from a true place of light. "Don't you dare. My friends call me Tanya."

He stopped and looked at me. His look measured me. "Thank you. Then I shall call you Tanya, Your Highness."

He kissed my hand, and we resumed our progress.

As we neared the house, I reminded him that, in the circumstances, it would be better if he was not observed with me, so he helped me to dismount as we entered a small thicket. As I began to walk towards my wing of the house, I saw Lieutenant Tudor canter away at an angle to me. Instinctively he knew that it would distract anyone looking. As he disappeared, he looked back for a fraction of a second and our eyes locked. It was a brief moment of eternity. I paused, considering the implication, then resumed my course home. [10]

7th June 1920 – Sandringham
1.40am
Dreamed I was back in St Petersburg. At the Kazan Cathedral. Mama, Papa and the others were there, but Anastasia's face was oddly blurred. I tried to walk towards them, but as I got closer, they seemed to be forever receding. The frustration of not being able to be with them was overwhelming and I woke up screaming and pounding my pillow. The footman knocked on my door, to ask if I was all right. I answered in the affirmative. Another lie ... to compound all the others.

Later that night...
Dreamed I was in water, choking, fighting for air. Someone hauled me onto the bank. There were industrial buildings near me, and a lot of shouting in a language I recognised as German.

Part II

Owen

March 1921 - August 1923

2nd March 1921 – Sandringham

The rain today was terrible, but I just had to get out. The feeling of the water on my face woke me up and made me feel alive! Yes! Alive! For almost the first time since I came to this country I am beginning to feel whole and not as if I'm in shock, with some weird part of myself floating away like a balloon on a string.

I decided to visit the horses. Cousin George has just bought me a new hunter called Phoenix. He is reputed to be very difficult, but I was curious and just wanted to see him. When I got there, he was not in his box. The groom told me he was in the indoor school with a man from the army who was trying to break him in. How dare he! This is *my* horse. *I* shall break him in. Father Grigory taught me how to communicate with horses when I was twelve and I've never forgotten the skill. I know His Majesty means well, but he can be awfully patronising, especially towards women. I've noticed this reflected in the behaviour of his sons too, especially David. To think we once joked with Olga about him! I really don't think he will ever know the true meaning of love. To him, women are pretty things he sticks on his arm at a ball or soiree, or conquests he has in his bed. We don't exist as flesh and blood people with opinions and ideas of our own. Oh no! That would be unheard of, or, dangerous. Well, perhaps I should show him just how "dangerous" I can be.

When I got to the indoor school, I saw the strangest sight. Lieutenant Tudor was standing in the centre of the arena, with his eyes closed, concentrating, while my horse stood uncertain, snorting and pawing the sawdust in the corner. He is a most magnificent chestnut stallion, with a small white flash on his nose, and he seemed to be engaged in a silent battle of wills with Owen. I stood at the rail, transfixed. It was as if they were locked in telepathic combat. Very slowly, Phoenix stopped his pawing of the ground and began to walk slowly around the edge of the compound. Owen did not move, but stood, motionless, eyes closed, concentrating. Suddenly, Phoenix turned and charged straight at him. I was too startled to cry out in warning. Just as he was about to run Owen over, Phoenix swerved to one side, coming to a stop behind him, breathing heavily. Owen had not moved. The same occurred again, only from the rear! Again, Owen did not move, but stood, rooted to the spot. A third time, Phoenix charged. A third time Owen stayed motionless. Phoenix paused for breath, and slowly went back to patrolling the edge of the arena. Then, the drama started again. This recurred three times. Finally, Phoenix stopped, directly opposite Owen, where he could see him head on. There was a very long pause. This had now been going on for nearly half an hour. Only now did Owen open his eyes. He had not seemed to notice me at all. He stared straight at Phoenix, locked eyes with him, and walked very slowly up to him. Reaching out his hand, he stroked his face. Phoenix snorted loudly. Then, a seeming miracle. Owen began to walk around the edge of the arena. Phoenix followed. Absolutely docile. At a point directly opposite me, he stopped and led him across to me.

Our eyes met and the smile in them gradually spread to his lips. "Would you like to try him? I'll saddle him for you."

How had he known I was coming? There was indeed a side-saddle on the rail on the opposite side of the arena. I must have looked apprehensive.

"Don't worry. He's quite safe now. And I'll be here, just in case."

He saddled Phoenix, helped me to mount, and handed me a riding crop. I touched Phoenix lightly on his side.

"Walk on."

Smoothly, we walked around the arena as Owen held us in his gaze. At the end, we turned and walked the other way. It was bliss. I couldn't wait to try him at a faster gait. I looked at Owen. How I would love the others to have met him, especially Olga and Father Grigory. As he looked at me, I knew he was one of us. From that moment, everything in my world changed. A new sun

187

is rising. But what will the day bring, sunshine or rain?

10th April 1921 – Balmoral
Being lost in the Scottish countryside reminds me so much, in peculiar ways, of home. The smell of the trees, the lochs, even the actual shape of the land itself is reminiscent. I see a steamer pass by in the distance on its way up the loch and it reminds me painfully of our times on the Standart exploring the Finnish islands. How I wish I could return there. But the return is to a feeling, not a place or a time. Isolated here, even among my relatives, it is difficult to capture much of the aura I once knew. But today, for a moment, there was a suggestion of magic.

I was walking among the trees in one of the small forest groves here. I find walking increasingly difficult, but, among Nature's wonders, I feel at least partially restored. I had stopped by the stump of an old oak tree, lost in thoughts of home, when a small bird landed on my shoulder. Its blue-grey plumage revealed it as a nuthatch. I held out my hand in expectation, as I used to do and it hopped onto it, turning to look at me. In an instant, as of old, I was lost in contemplation of this beautiful creature. It was as if Mother Earth Herself smiled at me.

From nowhere, I heard Olga's voice saying, *"All will be well. Trust me."*

Suddenly, in a strange way, I could feel that she was right and all the tension and pain I had accumulated over the preceding weeks began to dissolve. As the bird flew to land on a nearby tree, I realised again, and for the first time for many years, how well God watches over even the smallest and most insignificant of us. All truly is well and there is nothing to fear, except fear itself. I walked on, into the dewy air and warm breezes of a new spring day. In the distance, the double headed eagle of Peterhof's Heraldic Pavilion shone proudly and I caught sight of Olga waving excitedly to me.

11th April 1921 – Balmoral

A bad day. Nightmares woke me several times. The same pictures. All blood and fire and pain. Aircraft noises and people shouting. I awoke exhausted and sweating, aware only of the increasing pain in my back. Then the remembrance that I am the only one left. All I can do now is cry. I don't even have Ortino for company. Remembering him makes me feel even worse. All I want to do is go to sleep and never wake up again. I spent the whole day in my bedroom. I did not go out and did not answer any calls from either the servants or King George. He seemed genuinely concerned for once. But, in truth, he is as helpless as everyone else is. I am a wreck and a relic. I do not belong here with these people. It would be much better if I died. Then it could be said that all of my family died in Ekaterinburg. For it would be nothing but the truth. Going on is a hollow joke. What *ever* did I think could be achieved by this miserable loneliness?

4th May 1921 – Sandringham

Unexpectedly today, received a letter from Lieutenant Tudor. My cousin has apparently given him permission to write to me. This has come about through his uncle, Admiral Tudor, who was head of the Royal Navy's Japan Station at the time of my rescue and has always taken an interest in my case. I was introduced to him back in 1919 when I was first at Sandringham. He is, in spite of his rank, a very nice gentleman, kindly and courteous. I can see where his nephew gets his manners. The letter asks if we may meet next Monday for a ride. I think it will be very pleasant at last to have a companion my own age that is not a minder of some kind. I shall answer in the affirmative.

9th May 1921 – Sandringham

Riding today with Lieutenant Tudor. I must say he is a very handsome man. He sits very well in the saddle, and has a very lean and athletic body. I dressed my best, so I hope he didn't think

I looked too run down. He was very attentive, aiding me to mount and dismount, and the conversation was very natural and unforced. He was also very funny. I haven't laughed this much in a long time. It left me with a beautiful feeling of gentle sunshine in my heart.

Night.
Slept very well. First time in months I haven't woken up in the middle of the night and not been able to get back to sleep.

11th May 1921 – Sandringham
Letter from Lieutenant Tudor this morning. Apparently he enjoyed our ride as much as I did. He is on leave for the next ten days and wants to spend some afternoons with me. I wrote back straight away. Yes! Yes!

14th May 1921 – Sandringham
Riding again. It was raining gently today, but we didn't mind. It was lovely to be out in Nature. We stopped in a small glade and sat on the ground. He asked me about my life in Russia and my family. It felt good to talk. I haven't been able to talk to anyone properly since I came here. When I was first on the estate, things were still too raw. Lalla was very nice, but talking to her about intimate things was not terribly appropriate. Lieutenant Tudor is different. He feels more like an equal somehow, and, seeing him with the horses has convinced me that he is "one of us". We talked about what he does. He referred to it as "horse whispering". A strange term, but appropriate. In turn, I talked to him about Father Grigory and how he had taught us all to communicate with Nature. As I stood up to go back to my horse, a robin landed on my shoulder and sang.

"I wonder what he's trying to say?"

"That it's time for his tea."

"And ours too. I'm famished."

The little chap trilled as if in confirmation and flew off into the trees. He was even flying in the direction of home. We both laughed. Tea and cakes in my study. He kissed my hand as he left.

Later, as I was dressing for dinner, I saw Olga in the mirror behind me. She was smiling. I turned to say something to her, but when I did, she was gone, and I felt so sad. I would love to be able to share this growing warmth with her. At night, cried myself to sleep. The loneliness is so deep. It won't go. No matter what I do. No matter what anyone does.

15th May 1921 – Sandringham

Riding again with Lieutenant Tudor. I like it when he calls me "Tanya". It makes me feel safe somehow. Sunny today. At one stage, rode absolutely flat out. And I beat him. He was really trying. And he lost. As I thought. Russians are really the world's best riders. (And dancers, composers, musicians, poets, writers, emperors… you name it!)

16th May 1921 – Sandringham

Did something very silly today. I rode Phoenix straight at a hedge. Owen shouted at me in alarm, but I went for it anyway. Phoenix jumped it, but I hadn't anticipated the ditch on the other side. He landed awkwardly, stumbled and fell. I was thrown off and landed. Hard. I blacked out. Woke up in bed, surrounded by nurses and doctors and a very concerned looking Owen.

The worst of it was Cousin George. He was standing next to me, with his hand in mine, and a look like thunder on his face. "Tatiana, that was extremely stupid. You could have died."

I felt too weak to respond. He turned and vented his fury on Owen. "And you, sir, are a bad influence. I think you had better leave."

Owen made to come towards me. It had not been his fault, but he wanted to apologize, and I saw something else in his eyes.

Something which made my heart beat a little faster. A look passed between us.

The King saw it and cut him off. "I will look after her, sir. I think you will find that your pass has been cancelled. I would return to your regiment immediately, before they think you absent without leave."

Owen made a hasty exit. I reached my hand after him, but it closed only on empty space.

21st May 1921 – Sandringham
In bed still. In pain still. I didn't break anything in the fall, thankfully. Nothing, that is, except my heart. Why was I so stupid? I know why. I think I'm in love with him. I jumped Phoenix over that hedge because I was elated. It was at that moment that I realized it. Oh, how I want to see his kind, strong smile again. He is so wonderful. He was my connection to life. And now, Cousin George has taken him away. Why am I cursed like this?

Admiral Sir Frederick Tudor - 24th May 1921 – Buckingham Palace
"Constantinople? That's a long way, sir."

"Far enough for him to forget her, with any luck."

"With all due respect, Your Majesty, you underestimate my nephew. You also underestimate her. She is very strong willed."

The King smiled wryly. "Like her entire family. Her parents were no different. In the end that was their downfall, too."

"Unlike your family, sir, who adapted to changing times."

The King missed the subtle sarcasm in Admiral Tudor's voice. "Quite."

"The order has gone down anyway. And it's a promotion for him. He can hardly object. And you never know. He might meet a nice dancing girl and settle down."

Admiral Tudor laughed. The laugh was hollow. There was a pause. "How are things in Russia, sir?"

"Touch and go. Our top man is there and has made progress,

but Lenin and his men are very determined. Have you seen his writings? He is a very subtle man. Typical politician. He can read what people want, and appear to give it to them with one hand, while, behind their backs, he takes it away."

"He has also said that the only way to maintain a revolution is with the exercise of terror. What of the Government in Exile, sir?"

"Willing to move at a moment's notice and implement the new constitution as soon as we tell them to" – he paused - "should our latest moves succeed in destroying the Bolsheviks from within."

"When will you tell her, sir?"

"Not a moment before the Kremlin is in democratic hands. Until then, she is to be kept completely in the dark."

"As Your Majesty wishes."

Admiral Tudor left the King, contemplating the danger Tatiana was in, and the cruelty with which her life and that of his nephew were being treated. Unfortunately, he thought, sometimes cruelty was necessary, especially where the fate of a nation was at stake. In such circumstances as these, human life can suddenly count for very little.

Tatiana's Diary - 10th June 1921 – London
My 24th birthday today. Got a card from King George and Queen Mary which was as cold and humourless as they are. Got another one from Prince George. This was much better. He knows of my fondness for teddy bears. This one shows a bear posting a letter. It was very sweet and I have written to tell him so. No letter or card from Owen. I think they're keeping us apart. Deliberately. My staff made me a cake and I insisted that we all sit and eat together. They all seem to feel very relaxed with me. That's just as it should be.

Read in the paper today about the plight of war orphans. I would love to set up a committee again to look after the lost children like I did at home. I shall suggest it to His Majesty. I need something to do. I like reading as much as the next person. But not all the time!

21st June 1921 – Sandringham
Intense disappointment. King George has refused my request to set up a committee for the war orphans. Or, at least, it will run, but without my participation. The Princess Royal will head it instead. He made the point that I cannot be seen in the world yet. Why, I don't know. What is being achieved by all this secrecy is beyond me. There must be a purpose to it, or it becomes nothing but an act of sadistic cruelty.

July – September 1921
Nothing has happened at all. I just sit and read for most of the day. No letter from Owen. Nothing to do except sit here and turn into a vegetable. Very slowly. Life is so boring. Riding is my only solace. Without Phoenix for company, I don't know what I would do.

December 1921 – London
I've felt too numb and exhausted to write for several months. Every day now seems greyer than the last. There is one small ray of light, but it is extremely small and I don't know if it's just me clutching at straws, so I won't say any more about it for now. I seem to be drifting half the time in a dead landscape. All the people seem to be made of paper, two-dimensional. Everything is well mannered, but utterly false. They have no idea how excruciating I find this. It feels as if I'm being slowly torn apart from the inside. I barely know what day it is any more. Everything is boring and hopeless. Yesterday, I tried to ride my horse and had to give up, as I couldn't mount him. I don't think I shall ride again. Another loss of freedom. Drip by drip, the water of my life is flowing away and the walls of my dam can no longer contain

it, or cope with the widening cracks in my physical form (and my mental one, I suspect).

1st January 1922 – Balmoral

I did not celebrate Christmas or New Year. What would have been the point? In bed all day with a fearful headache. The only bright spot was the delivery of a humorous New Year card from Lieutenant Tudor. The small light grows. The card was in Turkish, but he wrote a translation, and the picture spoke for itself. They do say that laughter is the best medicine. For a moment today, I believed it.

15th February 1922 – Balmoral

Out walking (or should that be hobbling with my stick), I came across the statue of John Brown, Granny's Gillie, who used to bring her messages from Prince Albert. If only he were still here. I could ask him about Olga, Papa and the others. Any messages I used to get are silent now and I'm becoming increasingly sceptical about it all. Having said that, I have to comment that Olga used to say that she had a vision of me walking by a river using a stick, and that I was alone. If that was right, it implies that everything else was too. Maybe things might be salvaged yet...?

23rd February 1922 – Sandringham

Cousin David. Urgh! The very thought that he will one day be king of this country is horrible. Watched him yesterday larking about on the estate with some of his "chums". He was driving his new car around the estate roads much too fast and frightening all the animals (and humans!) unlucky enough to come within range. Carousing at night getting much too drunk and firing off his shotgun outside my window, just to annoy me. Actually, I felt more like killing him. That sound has some awful associations, which you can guess. Between Cousin George and his infernal stamp collection (I've had fantasies about throwing it on the bonfire next November 5th) and Cousin David and his drinking, I think the entire British monarchy is in for a spectacular fall one day... They're all deranged. Poor Johnny was the sanest one of them. I like Georgie too, but I never see him now, he's always away in the Navy. As for Bertie, he can't stop stuttering. Mind you, if I had a father as prone to rages as Cousin George is I think I might have developed one too. All he needs is a good wife to get him away, and love him, and make love to him, and he will heal and the speech will right itself. He has a very good heart. To think we once teased Olga about David. But she didn't like his cat, and besides, my darling always wanted to marry a Russian. I wonder what ever became of Lieutenant Voronov, the Standart officer she fell in love with?

14th April 1922 – London
My back is quite painful today. I'm using my stick more and more just to stand up straight and my alarm at the loss of feeling in my lower legs is growing. I saw King George's doctor yesterday and he informed me that there was nothing he could do for me. He suspected spinal caries as long ago as 1920, given the wounds in my back and all the bruising incurred in the rescue, but hadn't wanted to tell me in case he turned out to be wrong. The injustices of life just keep on coming. Papa always said that he felt like Job and now I can see what he meant. My escape and new life, which had all seemed so full of promise, are now apparently to be brought to nothing. My silly body! I never thought it would let me down like this. Well, I'm determined not to leave this life with nothing. Marie always wanted a husband and children.

"If only I could just be normal and marry one of Papa's officers."

Well, maybe I can do it for her, for all of us. I have been aware recently of an increasing love for Owen. I still remember vividly our first encounter and how it filled me with a feeling of gentle light. It was small at first, only a suggestion of a feeling, but it has gradually grown into regard and affection. Seeing him with the horses was a revelation. I really felt for a moment that he was one of our family, and not English at all. Father Grigory would have been fascinated to see him work. His bond with the animals was almost psychic. Certainly he always seemed pleased to see me, and I felt very good with him too. It has recently become something more than good, at least in my dreams!

We have kept in touch by letter, lately with increasing frequency. His Majesty has allowed us to correspond again, and it seems that his time in Turkey has not dimmed his feelings for me one bit. I do hope he is allowed to see me again when he comes home on leave. I asked my cousin about it, and he intimated that he would possibly allow it, but, after the last time, we would have to be watched over. That was very annoying. It seems I can't go anywhere now without a bodyguard of some kind. You know Owen is the only person I feel I've truly connected with since I arrived here. England is a very beautiful country from a physical perspective, but the people are on the whole cold and unresponsive. I have felt the need to be lost in Nature more and more, but now that my legs are increasingly useless and I can no longer ride like I used to, I am reduced to walking everywhere and, at least for now, hobbling with a stick. Sometimes I can feel the anger welling up inside me like a powerful whirlpool. It is like a maelstrom. There is a lot hidden underneath and I'm afraid of what may happen if I let it go. It would seem that Olga's suppressed rage is now a part of me too.

But maybe I can use the energy to power me through one last act before I die. I know I will now. I saw it in the doctor's face although he wouldn't tell me how long I have left no matter how much I pressed him. In my heart, I know it cannot be many years. So I will put them to good use. These pages that I have been scribbling will form part of a record of events that I will save for the future. I have already noticed the distortions that are surrounding our story. Let the liars talk. I will not tell what I am doing and will write in secret when my minders are not watching. One day everyone will be able to read the truth about Mama, Papa, Alexei and the rest of us. And in this, I include Father Grigory. He was one of us. In some ways the most important one.

The English have a quaint saying: "Don't shoot the messenger."

Well, that's precisely what they did to him. His prophecy about our family has proved more accurate than I either wanted or intended it to be. It would seem that I died effectively on the day that I was rescued. Which actually, now I think about it, makes Father Grigory totally accurate in his assessment of our future. But I still can and will salvage something from the ashes

12th January 1923 – London
I've accepted Cousin George's suggestion that I have increased physiotherapy for my legs and back. Also, I'm to try an Indian technique called Yoga. Maybe it will slow down my mind a little. Also, the breathing exercises will help my lungs, and my circulation.

14th February 1923 – Sandringham
I've been meditating as an adjunct to my Yoga exercises. The strangest things have begun happening. I have been "seeing" pictures in my head from perspectives that are not my own, and I'm sure I've seen Masha's face now several times, along with sensing a faint suggestion of her perfume. Maybe it's just a memory of her. But it felt real. I think I'll take it as such. It feels better like that.

Received a Valentine's Day card today. It was anonymous, but the little drawing of the horse gave away the sender. It can only be one man.

Night
Dreaming. Woke up touching myself. First time in years I've done that. I won't tell what I was doing in my dream, and what made me wake up with such a start. It was very nice though.

12ᵗʰ March 1923 – London
I'm riding again! The physiotherapy, Yoga and meditation have worked! Oh, the exhilaration. I screamed for joy. King George and Queen Mary came to see me try. I think I may have been wrong about them, just a little. I've never seen Queen Mary smile, but when I got off Phoenix, she came to me and took my hand, and positively beamed. I felt the warmth in her heart. Slept very deeply. Woke hearing a Russian lullaby that can't possibly have been there, nor can Olga, whom I heard singing it.

30ᵗʰ May 1923 – London
Received another letter from Owen this morning. I must say that reading it gave me an awful lot of pleasure, the kind that I haven't felt in a number of years. It sort of starts with a tingle in your tummy (no – I'm not suffering with indigestion!) and moves all the way up your back until your head feels on fire. The pleasure came in waves and made me a little short of breath. He proposes we meet next week for a short walk through Hyde Park. Not sure what His Majesty will think. He may let me, like last time, but with a minder – again. I'm getting better all the time, and these restrictions are beginning to get on my nerves. It's been going on too long.

All the "ordinary" people I see around me. How I envy them their anonymity. They don't need minders, and are free to think, feel and act as they please. I remember what pleasure Olga and I got from going into Petrograd to see the families during the war. Somehow, that was different. We always managed to escape our minders then, and Papa really didn't mind at all. Surely that is the ideal. I'm trying to grasp something, a principle. I know Olga would know instantly what I mean, and would even be able to put it into words for me. But I instinctively feel something is wrong here, in England. Somehow, I'm not part of "this" family. Maybe Papa, Mama and the rest of us never were…

5th June 1923 – London

Walking arm in arm with Owen through Hyde Park – our shadow is never less than a hundred yards away. Hateful. It's Nastya's twenty-second birthday today (in our old calendar), and as I see the creatures here, the birds and the squirrels, I'm reminded irresistibly of her. I half expect her to come rushing up behind me, as she always did, grab me round my waist and spin us both round in circles. She would have loved London, especially the concerts and ballets. And if she could ever have disciplined herself enough, she would have made a very good pianist too, maybe good enough to study at the Royal College. Sergei Vassilievitch loved her very much. He was always playing jokes on her in lessons and they had great fun with musical puns, which he loved to tease her with. She was becoming an excellent musical mimic, with a great ability to imitate the styles of her sisters, especially Olga.

I remember the last thing I ever heard her play. It was a study by the American composer Edward Macdowell. Nastya loved his music, especially the piano concertos, but she wasn't yet advanced enough to play them. The study, she played with exquisite tenderness. I was entranced. Her technique might not have been as good as either Olga, or myself, but she was more than our equal in expression, especially the wistful kind. Not what you would expect perhaps, but she hid many mysteries in her soul. I miss her more than I can say.

Life here is stifling me. I must and shall make a break for freedom, or I will surely die, either by illness or my own hand.

6th June 1923 – London

There is a member of my staff, just one, whom I trust. His name is John Robertson. He has been with the King since 1911 on his staff and has known him since he was a boy. But, even more than that, his mother was Russian, and served Papa's Grandfather, Alexander II, so, through his mother, he is loyal to us. I think he is a little in love with me. That will prove useful. He sees daily the restrictions on my movements and has also observed me with Owen. I have asked him to act as go-between for Owen and me, as I know now that our "official" letters are being intercepted and read. All so far has been under King George's control. Secretly, John has now been delivering our messages. Personally, I think he enjoys the risk, and also, seeing the look on my face when a reply comes from Owen. Together, we have begun to hatch an escape plan. I want to get away from here with Owen and be with him. Forever. I won't say how, but I have with me the means for us to be safe.

Meanwhile, I shall go through the boring daily routines as usual. The agreement with Cousin George is that if Owen and I behave ourselves, we can continue as friends, meeting at the discretion of the Palace, and Owen will not be sent abroad again like he was in 1921. They thought then to keep us apart. It hasn't worked. (Yes! I'm that unforgettable. Ha ha!) I feel so excited I can't tell you!

8th June 1923 – London

Sat in the garden at the back of Buckingham Palace reading War and Peace. In Russian. Most of my books are in Russian. I know I speak English as well if not better than everyone else here, but somehow, although we all talked together in English at home, especially with Mama, it's not the same here. The atmosphere is wrong. If I want to recapture some of my old feelings, I read in Russian. The musical rise and fall of the language is soothing to me, like a distant lullaby or the feel of a forgotten memory of love. Nothing else will do. Fell asleep.

As I woke, saw the back of someone walking away from my tree, where I was lying. It looked like Olga, but as I woke fully and went to call her, she had vanished into the violet-hued haze of the summer afternoon.

Evening
John brought me a note from Owen. It will be the week of July 14th. He has leave coming. The week of the fifth anniversary…

14th June 1923 – Sandringham
I've been confined to my room on Cousin George's orders. This morning, while out riding, I stopped to complain that my minder was too close to me. As I rode on, he remained too close. Each time I politely asked him to move back, he replied with a stony silence and carried on as before. At least in Ekaterinburg, the guards were communicative, even if they were surly and drunk half the time. Eventually, I got so angry that I deliberately turned Phoenix round and rode straight at him, lashing out with my riding crop. I'm afraid I hit him in the face, knocked him off his horse, and rode off into the park. When I got home, I was summoned.

"What is the meaning of this assault on one of my people, young lady?"

"He was too close. I could almost feel his breath on my neck. I had asked him to ride even a little further away, but he must be deaf as well as stupid. He wouldn't listen."

"So you assaulted him with your whip…?"

This was too much. The anger seemed to come roaring up from deep within me. And there was no stopping it.

"How would you feel? Confined. Kept prisoner like this. You promised I would be free when everything calmed down. But when will that be? Not this side of 1930, I think. And why am I in this stupid position? Because you could not be bothered to send a ship for all of us when you promised to. You, sir, are a liar and a coward. Why my father ever felt affection for you I'll never know. I've lost everyone because of your stupidity. You are unfit to be a king or a father; look at how you treated your own son!"

I had advanced on him and was now looming over him like a vengeful shadow. It helped that I was several inches taller.

"You and that equally vacuous wife of yours should have been in Ekaterinburg, not us. Papa was gentle and kind, and you murdered him. You murdered all of us! And all you can think about are your privileges and your stupid, stupid stamp collection!"

I was now standing over him screaming at the top of my lungs. At that last, I took hold of the book of stamps he had been studying and threw them on the fire. I also cleared his desk with a sweep of my arms. This anger was not just mine.

In floods of tears I stormed out and went back to my own room. As I lay on my bed recovering my self-possession, I heard the lock on the door being turned. I should have expected as much. No answer. No admission of guilt. No apology. Just cold, calculating self-serving actions from my cousin and his wife. These are not people. They are monsters disguised as human beings.

15th June 1923 – Sandringham
My door was finally unlocked at 3.00am. I was awake and heard the click. Summoned again at 9.00am by King George. He was sitting at his desk perusing his stamp collection again. For a moment I thought he was doing it deliberately to annoy me, but when he saw the look on my face, he hid the book hastily.

"I've been thinking… having you in the house, even sequestered off in one wing, is too public… and lately I've been hearing some disquieting rumors from Russia. It seems Trotsky's intelligence men may have got wind of the possibility of your presence here."

He looked up. His eyes were unreadable. At that moment, a very large man in what I assumed to be a guard's uniform came into the room.

"For your own safety, I have decided to have you escorted to the old farm. Your staff will go with you, of course. You are to remain there until my intelligence people tell me you are safe. We have to somehow quash the rumours."

He looked into my eyes. I didn't like his look at all. He spoke the next sentence very slowly and deliberately.

"Let them believe you are dead."

There was a long pause. I didn't react. The presence of the bully behind me made resistance futile. Cousin George smiled. But his eyes were far from affable. "The sergeant will escort you out."

This horrible stranger was, by this time, looming over me. After the tensions of yesterday, and a terrible, sleepless night, I felt far too exhausted to comment. As I left him, I saw King George V carefully get out his stamps and begin examining them with a magnifying glass as the door closed behind me. [11]

16ᵗʰ June 1923 – Sandringham
Back on the farm, as in 1919. Ekaterinburg all over again. Two guards posted outside. A desperate letter to Owen. John has carried it for me. Unknown when or if I will get a response. We must do something and soon, or everything I have been through will be for nothing.

17ᵗʰ June 1923 – Sandringham
No reply yet. Rain. Outside and inside.

18ᵗʰ June 1923 - Sandringham
Pain in my legs intolerable this morning. Barely able to get out of bed. Pain in my chest too. No reply from Owen. Sat reading War and Peace in the kitchen all day. Went and sat outside in front of

the farmhouse in the evening, playing Tchaikovsky's B flat minor Concerto on Johnny's gramophone, very loud. I think I annoyed my watchers sufficiently, that they went away to a greater distance.

Night

Dreamed Olga was kissing me. Woke up to the scent of Rose perfume. The room was filled with it. It went very quickly though. I was left feeling much more peaceful than I have in months.

21st June 1923 – Sandringham

At last, Owen has replied. His letter was obviously written in haste, but he has declared that he will be with me or die (me too!). He says he will write again soon with details of a plan to escape. For both of us. John has provided him with details of Sandringham's estate layout. For now, he suggests I apply to King George to be allowed to ride again. This will be a key element of the escape, I think. I sent a letter to His Majesty at once.

24th June 1923 – Sandringham

Cousin George has replied. Silently. This morning I awoke to find Phoenix and his groom, and all my riding gear at the stable. Interestingly, the one thing the King has not returned is my riding crop. I wonder why?

Afternoon

Went riding. With a shadow. That big brute of a sergeant obviously rides too. I wish Olga and the others could see him. They'd laugh themselves stupid. A stone with a face like a squashed pudding weighing down his poor mount. I would shoot him and put him out of the poor horse's misery. I did not object to his closeness and was the very model of diplomacy.

25th – 30th June 1923 – Sandringham
Each day the same. Get up. Wash. Dress. Eat breakfast. Read.
Ride. Read. Eat dinner. Listen to gramophone while reading.
Undress. Bed. Sleep.

Sleep is best. Every night lately I've been back home with my
family and we've all been together, like it was when everything
was happy. I've even had Ortino for company. Strange. Waking
up is hard and painful, and twice I'm sure I've felt Ortino
sleeping where he used to, curled up like a cat beside my right
arm. I've even heard him snoring. Thinking of this makes me cry.
That's all long ago and far away, and my family are now no more
than dead phantoms. So why do I find the dreams to be so real
and comforting? They are not replays of past events, but everything is new. Masha even looks more beautiful than she did, and
more mature, although Papa and Mama are the same and even
look younger and healthier than they did. Always, I see Olga
smiling at me, the look in her eyes at once both reassuring and
sad.

1st July 1923 – Sandringham
Suffered a serious fall this morning. Coming out of my bedroom,
my right leg collapsed under me and I fell down the stairs into
the kitchen. Happily I was only bruised, nothing was broken, but
the shock has exhausted me. The doctor has insisted that I use a
stick from now on permanently when walking. I will not let this
spoil our escape plans. Expecting a letter from Owen this week
about it. It cannot come soon enough. I'm dying in this confined
space...

5th July 1923 – Sandringham
Owen's letter. It's to be the seventeenth. The signal will be the
ringing of the telephone four times in the early morning. He has
the number from John. I'm to change my riding schedule and
begin taking Phoenix out in the morning. If I do this over the next

twelve days, it will give time for the routine to sink in and lull my watchers into a false sense of security.

8th July 1923 – Sandringham
My bruising has come out properly now and is very painful, particularly my chest, which really hurts when I breathe. Walking is more difficult than usual. Coughed a little this morning and found a bit of trouble breathing. Not serious though.

11th July 1923 – Sandringham
Walking easier today. Finished War and Peace and began Anna Karenina. Morning ride very pleasant. The Pudding fell off his horse when I took Phoenix under a tree with low branches and he took the concept of "close watch" a little too literally. If my chest wasn't hurting so much, I'd have laughed until I was sick. What was really scary was that he arranged himself and got back on his mount without so much as a change of expression. No laugh, no smile, no nothing. It all made me shudder.

14th July 1923 – Sandringham
A fright today. John could not attend me. The Pudding informed me that he was ill and had to stay at home. The Pudding also went further and sat at breakfast and dinner with me, as well as coming for a ride as usual. At one point I half expected to find my toilet door removed so he can watch me pee as well. But thankfully they have not gone that far. Yet. Give it time.

Night
More terrors. Went to the toilet and literally fell over the Pudding, who had stationed himself outside my door, saying, "For your safety, *Your Highness.*"

I really didn't like his emphasis. His sarcasm is as unsubtle as his appearance.

16th July 1923 – Sandringham

Pudding replaced by Stoneface (a corporal) today. I was diplomacy and charm incarnate. John's absence is worrying. The Reds did this to our friends in Ekaterinburg, taking them away, just before they killed us (yes… I feel as though I am a walking corpse too. I should have been there, and not here. This "escape" to England was a mistake). Jewels securely in my dress. All is ready. It is tomorrow. Freedom, or death. I have decided that if this fails, I will commit suicide. I would rather not remain in this prison any longer. If it comes to that, then I shall really escape – either to oblivion, and peace, or to my family, and joy. The rest, and our story, will have to wait for a later time.

17th July 1923 – Sandringham

Owen. My darling Owen. Today, our plan swung into action. The phone rang at 9.00am, four times, as Owen had promised, but ceased just before Stoneface got his paws on it. I got quite a fright as I saw him descending on the receiver to lift it, but the rings stopped just in time. I took Phoenix out at 9.30am, as usual for my morning ride, but, at a certain point, diverted him away from the usual route and took off at full gallop. These English are not as skilled with horses as we Cossacks! I lost Stoneface, who was following me, with ease. It was so exhilarating. For a short instant, I was back at home again, riding with Olga through our estate in the Crimea. We were at full tilt, Olga had lost her hat and her head was thrown back. I will always remember her screaming with joy again and again at being in such close communion with the horse that she was almost one with him. Father Grigory would have understood. Time was short – so horribly short. Then, and now. I must do this, or die. Owen was waiting at the park boundary. He helped me dismount, and then, we were in his car and off!

Afternoon
Reached our first "bolthole". In bed all afternoon. Oh, the beauty. We took each other again and again, without stopping, for what seemed like hours. Felt all my tensions and sorrows draining away. Lost in bliss, I cried, screamed and laughed. Oh, how we laughed!

Afterwards. Oblivion. Total and complete oblivion. If this is what death is like, then I will welcome it with both arms wide open. There is nothing to fear. All is beauty, only beauty. But, please God, I won't go there just yet. Not yet. I lie in Owen's arms and stroke his face as he sleeps. He has risked much for me. It must not be in vain. I shall help him to win too. The game's not over. I have moved the first piece. Let's see what happens next.

19ᵗʰ July 1923 – York
Owen and I are heading North. We have been posing as "Mr and Mrs Johnson". That was my idea. I thought "Jones" was too obvious, in spite or perhaps because of it being Owen's original family name. Anyone looking for us would spot the name at once. You may ask what we are doing for money? Well, before my escape I stitched a lot of my diamonds and other jewels that are a part of my inheritance, and which King George had been obliged to give me when I demanded them back a month ago, into my dress and riding habit. In Ekaterinburg, those jewels had saved my life when I was injured by that second grenade. As there, no-one knew what I was doing. After all, how often have you seen any of my English relatives in captivity with nothing but two sticks to rub together? Anyway, selling just one of the stones has given us plenty of money to be going on with. Enough to last us nearly a year. So we are quite safe, for now. I have told Owen that when we are really safe at last, I will sell all the jewels I have and we can live comfortably for the rest of our lives. I know that he feels uncomfortable about this, less of a "man", but more may happen yet, and, above all else, we have each other. In

the end that is all that counts, or lasts.

York is so beautiful. We spent hours in the Minster and close surrounding it. In the evening, went to a choral concert. The music sent my spirits soaring. One thing though. English basses are no match for Russian ones, and although I greatly enjoyed the Evening Service by Stanford, it still was no match for the passion of Russian liturgical music. Try listening to the Vespers of Rachmaninov or any of Grechaninov's wonderful music for the liturgy and you'll see what I mean at once. It is not words and pretty phrases which carry meaning, but passion and feeling.

Night

Oh how he loves me! Fire – Beauty – Oblivion – Death – Bliss! I am also in no pain now. I'm breathing better and walking upright without my stick. All is going well.

27ᵗʰ July 1923 – Keswick

We've changed our name now to Philips. This was Owen's idea. Yesterday, it occurred to me that King George and his people couldn't send out anything official about us, as then it would all come out about me being here, and worse, how I got here, and what the circumstances were. Any search for us will have to be as covert as we are being ourselves. We really have them "over a barrel" as the saying goes here.

Over the last three days we have been to Lake Windermere, and then Grasmere, to see Wordsworth's home. We went for a ride on a steamer on Lake Windermere. The scenery was wonderful. It brought back many memories of home. Too many. I'm afraid Owen's experience of the trip will mostly be of me crying on his shoulder. Some of this was set off by seeing a lady with a black French Bulldog. It was too much to bear.

Grasmere was interesting, but Wordsworth's house was very small. I was reminded slightly of Chekhov's house near Livadia. I think I prefer his. Also, I know Owen admires Wordsworth, but, like most English, he doesn't seem to really feel his emotions. Most of the poetry I've read of his sees him simply observing his own feelings, rather than really being a part of them. Therein lies a lot of the English "problem". All head. No heart. Owen seems an exception to this. He understands me so well. I've not felt like this except with members of my family. Perhaps I like being with him because somehow his energy reminds me of them. It's like being home again.

30th July 1923 – Manchester
Went into a shop on Deansgate called Forsyth Brothers. On the first floor they do pianos. Had a go on a new Steinway. Bliss. I've not played on a really good quality grand piano since the summer of 1917. Cousin George does not keep the pianos at Sandringham in sufficient working order, in spite of their looking clean enough. Somehow the D above middle C is always out of tune. Played two preludes by Rachmaninov (No's 6 and 23), and a portion of Chopin's Third Sonata. I'm surprised I remembered it all. Owen just stared in amazement. How I wish that I could have just had a "normal life" and followed a profession like everyone else. If I had been born to an everyday family, ballet or music would have definitely been my preferred choices. The sadness of my reality was never more starkly displayed to me than it was here, surrounded by all those beautiful instruments. Owen gently stroked my hair as, after I had finished playing, I felt the tears fall gently over my cheeks, another act of useless mourning for a life that never was...[12]

2nd August 1923 – Chester
Had to flee here from Manchester in a hurry last night. Heard a commotion outside our hotel window, saw a car and some men get out. Instinctively recognized secret police men. They have the same aura the world over. Escaped down the back stairs, but please God I don't have to do any of that again. My legs and back

are killing me, and I had a coughing fit when we reached Owen's car in a side street nearby. Didn't tell him, but the phlegm contained a small trace of blood. My heart sank. There is only one thing that can mean. The stress of this last day, running, and the unconscious stress of knowing we are on the run constantly now, has obviously taken its toll. If I were a fish in a river, I would now say I was on the verge of being reeled in. The hook is in my mouth. Soon, I shall be hauled onto dry land, where the air will choke me.

6th August 1923 – On the move

One guesthouse to another. Changing names all the time. No time to change clothes, or even wash now. I'm beginning to smell. Owen looks dishevelled and tired by it all. They are definitely closing in on us. Only one chance now. To London. We will marry, quietly in a register office, me under an assumed name. Then, King George and the others will have a fait accompli. They will have to let me go out into the world.

Colonel Richard Meinertzhagen - MI2(c) HQ, London. 9th August 1923

Colonel Richard Meinertzhagen looked deadly serious. "I mean it, sir. I will not carry out that order."

His boss glowered at him. "The trouble with you, Meinertzhagen, is that you always think you know better than the rest of us what should be done. Killing them both would remove a painful embarrassment from the Sovereign. You know that as well as I do. And besides, since the end of the civil war in Russia, any hope for restoring a constitutional monarchy has gone. She may as well be dead now, and that disobedient pup of a lieutenant, too. She's been officially dead for the last five years anyway, so it'll be no loss. Looking after her will simply squander resources and throw good money after bad."

Meinertzhagen planted both his feet squarely on the floor and confronted C, choosing his next words very carefully; knowing that his boss had just described the circumstances of a prisoner on Death Row. Tatiana didn't know it, but her life was now in the colonel's hands.

"I know this young lady quite well. She will not go without a struggle. And I think she will also have a plan in place in the event of her death. Killing her may well wind up being just the beginning of the embarrassment. For us all. I think it would be better to catch up with them, find out what has happened, if anything regarding a marriage, and then try to contain the problem. I will not carry out a cold-blooded murder of this girl, sir, for you or anyone."

"And you think she can be contained?"

"If I know her like I think I do, then, yes, there are possibilities. Let me get to them and find out, then we can decide what to do."

C gave him a look. Weighing up his determination. The scales were swinging. Meinertzhagen hoped he had done enough.

"Very well. Your orders now are to get to them and contain them, before she is officially recognised and the news becomes public. Do whatever you have to. But this problem must be solved soon, or I shall have no choice but to ask someone else to carry out my previous instruction, and terminate them both, as quietly as I can."

"Yes, sir."

Meinertzhagen left C's office to carry out the orders before his boss had a chance to change his mind. Trouble was, he knew very well that C could go behind his back and order them both killed anyway. Being refused had not pleased him. Meinertzagen had to act fast, and pray he reached them, and then the King, in time. That was the one connection even C was unaware of. It was his last card. He hoped he would be able to play it for her.

Tatiana's Diary - 10th August 1923 – London
York Hotel, Mayfair. We always seemed to manage to keep one

step ahead of our pursuers. Marriage tomorrow. Then back to Sandringham to face King George. Spent the night making love. The marriage ceremony is nonsense. Two such as we are already married, in the eyes of everything Holy. Truly Holy, that is. As I came, kneeling on all fours, I saw Olga, just at the side of me. She reached out to touch my hand, resting on the bed, and I felt her kiss the side of my neck. The feeling was electric. It was like being hit by a bolt of lightning. I screamed and passed out, surrounded by the most ecstatic feeling of joy I've known in many years.

11th August 1923 – London
After last night, I thought all our troubles were over, but they seem, in fact, to be only just beginning. This morning, we headed for the local register office. We had grabbed two passers-by and were just about to enter the building, when a man in a long black overcoat came up behind us, put his hand on Owen's arm and requested that we go with him to a waiting car. Owen reacted by punching the man hard in the head. As his accomplice came out of the car to try to help his fallen comrade, I got in a great shot to his stomach with my foot (it hurt!), and we stole the car and headed off to the hotel.

Unfortunately, when we got there, we were in the middle of packing, when two men entered our room. One of them I recognized at once. Colonel Meinertzhagen. I had spent considerable time with him and his wife Amorel in the autumn of 1918, just before I went to Harrogate. His friend I had not seen before. Owen evidently also knew the Colonel. He pulled Owen into the bedroom, while the other one kept watch on me. There were raised voices, mostly Owen's, but I couldn't concentrate because I could feel the blood rushing to my head, and I felt very dizzy. I started to cough. Hard.

Owen came rushing out of the bedroom and held me as I retched. "Have compassion, man. Can't you see she's dying?"

Colonel Meinertzhagen looked at me. There was blood on my

lips. He smiled. And, for once, I think the smile was genuine. It was as if a light had come on. He crouched down and put his hand on my arm. The look on Owen's face was fierce.

It was the Colonel who broke the tension. He addressed me, using my title. I hadn't heard anyone utter it in nearly seven years.

"Your Imperial Highness, I think I've got an idea. But I'll need to sell it to the King, and I need to act fast before... other measures are taken."

He looked at me deeply. "I need you to promise me that you and Lieutenant Tudor will not leave this room. Everything depends on you keeping your word and not trying to run again. I warn you, if you do, there's not a thing I will be able to do to help either of you. Might I remind you, you, Your Imperial Highness, are officially dead. You have been since 1918. And as for Lieutenant Tudor, he is currently AWOL. You can both be made to disappear as conveniently as anyone pleases. But, if you trust me, all will be well."

For half a second, I saw a look in his eyes, which reminded me of a parade ground long ago and far away, and I was trying desperately to adjust my hat.

Owen was going to be defiant. On a hunch, I stopped him. "Very well, Colonel. We will await you."

"Your Imperial Highness is very gracious. I shall leave two of my men outside for your protection". He kissed my hand, as politely as any courtier did, but the look in his eyes was serious. He was protecting me, but from whom? We had reached an understanding. At night, I slept well. I was playing in the Imperial Park. And Ortino was with me.

King George V - 12th August 1923 - Buckingham Palace

"Good God man, she's the heir to the Romanov throne. I can't have her marrying *him*. He was just detailed to look after her, and as an amusement..."

"With respect, Your Majesty, they are now very obviously in love. And remember, she is her father's daughter. The Emperor married for love. I don't think I'm presuming too much to say that in the present circumstances, he would at least respect her choice."

King George paused, allowing Colonel Meinertzhagen's words to sink in. Then, making a decision, he said, "If I allow this, what's your plan? She must be out of the way. Somewhere she cannot be recognized, but also somewhere from where she can be taken away to safety if necessary."

"I've already thought of that, sir. There is one place that fits all our requirements."

He went to a large map of England that he had already placed on the table where the King usually looked at his stamps. He pointed to a small town on the Kent coast.

"Lydd, Your Majesty. Home to the new 3rd Royal Tank Corps. They're looking for a promising new lieutenant. They can stay there. In case of any attempt by Lenin's men, there's a whole army camp to protect her. But also, she'll have to be placed in a house right on the edge of the camp, but enough away that they won't be seen regularly by the men. This is just a contingency. Lydd is on the coast. A boat could take her across the channel at a moment's notice."

"And if her illness gets worse?"

"In the event of her death, Lieutenant Tudor can be transferred back to his old regiment with no loss of face. His transfer to Lydd can remain temporary, and off the record, while we see how the land lies with her. No need to make it official yet."

The King was thoughtful. He went to the window and looked out. The colonel couldn't see it, but there were tears in his eyes.

"If only I hadn't been so afraid of the media in 1917. She would be surrounded by her family now instead of being a fugitive, trapped and ill, waiting to see what will happen next. We had some misunderstandings. But I was simply trying to protect her. Just in case our missions succeeded and she was needed again back at home. That was the whole reason for keeping her quiet here."

"Perhaps, sir, you should have told her."

"Perhaps," the King sighed sadly. "Another error of judgement." There was a long pause. Then the King drew himself up to his full height and turned to face Richard Meinertzhagen.

"Very well. You've convinced me. Let them marry. But I'll have them wed in that chapel where George III's son Augustus married his mistresses. We can keep it quieter then. Transfer Lieutenant Tudor to Lydd, but don't make it official. Have your men recovered her jewels?"

"Yes, sir."

"I want them banked. She may need the money later. Make sure that where they are, there's an intelligence watch on them round the clock. We don't know how far that Manchester report might get."

The Colonel bowed and prepared to leave. As he reached the door of the King's study, King George spoke again, quietly, and with more warmth than Meinertzagen had ever heard him use before.

"Colonel, I want her looked after properly. She is a member of my family, and I loved her father like a brother. It's the least I can do for them now."

"Yes, sir."

"And Colonel, make sure her horse is stabled nearby. It will please her. And Lieutenant Tudor can ride him into the camp. After all, he was trained by him. And Colonel..."

"Yes, Your Majesty?"

"Thank you."

Colonel Meinertzhagen bowed and left the King looking out of the window, thinking of a time long past when two look-alike men had stood arm in arm, laughing and joking while a photographer took their picture...

Tatiana's Diary - 15th August 1923 – London

I hate intelligence men! Even the title presupposes something most of the ones I've met are obviously short of. Captain Watson arrived in our hotel room to give Owen a "pep talk". He and Owen know each other very well. After all, they served together in Constantinople. But Owen told me long ago that he was also something else. He is a member of Colonel Meinertzhagen's unit of British Intelligence.

Captain Watson took Owen into another room and after a few moments, I heard raised voices, mostly Watson's. Owen kept pretty silent, except for one very loud "no", which I heard from him. When they came out, Captain Watson was highly flushed and obviously frustrated. Owen winked at me as he showed him out, but, after he had left, Owen slumped on the chair by the bed, tired. Yet when I knelt at his feet and lifted his chin, he had a look of fierce victory on his face. I stayed on my knees for a while. I remember the warmth of his hands on my head as I moved and the feeling of starlight in my soul that briefly made me want to cry with happiness.

16th August 1923 – London

Well, I've done it. Owen and I were married this afternoon. There were only three other people there at the Church besides the priest and us. Owen's best man, Colonel Meinertzhagen and two witnesses, one of whom is a very silent man whom I take it is Colonel Meinertzhagen's boss. The cover story for us is already in place. I am to be passed off as, wait for it, a belly dancer from Constantinople! My name is Larissa Haouk. I chose that deliberately (the name, not the profession – I would obviously have preferred ballet dancer – maybe they misheard me – belly/ballet?) as the Von Haouks are relatives of Mama's. Owen is to be transferred to the Royal Tank Corps in Lydd in Kent. I've seen where it is on the map. It's really out of the way, which will probably suit my cousin and his intelligence people admirably. While I think about it, whatever became of the promise that I would be let out into society again once all the smoke cleared? I have suspected for a year or so now that they never had any intention of letting me do that. Yet another English lie. They seem almost as good at it as the Bolsheviks... Now there's a thought. I shall be glad to be as far away from all of them as I can. As I probably don't have long to live now anyway, my fate should no longer matter to anyone, least of all to me.

Owen is a good man. He is decent and sincere and I stand little chance of achieving my purpose in any other way now that my physical beauty is rapidly diminishing. I caught sight of myself in the round window of the gallery landing outside the chapel. I may be only twenty-six, but I am no longer young. I am bent at the waist, my spine is curved and my hair is now, in places, prematurely grey. Add to this the constant pain I am in, in spite of the physiotherapy and Yoga exercise and the fact that I am increasingly unable to feel my legs and I think you see the truth of my situation. The marriage has only been given "the nod" as they say in this country because I patently do not have long left. We will live somewhere safe until I die. Then I can be buried somewhere obscure and safely forgotten. Officially, I will have died in 1918. Why does this remind me uncomfortably of Prince John? But I will have a surprise waiting for them.

"In my end is my beginning."

PART III

WE SHALL REST

SEPTEMBER 1923 – JULY 1926

3rd September 1923 – London/Lydd

Nestled in Owen's arms... we made our journey by train to his new posting on the Kent coast. Famous, apparently, for the testing of an explosive called Lyddite (how original!); it also boasts a very beautiful coastline. The army camp which Owen has been posted to is the new headquarters for the Royal Tank Regiment. But, curiously, contrary to what I originally thought, Owen is still going to describe himself as being in the Hussars. I found this out quite by accident. He had gone out to the paper shop to get some tobacco. While sat at the dressing table, doing my make-up, I opened the desk drawer to find in it a letter he had concealed hastily when I came into the bedroom from the bathroom. This letter confirmed he was "on loan" to the new regiment for an indefinite period. Some "indefinite" period all right. It will end when I die, of course. After a discreet period, he will return to his real regiment as if nothing had happened.

I angrily wondered how much of our "marriage" was love and how much a job. Given him by whom? Cousin George? After he returned, he saw that I was angry and, discreetly, comforted me in that delicious way he has. I remembered, for a moment, why I had fallen for him. It was difficult, but he took me and I redis-covered oblivion, silence and a kind of peace.

Arrived in Lydd about fifteen minutes before 4pm this afternoon. The air here is dry. It is easier to breathe than in London. Coming to our new home, a small Edwardian house called Ferndale, we pull up alongside the most wonderful, massive green, right in front of our house. While Owen takes our luggage in, I spend time just walking up and down, luxuriating in the sheer space of it all. As I stand in front of our doorway, in the distance there are some tents, from the army camp, I later discover, and, a windmill! I hope there are more nice surprises here. Living in Lydd may not prove to be so bad after all.

The house is comfortable and has a nice feeling to it. We sleep on the first floor at the front. Getting up and down stairs is not too bad at the moment. With my stick it is all right. But what of the future? Dare I hope for a miracle? Life seems bearable just now. Maybe I would yet like a little more of it.

14th September 1923 – Lydd
Journey with Owen out to the see the churches of Romney Marsh. Out here the air is so beautiful and clear. My lungs and chest are feeling better all the time. The churches are very interesting, but a little drab, not like our Russian Orthodox churches. I miss the colour, the singing, the light streaming in through the windows and the light from the thousands of candles lit by the believers. But there is one thing here I have not known these last years. Peace. It is everywhere. It seems to surround one out on the Marsh. Also, I have seen today a pair of marsh eagles. I shall have to write to Colonel Meinertzhagen about them. He is a keen bird watcher and would love my description of them. The eagles also reminded me of Olga somehow. Beautiful, majestic and deadly all at once, and deep as the Universe. I feel safe thinking of her. Remember, the eagle is also a protector...

17th September 1923 – Lydd
Today's excitement was the delivery from London of a new Bechstein Upright piano. It has a lovely tone, and the action is quite light. Fortunately I have quite a light touch. Immediately sent to London for some of my favourite pieces, including my absolute joy, the Rachmaninov Second Sonata, Chopin's Preludes op.28 and Scriabin's Sonata No.7. I can't wait to get playing again. I just hope someone will be around to page-turn for me!

19th September 1923
Darling Owen. He really can't keep his hands off me. Woke this morning to the feel of him taking me again. He does that a lot. Always when I'm turned on my side, or on my tummy. What's really delicious is that he kisses the scars on my back as he enters

me. I feel him, strong and beautiful, and my wounds always tingle to his touch, as if his ministrations are silently healing them. Father Grigory always said sex was healing. I definitely think he was right.

4th October 1923 – Lydd

I missed my period today. Oh, I am scared. And elated. What if Owen and I were to have a child? He or she will be the last of my family. And how will Cousin George cope with the idea of protecting it? I do hope my child can have some freedom, and not have to hide away like its mother is having to. Me, a mother! How jealous Masha would be. She always wanted a baby, and when she was little was always playing with her baby dolls.

Night.

Told Owen when he came home. He knelt and kissed my tummy. We made love ever so gently. He allowed me to rest my front and head on the pillows while he took me from behind. I love being passive like this, and just feeling the love as it rushes through me like a sword. When he loves me, all my nerves come to life again and I feel healed, if only briefly. Oblivion is bliss. Waking to find him loving me again. My darling heart!

8th October 1923 - Lydd

I have definitely missed my period now. A doctor will call later today to take away a sample to test, and we will see if it is confirmed, but in my heart, I know I am to have Owen's child. When he is born, he will be the last real Romanov. Maybe, in his lifetime, Tsar?

King George V - 10th October 1923 – Buckingham Palace

"A *child!* How long before it is born?"

"Seven months, Your Majesty."

The King turned away from his private secretary.

"You realise, sir, that this makes her protection even more imperative than before. The child will be the only survivor of her line, especially if Her Imperial Highness does not survive long…"

The King turned to face Stamfordham. "Will she carry the child to full term?"

"Impossible to say at present, sir. She is young, but her spinal caries is now combined with TB. She could have ten years, or ten months. It all depends on how strong her will to survive is."

The King walked over to his desk and sat down. He put his head in his hands. After a moment, he took a deep breath. "Have measures put in place to take care of any child, should one be born and should Tatiana die early on. And have the doctors monitor her frequently. I want weekly reports on her condition."

Stamfordham bowed. "Your Majesty."

And he left discreetly, leaving the King contemplating this new complication in his life. He hoped for a child. But he was scared for Tatiana. Her condition was fragile and was bound to worsen. For one of the few times in his life, he found himself praying, unbidden, to a God he did not believe in.

Tatiana's Diary - 18th October 1923 – Lydd
A new family have moved into Ferndale this morning. They are called Bishop. There are just the three of them. They are a medical family, apparently sent by Cousin George, or so Owen told me at dinner. Mr Bishop is a gynaecologist and has been asked to provide frequent reports on my condition. His wife is a nurse and midwife. Their son John is an obnoxious little boy who runs around too much and jumps on all the furniture. At least I will be protected in the event of anything going wrong, and Mrs Bishop will be here all day. Trouble is, flattered though I am by all this "protection", I'm beginning to feel stifled again. There are too many people around me all the time. I have no space to myself. Maybe I can change this in time. Let's see.

17th November 1923 – Lydd

I'm being monitored weekly. Treated more like a prize horse, in fact. I don't mind being looked after, but this is really beginning to get out of hand. I'm being cosseted so much that I sometimes feel I'll wake up in the night to find myself being probed in an unmentionable place by Mr Bishop. I really don't like his eyes at all. He is a surly and uncommunicative man with a rotten bedside manner. I think some of his patients might consider dying simply to get away from him.

18th November 1923 – Lydd

Snow and ice today. Apparently unusual for Lydd. Owen told me the windmill on the Rype had icicles on it. Just like back home (only we didn't have the windmills, just lots of icicles). I longed to go outside, but Mrs Bishop wouldn't let me. I had to consider the baby, and my condition, with my legs being a little unsteady, was ripe for a fall. Not what *we* want at all.

24th November 1923 – Lydd

Nightmare. I'm hanging by my neck from a gallows. My hands are tied behind my back and I'm wearing a simple white dress, and barefoot. I'm being watched and I'm struggling but not dying. Gasping for breath, but not strangling completely. It's as if the situation is going on and on.

Around me there are people in white coats with clipboards, making notes, and nobody seems in the least concerned with me writhing in front of them like this. The humiliation and pain is terrible. I pray for death and it doesn't come. I beg to pass out, but somehow I can't. The warm feelings that I expect, the euphoria and dizziness don't come. Instead, there is a feeling of emotional remoteness coming from the people around me. My chest feels like it will explode, as does my head, but still the ordeal goes on. It is a twisted parody of the experience of the Firebird Girl. Now, I am ridiculous and there is no Goddess to save me, to kill me. It is as if the whole experience is being analysed and mocked.

But just as I feel that it will be like this forever, I feel a pair of strong yet soft, feminine hands grasp my ankles and hold them together. This soothes me. As my struggling diminishes, one of the hands briefly caresses my ankles and feet. Then, so fast, I have no time to think, the hands pull down on my ankles. Very hard. I feel my neck snap and finally, the world goes black, then white and I'm floating, floating, into an overwhelming light. I'm bathed in love, a love which surrounds and penetrates me. So much so that I have an orgasm. Finally I really do pass out, surrounded by the scent of roses and jasmine flowers. Distantly, I am aware of applause coming from the people in the white coats. Perhaps they have learned something about the deep nature of true love after all?

4ᵗʰ December 1923 – Lydd
Coughing attack this morning. The amount of blood was small, but it was still worrying. My tummy and legs hurt afterwards. I was also sick in the afternoon, and felt dizzy. Writing this at night when I'm feeling a little better.

7ᵗʰ December 1923 – Lydd
So dizzy I can't get up. Woke at 1pm to see Marie by my bed.
   "Hello, my darling."
   "What are you doing here? Aren't you dead?"
   Masha laughed. *"Silly. There is no death. Just change."* She caressed my face. *"Look beside you."*
   I looked to my right. There was Olga. But she seemed to shimmer somehow, as if she wasn't quite real.
   "Beloved."
   She took my hand. *"You can come with us now, if you wish, or play this out until the end. If you come now, it would be better. A delay will only harm you."*
   "But my baby..."
   Olga looked at me with deep compassion. Marie was stroking my arm. I could feel them both, more than see them. Strange duality of experience, especially one so vivid as this.

"Always reaching for victory. Even when defeat is inevitable."

Suddenly, I remembered my dreams of the Firebird Girl and the gallows. The realisation hit me. In the dreams, Olga was Goddess of Death. It was she who had killed me both times, released me from my torment and taken me into the light. But where I felt joy and communion there, here I felt instead only confusion and fear. This was the wrong time. I was angry now. Bursting into tears, I said, "Go away! You won't take my baby. You're not having him. You're not. He's mine. Do you hear? Mine!"

I came round this time, to find Owen with me. For a moment I could not work out if it was real or just another dream within a dream.

"Hush, darling."

I was struggling against him. He was where Marie had been. Mr Bishop was on the other side, where Olga had been.

"You've had a nightmare."

No, it wasn't, I thought. To go with my dearest loves would have been a release from this horrible world, but I didn't want to lose our baby. It was more important to me now than anything. And why had I called him a "he"? Somehow, that didn't feel right.

I sank back into the pillow and cried. As in the nightmare, I was caught between life and death. An intense desire to pass away, to rejoin those I loved most dearly, and yet... feeling strangely connected through the child inside me to them, and something else as well that I could not even begin to define...

8th December 1923 – Lydd
Dizzy and sick all day. A horrible roaring in my ears too. Legs and chest intolerable.

9th December 1923 – Lydd
Seeing phantoms. Masha, Olga, Mama, Papa, Alexei, all around

my bed. Papa was praying for me, and the others were singing. But shall I live or die?

10th December 1923 – Lydd
Coughing attack. Chest hurt all day. Unable to eat at all.

11th December 1923 – Lydd [13]

Medical Notes – HIH Grand Duchess Tatiana - 11/12/23
Resuscitation 10.32am. Called for priest 10.40am. Second resuscitation 10.55am. Heart rate, blood pressure and breathing stabilised at 11.05am. Priest arrived from London 4.55pm. Administered last rites. Condition stabilised gradually during the day, but still critical.

12/12/23
Condition remains critical. No significant change from last night.

15/12/23
Condition worsened again overnight. Breathing shallow and slow. Lungs beginning to fill with fluid. Blood pressure dropped to dangerous level. Decision to be made. Critical now. Must get heart back to single, rather than dual control, or patient will not survive.[14]

Owen Tudor - 16th December 1923 – Lydd
"Lieutenant, we will lose your wife if we do not induce a miscarriage. Too much of her energy is being taken sustaining the child. But she is rapidly losing the struggle with her influenza. Her body is already weak. As you know we have already had to resuscitate her twice, and she cannot cope with this unholy assault on both sides. If we induce, she might survive. If we don't do it now, we are certain to lose them both."

"How long?"

"A week, or much less, if we do nothing. If we act now, she may pull through, but it will be touch and go, even so."

There was a long pause. Owen Tudor turned away towards the fireplace. He spoke very quietly, knowing how much his decision would break Tatiana's heart, but so wanting his wife to live, for however long.

"Do it."

Bishop nodded and left. Owen Tudor sank to his knees, put his head in his hands and wept like a child. In his heart, he knew this was the beginning of the end. How long that end would be depended on fate, a fate that had been already too cruel, and now was set to take away even that vestige of happiness that had been so tantalisingly held out to them all those months ago, in what now seemed to him like another lifetime. He could still see Tatiana's face as they made love on that first day in July. In anger, he got to his feet, picked up his wineglass from the mantelpiece, threw it into the grate and roared as the glass shattered into a million fragments of musical light.

Owen Tudor - 17th December 1923 – Lydd

"Is it over?"

"Yes."

"What was it?"

"A girl. There was no chance of her surviving at this early a stage."

"How is my wife?"

"Dying. I don't think she will last more than a day. Possibly two."

"Can I see her?"

"Of course."

Owen went upstairs. As he opened the door, he saw Mrs Bishop sitting by Tatiana's side. She got up quickly and left the room.

"Call me if anything happens, or when you leave."

He sat beside his wife and took her hand. She did not grip. Was not even aware of him. Her breathing was laboured and slow, and her lungs were gurgling badly. She had lost so much weight. Her face was a shell, a shadow of her beauty. But even that shadow was more magnificent than any girl he had ever seen, or would ever see, he thought. He stroked Tatiana's hand. Her breathing was so slow...

Grand Duchess Tatiana - 17th December 1923 – Lydd

"Hello. Who are you?"

"Your daughter."

Tatiana looked into the little girl's eyes. They were such deep blue, almost hypnotic in their intensity.

"You do know me. Look closer."

Tatiana seemed to drown in the little girl's eyes. Suddenly, there was a spark of recognition. The little girl jumped up and down.

"Sorry, Tanya, but I had to try."

Tatiana gripped the little girl's hands. She was about to run away.

"Owen's really nice. I'm glad you've got him. I'll have to try the other way now."

"What other way?"

*"You'll see. Olga doesn't approve. She thinks it's unethical. But I **will** have my life back. Thank you so much for trying with me. I love you."*

The little girl faded from sight, leaving only the faint memory of her golden hair behind her. The tears were streaming down Tatiana's face. Her chance had gone. And Anastasia's too. What would become of them both now?

Tatiana lapsed into oblivion, and spent most of the next two weeks fighting her way back from the brink of death. Mr Bishop and the two other doctors who attended thought it was no less than a miracle. Owen was delighted to have his wife back. But his delight was tempered by the knowledge that she would never walk again, unaided. The disease had weakened her system beyond repair. From December 1923, it was no longer a question of if Tatiana would die. The real question was how long and protracted the decline would be.

King George V - 27th December 1923 – Balmoral

"She's out of immediate danger, Your Majesty."

The King slumped down in his chair. "What is the prognosis?"

"She still could die within the month, sir. Her heart has been considerably weakened. It will accelerate the diseases she is already carrying."

There was a pause.

"Should she survive, shall we carry on looking after her and sending reports to you?"

King George looked up. He was distracted. His mind was somewhere else. "What?"

"Do you want us to carry on looking after her and sending reports to you, in the event she survives her ordeal?"

There was another long pause

"By all means, look after her. But you read the reports from now on. Only tell me if things worsen, or if she is close to death. And…"

"Yes, Your Majesty?"

"Remember, she is of the Orthodox Faith. Begin to make burial arrangements. She will have to be buried in Lydd under her assumed name. Telling everyone about it now will only bring unnecessary embarrassment and complications, and questions I'd rather not be forced to answer. When the time comes, bury her with all the rites of her Faith, but make sure she is put well out of sight."

He paused, before saying, "For now, let her live the remainder of her life in what comfort she may. Let me know as and when things become worse."

Stamfordham left the King contemplating a book of Orthodox Prayers he had found in his library. Nicholas II had given it to him during the family's last visit in 1909, but he had forgotten it until now. He opened the page at random. It read:

"*Kontakion*

Neither grave, nor death had power over the Mother of God, who resteth not in her intercessions and is a hope that faileth not in her protection: for the Mother of Life hath been brought into Life by Him who dwelt in her ever-virginal womb."

Tatiana's Diary - 17th June 1924 – Lydd

Bright and sunny today. 21 degrees. Went out onto the Rype in the afternoon. Sat under a tree and had tea brought out by Mrs Bishop. My two sticks made progress difficult. Read Anna Karenina. Dozed. Woke a little after 4pm to find Owen leaning on my tree, watching me sleep. It reminded me of our first meeting.

"May I escort you home, sir?"

In spite of myself, I burst out laughing.

He picked me up in his arms. "Light as a feather, you are now." He looked at me with that dear concern of his.

"All the better for you to pick me up in your strong arms." I kissed him. "My Hero."

We both laughed ourselves silly as he carried me indoors.

24th June 1924 – Lydd

Tried to get out of bed this morning. My legs would not respond to commands. Yelled for help. Mrs Bishop came and helped me to the dressing table chair. Doctor came mid-afternoon. Told me quite starkly that my condition has worsened. Feeling in my legs is almost gone. All that is left is a vague tingling. My cough is worse too. Shall need a chair to get about in now. How humiliating. And someone to carry me up and down stairs. Owen will have to do that in the morning before he goes out. Then I shall be stranded until he comes home. But I shall get by. If I have my supply of books and writing paper, I shall be happy.

13th July 1924 – Lydd

Heard a performance of Tchaikovsky's Symphony No.6 in B minor on the radio. It was so beautiful. I wished I could put my Pointe shoes on again and dance to the second movement. I remember Olga and I devising choreography for our plays. Once, she, Marie and I did an impersonation of the three graces. I've never felt so beautiful. I closed my eyes and imagined the three of us dancing. It was heaven. When I die, I hope we can be together and dance again. Beethoven, who was deaf, wanted to hear again. Well I, who have lost my legs, want to dance again. Beauty is all that matters. In this life or any other. Remember this. Beauty is all there ever was. Beauty is love and love is beauty. Forever…

23rd August 1924 – Lydd

Finished Anna Karenina today. Anna's suicide seems curiously attractive to me. I feel as if I have outlived my time now. Perhaps I should have gone with Masha and Olga when they came for me at Christmas last year. Owen would be free then to get on with his life and career. I'm just holding him back. Anna killed herself because she thought she had lost Count Vronsky's love. She also thought, as an older woman, she was holding him back. I am the older woman, and I am holding Owen back. If I had a gun, I would go to bed and blow my brains out, but I don't and can't get one from Owen, he's very careful not to bring his home with him. Hanging myself would have been my preferred method. But I no longer have my legs, so that's not an option. I would never be able to stand on a chair with a rope around my neck and kick the chair away. And I hate pills. All that swallowing and feeling fuzzy. UGH!

Of course, I could still let nature take its course. If I do, perhaps there might be time left yet for one last flourish. The one thing I'm enjoying is my poetry. I feel so close to everyone when I'm writing. When it's finished, I think I'll call the collection

"Russian Snowflakes." If anyone ever sees it, it'll broadcast our love all over the world. Maybe that may change things. I know now that politics never will. Love and compassion are the only things that ever change minds and hearts. If people look to each other with the eyes of God, there will never be any need again for a State. Maybe Heaven is like that. Soon, my family will tell me. I'm sure.

I've decided. I will go when it is my time, and not before. I'm ready, and not afraid. Until then, I shall write of Beauty and Love while I still can. That is all that is left. All that ever was…

25th December 1924 – Lydd

Christmas Day. Sleeping by the fire after what passes for Christmas lunch. Waking, I become aware of a familiar sound. The piano is playing. The music is a prelude by my former teacher, his Prelude No.23 in G sharp minor. When I was well it was one of my favourites. Olga was always infuriated by it. It requires a very subtle technique, which she never quite mastered. My eyes open and become accustomed to the dim light. Sitting at the piano is… Sergei Vassileyvitch! I burst into tears. His beautiful presence is too much for me. As I begin to convulse with sobs he ceases playing and comes to me, takes my body in his arms and holds me so tenderly. I cry freely for the first time in years in his embrace, and for what seems like an eternity we both exist outside of time.

He tells me he is in England with his wife visiting a composer friend of his who is currently staying in London, Nicholas Medtner. A letter I wrote to him had reached him in America where he now lives, but the Royal censor had deleted the address and he had to use all of his prestige and an appeal to Cousin George before he was allowed to come to me. Seeing him transports me back home, if only for a little while. We spend two hours talking together in Russian and I feel healing energy all around. He tells me about his silence, why he cannot compose since he left our Russian homeland. At this, I cry again and we hold hands. For a long time, there are no words between us, only a communion of the soul that speaks louder and goes deeper than speech ever could. Then, he tells me about his plans for a fourth piano concerto. It sounds exciting and I feel frustrated that I will probably never live to hear it. Gradually, I feel warm and at peace, but exhausted. Owen comes in, I introduce them and they spend awhile talking together. I doze…

In my dreams, I see Nastya. She runs towards me, and hugs me tight, looking at me with that wry grin of hers.

"I've done it Tanya! I've really done it!! And I'll come and see you soon. Trust me. Don't be sad about leaving me. It was all right you know, and in the end I've got a new body. Just you wait and see. I'm going to surprise everyone, just see if I don't."

Before I can ask her to elaborate, she twirls and dances away from me. The light fades and I'm left alone and sad, with just the faintest impression of Olga's presence. She seems to be smiling in my mind and I feel her warmth very distinctly.

Waking again later, Owen gives me the present my teacher has left for me. His new recording of the 2nd and 3rd movements of his Piano Concerto No.2 in C minor. My husband puts it on the gramophone and we sit together. As I listen I see again the halls of home and hear the laughter of my brother and sisters… Time is a circle … no beginning or end, just eternity … eternity…

3rd February 1925 – Lydd

Today I read a remarkable story in the newspapers about a young girl in Germany who claims to be … Anastasia! Apparently, this girl was fished out of the water in Berlin after having tried to drown herself. Those in the asylum with her afterwards mistook her for me (how weird!). But later she was found to be too small in height. Baroness Buxhovenden has been to see her and dismissed her outright, but other family members have seen her and asked her some direct questions about our lives and received answers that only Nastya would have known. What's really strange is that the paper has printed a picture of the girl, and it looks nothing like Nastya. So how does she know our intimacies in as much detail as she seems to? The other anomaly is that the knowledge seems to come and go. Sometimes it's there, at others she seems to be making it up.

I realise now that I've seen this in my dreams. The girl being hauled out of the water, the shouting in German, and then Nastya coming to me all excited about a new body. The girl had apparently attempted suicide. Could it be that this is what Nastya meant? Has she tried to take over this body? It would explain the fluctuations in the girl's knowledge after all. And Nastya said she would come to see me. I feel excited. But what if the body's original owner wants it back? Nastya will have a fight on her hands. And who would accept her as she is? She is evidently not one of us physically. I know what Father Grigory would say. It is the essence that matters, not the covering. With the permission of the body's original owner, Nastya and I could work together to spread the word about what really happened, spread Father Grigory's real message of love, healing and communion with Nature. I so want to see her. I get the feeling that if we meet, it will somehow seal Nastya's ownership of the new body as I feel I will be able to call her to me and help her to make her memories conscious. But will my body, which is now deteriorating, or my family ever let me out of this country to see her? I feel so impatient, I could scream.

2nd April 1925 – Lydd

Master John Bishop is the sort of boy who may one day grow up to be a murderer. Today, with a superhuman exercising of my will, I got up onto my sticks for the first time since mid-1924 and hobbled into the hallway of our house to find him tormenting a mouse he had caught in a trap. His behaviour was hideous and inhuman. I could feel the little thing's distress and it all but broke

237

my heart. Forgetting my condition for a moment, I rose to my full height and yelled at him in Russian. I used the expression Olga once hurled at our governess. You remember, Diary, the one that got her a caning? Well, John didn't understand the words, but he picked up my intent, especially after I threw one of my sticks at him. I missed and it flew into a wall light, smashing it. Simultaneously, reality hit, as did I the floor, hard.

The rascal ran off shouting, "The Russian woman has gone mad! She's trying to kill me!"

He was calling for his mother. She came running out to see what the noise was about and came to help me. I told her about the trap and the mouse as she helped me to sit up.

"That boy'll be the death of me. His father's always trying to stop him doing that. It's not just mice, he does that to any animal he can catch. I'm sorry you had to see it, Miss. Gets it from 'is grandfather he does. He was a gamekeeper…"

Gamekeepers should have more respect for the animals and the land. In the Old Times, man and animals lived together… in peace. Man took only what he needed, not what his greed desired. What would Father Grigory say! As I sat there and Mrs Bishop's voice diminished into the background, I was suddenly back in Spala. The year was 1910 and I was looking at a faun that was approaching me in the fading twilight of early evening…

14th July 1925 – Lydd
A gorgeous summer day. It's just a pity that I can't go for a walk along the Rype and out towards the Marsh. It's such a wonderful landscape that I'm sure would delight any artist and the sunsets are spectacular. My legs are now so completely useless that I have to be carried out into the garden in the afternoons.

Fortunately a young friend has been kindly obliging me. Herbert Prebble is a strong, handsome nineteen-year-old lad we have got to know. He is a journeyman and friend of Owen's whom I first saw about a year ago. He has been coming over after my nurse has left, and carries me into the garden where he leaves me, safely tucked up in my chair. I can spend all afternoon just gazing into the distance, watch the children playing and sometimes talk to them too. I'm sure a few of the young girls wait until Owen comes home to talk to him as he passes by. He still cuts a handsome, if somewhat curious, figure in his uniform. I'm also convinced that the uniforms in the British Army are not as handsome as our Imperial ones. They're all grey and green, with the occasional flash of blue. I know which I prefer.

I had a visit yesterday afternoon from Amorel Meinertzhagen. I haven't seen her since before Owen and I married. I was curious to know what she was here for. Her conversation was about "something and nothing" as they say in this country. I'm sure she was trying to find something out, but as to what, I cannot think. I have nothing to hide, and her husband and his colleagues finished with me a very long time since. So it was all rather strange. After an hour of nothing much and one half-finished cup of tea, she left rather abruptly and forgot to leave my husband her compliments. I mentioned the visit to Owen when he arrived home, but he was as seemingly puzzled as I. I did catch him later however with an unreadable expression after he got off the phone. Sometimes I wonder how much of his life he really tells me about and how much is fiction. But stuck in this dammed chair all the time I can't do much to find out...

Later...
Sitting here in the depths of night (it's 1.30am as I write this, and, by candle-light – aren't I naughty?) I sometimes feel, sitting in my wheelchair that I get a sense of déjà vu. As if it has all happened before, or will again. Time has been doing some very strange things to me lately. For instance, just the other day, Owen was wheeling me out to the shop just for a breath of air when I was convinced I saw Olga standing on the corner of the street up ahead. Not thinking, I tried to leap out of the chair. When Owen

asked me what was wrong, I felt foolish. And besides, when we got to the street corner, I saw it was a woman who didn't resemble Olga at all. Such silliness. I could laugh, but truly afterwards felt more like crying.

On the other hand, some things you see and hear are less easy to explain away. After Herbert had left me this afternoon, I was half dozing in the afternoon sun when I heard the strangest sound overhead. It was a deep roar, intensely musical. Some people might have been frightened, but I wasn't. I looked up and saw an aircraft fly overhead. It was clearly marked in British colours, but it was obviously one of these new-fangled monoplanes, not the old biplanes the RFC used to fly. The most striking things about it were its wings, graciously curved at the ends, and its speed. I thought I must be seeing things, but it was travelling at least twice as fast as any aircraft I had seen before. When little Molly from the farm next door poked her head over my gate, I asked her if she had seen the plane. Oddly, she didn't know what I was talking about, but someone must have seen the low-flying craft. Technology is definitely on the move in these "Roaring Twenties." [15]

15th July 1925 – 3.40am
I had fallen asleep at my writing desk when I was woken by a strong smell of Roses. I hadn't smelled that particular perfume for quite a while. Coming to, I saw a familiar arm and hand turning the pages of this diary. Looking up to my right, I saw Olga for real. Reaching out my hand, I touched solid flesh, warm, beautiful flesh and heard a familiar voice.

"I told you I would never leave you, my love."

I shut my eyes tightly. I couldn't allow this. The pain of seeing, and worse, touching her again now, was unbearable. I began to wail. Then, realising that I would wake Owen, I stifled it. Opening my eyes, I saw that the phantasm had gone and I was alone again. Which was worse? That, or the vision? I did not know how to answer myself. Hastily I hid the diary, wheeled myself over to the bed and heaved myself into it. Curious. I seem to be having difficulty breathing fully. I must just be unfit. That is all. Sleeping, my dreams are filled with the past, my family and a wonderful small black furry friend. All now shadows that don't exist. I wake up at 8am, crying for the umpteenth time. The pain will not go. I suppose there are just some wounds that never heal, no matter how much time or space you give for them. All my optimism is fading away. I feel so sorry for Owen. No matter how much he may think he loves me, and I wonder about that sometimes, I can *never, never* give him the love he wants in return. For once you have been truly, deeply loved, as I was, nothing can ever replace it and, once lost, it is gone forever.

17th September 1925 – Lydd
Today I lost Oscar. Anastasia's teddy. And yet, I think Nastya would have approved of what I did with him. Little Molly who plays at the back of our house is a very sweet and innocent little girl who reminds me slightly of Anastasia. She's only eight years old, but she still carries her teddy out with her when she's playing. This afternoon I heard her crying over our back gate and asked her to come and tell me all about it. Apparently she had been playing when a group of local farm boys had jumped all over her, taken her teddy and torn him to bits in front of her. The shock had been terrible and her mother had not been able to soothe her pain, so she had come to me.

I told her that teddies are indestructible and that no amount of violence can harm them. Her teddy was just waiting to come back to her. In fact, as it happened, he had already done so. I told her to close her eyes and put out her hand. She did so. I reached inside, underneath my blanket, where I always kept Oscar, lifted him out and put him into Molly's hands. I told her to open her eyes and when she did so, she could see Oscar's lovely lopsided smile looking straight at her. Molly burst into tears and hugged

Oscar tight. But she was smiling.

"There you are," I said, "Always remember. Teddies are forever. They never leave you. And if the light of the world should ever go out, they would still be there to show us God's Love and take us all home."

Molly hugged me as much as my chair allowed and ran home singing joyously. At that moment, I got a picture of Nastya in my mind. She was herself again, and she was smiling. My mind makes up some pleasing phantoms sometimes.

20th December 1925 – Lydd
Finished making the last of the teddies and rag dolls for the Salvation Army Christmas stall. It'll be held tomorrow. It took a lot of strength from me. But the looks on the children's faces, which Owen will tell me about later on, will be worth it.

22nd December 1925 – Lydd
Owen lied. He never went to the stall. My teddies were sold by Mrs Bishop. Where did Owen go? And why did he lie to me? Confronting him will be impossible. I don't have the strength. And he would probably only lie to me again.

25th December 1925 – 1st January 1926
Horrible. Strained. Was sick after Christmas dinner. In bed ever since. Did not celebrate New Year. Owen wasn't here anyway.

8th January 1926 – Lydd
Cough. Cough. Cough. That is all I do now. And spurt blood. I don't get up. I can't go out. Snow. Wind. Rain and loneliness. That is what my life has become. Empty. Empty. Empty. Owen is always away. I can't say I blame him. He probably can't stand the sight of me. All I see are nurses and doctors. No-one else. No. Not a soul. And sometimes I think they're looking for something. Possibly this diary. Perish the thought anyone should ever read it.

I hear life going on in the road outside, but it might as well not be happening at all for all I see of it. I'm not afraid of dying. But I wish that my body would just get on with it. This waiting is driving me crazy.

King George V & Owen Tudor - 4th April 1926 – Buckingham Palace

The King looked deeply into Lieutenant Tudor's eyes.

"I want to thank you, sir. This task was very difficult, but I understand from my Private Secretary that you have done very well. Your service will not go unnoticed."

Owen Tudor looked at the carpet. "Thank you, Your Majesty."

"Your old regiment is waiting to accept you back when the time comes, and you won't have any problems. I can promise you that. If you keep your word."

"No-one will ever know about this, sir. Not from me. Not even my family."

"I knew we could count on you. Your uncle convinced me in the beginning. He was right."

"And Tanya, sir?"

"She will be buried with all due ceremony, and then forgotten. But don't worry. I've instructed a firm of solicitors to handle the grave. It will always be well attended. She is family after all."

The lieutenant realised the interview was over. He got up to leave. As he reached the door, he said, "I did love her, sir."

The King was gentle for once. "I know my boy. Makes it worse, doesn't it?"

"For us all, sir."

For half a second, the two men's eyes locked and they were no longer King and subject, but Cousin and Husband, united in grief for the immanent loss of someone they loved.

Tatiana's Diary - 20th May 1926 – Lydd

I have very little strength left. Several entries in this diary have had to be destroyed as they were written on small scraps of paper garnered in odd moments when Owen and my "companions" weren't looking. Owen has been behaving very oddly these last few months, leaving me for very long periods in the care of some "people" he calls "nurses". These "carers" hardly speak a civil word to me and if I didn't know better I would consider them gaolers rather than the compassionate sorts they are supposed to be. Entries to this book have had to be surreptitious in the extreme and many have been lost, including some valuable remembrances of my family, which, I fear I will not now have the energy to rewrite. My breathing has been worsening and in the last few weeks I have begun to cough up blood in terrible quantities.

My time outside has been getting steadily less and I see no-one except Owen and his people. Why that reminds me of my captivity in Tobolsk and Ekaterinburg, I cannot for one moment imagine, can you? I suspect that the presence of these impostors, for yes, these nurses are undoubtedly that, as I now realise, my "husband" has been all this time, is to do with efforts to locate what I am writing. It is what I have kept from the past, all I brought with me from my home, beloved, eternal Russia, land of my dreams. I have had to conceal so much, so cleverly, that I now scarcely know who I am anymore and my strength has finally run out.

I shall conceal this beyond any hope of finding until many years have passed, so what I say to you, who find this, I say with love and with hope that you will remember me and my family in your prayers.

The record, such as it is, is now complete, or as complete as I have the strength to make it. I make no apologies for its content, some of which, some reading it may find controversial, but I wanted to set things down exactly as they happened so that we may not be forgotten. What we tried to do so nearly succeeded, but fate, as always, dealt the deciding hand. It is my strong belief that in centuries to come, when Eternal Russia becomes the country we meant Her to be, the country it could so easily have been, the standard of the Double Headed Eagle will once more fly over the Winter Palace and with Truth and Beauty in their rightful place in people's hearts, they will remember us with a smile and a prayer for our eternal rest.

This record I write with love in memory of my beloved family. Now I must set down my pen. Soon, I too will rest forever with them, sleeping in the Light.

Tatiana Nicolaevna Romanov 3.33 am May 21st 1926

16th July 1926 – Midnight
Entry by Lieutenant Owen Tudor – Placed in the diary in 1929
Those of you, who discover this work, treat it with tenderness and care. It is all that is left of my beloved Tanya. So much was taken from her in the last eight years of her life. I truly feel that, after 1918, life was over for her, although, I flatter myself to think, I made the end at least more bearable than it might have been. And, even if in exile here, she was at least free to be herself.

Last night, at around 11pm, I was with her in her room. How I wish I could take her in my arms one more time. But she is so fragile now, and all life is precious. I want every minute with her that I can. And she is fighting. Hard. I can feel it. She fights for life with every breath….every tortured breath. God, she is so pale now….so white. I was gazing at her face as she slept, when I became aware of a gentle breeze across my face. I looked up, and, out of the corner of my eye, and for a brief second, I saw a young woman bending over Tanya, touching her face. Her lips were moving, but I heard no sound. I saw her lay her hand in Tanya's and she kissed her. All this happened in a brief second or two, as if time was slowed to nothing; the events seemed divorced from our reality somehow. Then, she turned to me and I saw her full face, before she vanished, right in front of me. She was half smiling and I saw the glistening of tears in her deep, black eyes... Then she was gone. But she left behind the most beautiful smell of Roses I have ever sensed.

Diary Footnote August 1929

I hesitated to add this to Tanya's diary. But yesterday my Uncle showed me a photograph of her family. The smiling girl who was tending her was her older sister, Olga, who was murdered, as the rest of her family were, in July 1918. For a long time I held the picture and cried. My darling is home again, and I now know for certain that we all go on. Until we meet again...

Owen

14th August 1929

The diary of Grand Duchess Tatiana ends here.

Grand Duchess Tatiana - 18th July 1926 – 12.06 am

Coda – Just one more thing to do... Last night – she took my hand... Diary... I'm not here anymore... Feel like laughing... So much futility... they're not even aware of it...Wouldn't be even if you told them... the sound of your voice would fade away like a silent breeze into nothingness... nothingness...[16]

PART IV

MOBIUS

APRIL 1943 - NOVEMBER 2006

15th April 1943 – SS Vladimir Ilyitch - The Baltic Ocean

With his ship steaming slowly through a heavy swell, Seaman Pyotr Jordania cursed his luck for the fiftieth time. It was supposed to be an early spring day, but you wouldn't think so to feel the cold arctic blast coming from the wind across the crow's nest. One lousy game of cards. The lieutenant had caught him out, along with two colleagues, in the dead of night. What were they supposed to do? The Baltic was hell on Earth, crawling with enemy submarines. Everyone had been on edge. You couldn't sleep, so you played cards and tried to make-believe you were back at home. Instead of which, you wound up on a charge. Everyone was supposed to get the right amount of rest, all the better to fight the enemy, but how could you, stuck out here, worried because you hadn't had a letter from home in two weeks. Anything could have happened.

Suddenly, through the murk, a ship loomed up off the port bow. It came up so fast that Pyotr barely had time to blink before realizing that a collision was imminent. Frantically, he called out to the bridge and the collision alarm was sounded. The SS Vladimir Ilyitch lurched violently to one side and by some miracle disaster was averted. There was a lot of shouting from the men below at the idiots on the other ship. Surely their radar would have alerted them to a presence. But oddly, all the shouting and gesticulating seemed to have no effect. The sailors on the other vessel seemed to be totally unaware of them. The ship was also flying a very old flag from the stern. It was a Royal Double Headed Eagle on a yellow background, and as they passed the prow of the ship, in Russian could be seen its name in proud letters of gold: "STANDART". Pyotr froze. It was the old Royal Yacht, long since destroyed. He remembered seeing pictures of it when he was a boy and wondering quietly what it would have been like to sail with the old Tsar and his family. The ship and its Royal passengers were surely long dead. This was impossible. But how to doubt the evidence of his own eyes?

Snapping out of his reverie, Pyotr called the bridge and was about to call the ship's name to his captain when he looked up again... and the Royal Yacht was gone. All that was left was the icy wind and heaving seas of a Baltic Ocean in which super-powers were locked in a life or death struggle of pain and annihilation. There were no photographs to record the event and those who reported it were only able to confirm that they had been, like everyone else in April 1943, suffering from over-anxiety and too little, far too little, sleep.

12th *June 1955 – Leningrad*

12th June 1955 – Leningrad
Svetlana Brokhina had been ill for days. A little girl of only eight years, she had contracted a mysterious illness which the doctors could neither diagnose nor treat. Her grandmother tended her. She was all that was left of her family. Her mother and father had disappeared, arrested by the KGB for one of thousands of spurious offences with which the state was given to torturing its citizens, while her grandfather had died in the final assault on Berlin in 1945. Little Svetlana lay in her stupor, clutching her doll, the last present her mother had bought her, for her last birthday. Lyubov looked despairingly at the photograph of her husband, and, in spite of herself, she began to pray.

With her eyes closed, she felt, imperceptibly, a change in atmosphere in the room. It felt less oppressive, lighter, and, after a few moments, she smelled the fragrance of roses. This was unlike the roses in her living room. That was a more delicate fragrance. This smelled more like perfume, and expensive perfume at that. Lyubov opened her eyes. Bending over her granddaughter she saw a handsome man in a large military greatcoat. Kneeling beside her was a young woman of breath-taking beauty, who held her arm gently.

"Don't worry. Papa says that her fever will break today and she will be well."

The girl smiled. Her warmth made Lyubov tingle all over, as

if she was surrounded by dancing living sparks of electricity. Dimly, she realised that she knew these people, and, as the man turned towards her, recognition dawned. She grasped his hand in both of hers. It was warm and gentle.

"Thank you, Your Majesty. She is all I have left."

Nicholas II smiled. "You are very welcome. All shall be well for you now. Your husband sends his love, as do your daughter and her husband. Tell your granddaughter. When the time comes, you will see each other again."

The young woman rose to her feet. She was exceptionally tall, clearing her father's height by several inches. Lyubov realised that the perfume smell had been coming from her, but was now surrounding them all and penetrating the room in a cocoon of love. Tatiana smiled deeply. The sleeve of her dress was thin enough to reveal to Lyubov the shape of a tattoo on her upper left arm. It was very intricate, and she could not quite make out what it was. From one blink to the next, Tsar Nicholas and his daughter were gone, leaving behind the perfume and a feeling of the deepest peace. Lyubov slept.

When she woke, her granddaughter was awake, smiling and asking for something to eat.

Later, she said, "Baboushka, did you see the kind man and lady who came to see me? He touched me on my neck and told me I would be well. While you slept, the lady came back. She had a firebird with her. She touched your neck and told me you too would be well now. Who were they?"

Her grandmother smiled. She had been aware of pain in her side for several months and been afraid to seek help, not wanting to leave her granddaughter alone. The pain was gone now.

"That was our Sovereign Nicholas and his daughter, Tatiana. They have gone ahead of us, to where God lives. Where your grandfather and Mama and Papa are. They are taking care of them until we can all be together again."

The little girl had a distant look. "When the lady smiled at me,

I sensed Mama too, as if she was here as well, even if I couldn't see her…"

Little Svetlana slept. A doorway was opened. Little by little, the healing could begin. If people could have been aware of it, the air was filled with the sound of chanting, distant, harmonious and beautiful. Over the next years, it would become gradually more powerful, a silent, yet potent influence on what was to come.

28th April 1971 – Alexander Palace

Lieutenant Yuri Shenyets walked slowly away from his superior's office, taking in the sights and smells of this once beautiful palace. Now, for many years used as the offices of the Soviet Navy, the place still retained some of its old-fashioned charm. It almost oozed from the walls in places. Some of the old Imperial decorations had not been removed either. He took his time, savouring his visit. When he had told his grandmother that he had been summoned to the Admiralty, she had become excited, but not, it seemed, at the prospect of her 22-year-old grandson's promotion. She had ushered him into the back room of her small wooden cottage. It was a place he had never seen, one that he had even heard his mother talk about in hushed tones. Inside, once he had become used to the gloom, he began to see that the furnishings were like something out of an earlier, more elegant age. The walls were covered in old photographs. There were people in them that young Yuri recognised, but couldn't put a name to.

His grandmother pulled him towards one in particular, which she pulled off the wall and showed to him. "You see this place, that is where you are going. To be sure, it is called the Admiralty now, but when this picture was taken, it was the home of a very special family. You can see some of them standing in front of it, see, look closely."

She pushed the picture at him. To oblige her, he took it and looked. The picture was now fading and yellow at the edges, but the faces of the people in the picture were still strangely fresh, as if the picture had been taken yesterday. One face, in particular, caught his attention, that of a very pretty, tall young woman, with a white dress and hat on who was standing to one side of the front door and staring, unlike the other people, straight out of the photograph, as if at him. Her gaze was compelling and seemed to hold his. A silence was descending in the room as he stared at the picture.

"Beautiful, isn't she? She is one of the daughters of the last Tsar, Nicholas II. Her name was Tatiana. Murdered with the rest of her family in 1918 when the Reds decided they did not need them anymore. They were the saviours of our country and the demons murdered them. We have all been living in hell ever since."

Yuri was shocked. He did not know that his grandmother was a secret monarchist. Such information would have got her arrested at the very least and, in the Stalinist era, possibly even killed. No wonder his family had always discussed her in hushed tones.

"Come, come." She gestured to him. Over by the back wall of the small room was a chest of drawers, made in the old-fashioned peasant style. His grandmother took a small key from inside her dress and unlocked the bottom drawer. Inside was a small book. When she opened it, he saw it was full of photographs. The same family could be seen again, this time in ordinary clothes, with spades in their hands, digging plots of earth, wiping sweat away from their brows, wheeling heavy barrel water butts. There was a charming picture of a small boy playing with a very happy looking spaniel. Yuri laughed.

"The heir. He had a disease of his blood. He was a lovely boy. So gentle and kind hearted."

There was another one of the boy, this time with the same girl he had seen before. They had their arms around each other and were laughing. Her eyes held him once more.

Yuri began, inexplicably, to feel angry and then, as he saw more pictures, he felt tears welling up inside him. "Grandmother, where did you get these?"

"Look inside the cover."

Yuri opened the book. It was inscribed, with a postcard picture.

"To Lyubov Alexandrovna Yurchinka. Remember 1917."

It was signed, *"Nicholas, Alexandra, Olga, Tatiana, Marie, Anastasia, Alexei. August 13th 1917."*

"The family gave me this the day before they were taken away. They never returned."

Yuri gave his grandmother the book. There were no words. They were unnecessary.

Walking in this place, it was to Yuri as if he had stepped suddenly back in time. He felt floaty, as if his body and head were not quite joined together. This was the top corridor of the old palace. It seemed to go on forever, but he remembered from what his grandmother had told him that eventually, it turned into one of the wings. Reaching the stairs that led down to the ground floor, he was suddenly aware of a change in them. They looked somehow newer, and the gold was brighter than he had remembered it earlier this morning. As he walked down the stairs, he noticed that his feet were on red carpet. Strange. He had not noticed the colour when he arrived. In the distance, he heard a piano being played. Straining his ears, he quickly recognised the music. It was a piece he had himself always longed to play, but his devoutly communist teacher at the Moscow Academy had denounced it as "Decadent Tsarist crap!"

The offending piece was Rachmaninov's Piano Sonata No.2 in B flat minor. The finale was being played and he was instantly aware that the pianist was no beginner, for it was the finale of the original 1913 version that was being played. He knew few modern pianists would dare to tackle its Olympian heights.

Transfixed, he felt his soul begin to sing with the soaring second subject. The reading was amazingly poetic, as if the player knew the composer's feelings intimately. Such fire and passion. He felt himself drawn towards the sound instinctively. His spirit had a need to be in the presence of the music and performer. As he got closer to the sound, he realised he was on the deserted first floor of the palace. He knew from what he had been told that one of the rooms contained an old grand piano, but it was supposed to be in a sorry state of repair and had not been played for many years.

He arrived at the door behind which the piano was being played. Gently, so as not to disturb the player, who was now in the throes of the finale's coda, he opened the door, thinking to congratulate the pianist on a wonderful performance and maybe even find out who their teacher was, although he was certain that it was a Leningrad style he was hearing. As the door opened, a shaft of sunlight breaking through the clouds struck him, which all but blinded him. The piece was reaching its thunderous conclusion. When his sight recovered, he saw the room was painted in dark red and burnished gold and covered in mirrors. They all looked new. A roaring fire was in the grate and candles covered the walls, illuminating the room in a soft golden light. The piano was brand new, not old as he had been told and at the piano was sat the most beautiful girl he had ever seen. Poised, serene and tall as a weeping willow, she smiled up at the girl who was leaning on the piano and had been turning her pages, a girl who exuded the grace of a ballerina. He watched the two beautiful creatures kiss.

It was then that the pianist looked directly at him. Before he could utter a word, her eyes met his and his words of congratulation died in his throat. The girl looking at him was the same one he had seen staring out of the photograph he had seen in his grandmother's house two days earlier. Her companion was Olga, one of her sisters. Tatiana held his gaze for a long moment, then said something to her sister in a dialect of Russian he did not recognise, but it was obviously a statement of alarm. Quickly, Olga walked to the door of the room and closed it, an enigmatic half-smile on her lips. Just as quickly, Yuri re-opened the door wanting to protest.

The door opened on a room full of discarded and rusty office furniture and old filing cabinets. There had obviously been mirrors on the walls once, but now most were covered with old sheets and some were just as obviously broken. In the far corner stood what remained of an old grand piano. It was neglected now and uncared for. Its music had long-since died. As Yuri reached it, on the upturned lid, could be made out a name in faded gold lettering:

"Erard – Paris 1873."

Overwhelmed, Yuri began to cry. But he was pulled out of his reverie abruptly.

"Lieutenant, what are you doing here? This floor is restricted!"

It was the adjutant, Commander Rostov.

"I'm sorry, sir, but I thought I heard a piano playing in here."

"Don't be ridiculous. No-one's played that piano since before the revolution. I think you've been drinking a little too much celebratory vodka, eh?"

The Commander smiled. "Now, get on with you. I know you have leave coming. Go and enjoy it. Active service will come soon enough. I hear the Philharmonic has a good concert on tonight. Rachmaninov I think. Symphony No.2 and 2nd Piano Concerto. You're a pianist, aren't you?"

"Yes, sir."

"Richter's playing tonight. You won't get much better. Enjoy."

"Thank you, sir."

Saluting the Commander, Lieutenant Yuri Shenyets ran out of the room, down the dilapidated and tired-looking staircase and out through the old palace doors into the weak afternoon sunlight.

Soon it would be dark and he would go alone to the Rachmaninov concert at the Philharmonic. But his heart would not be in Leningrad and the pianist he heard playing the Rachmaninov concerto would not be Sviatoslav Richter.

29th November 2006 – Cathedral on Blood in Honour of All Saints Resplendent in the Russian Land – Ekaterinburg – Morning

First morning prayers were being said. Father Seraphim closed his eyes and contemplated the image before him of the Mother of God. The music, part of Rachmaninov's Liturgy op.31, filled the air around him, combining with the incense to create a very special air of spiritual upliftment. He could feel the people beginning to assemble, coming and going beside him as he raised his voice to intone the eternal words of beauty and fulfilment radiating from the choir, and lost himself at the gateway to Heaven.

Very gradually he became aware of a deep hush in the vastness of the cathedral space. This was not normal. People should be in constant motion throughout the service. The silence was different somehow. He could feel the presence of the congregation, but it was as if they had been stunned into immobility by something. Father Seraphim opened his eyes and was greeted by a sight that challenged his comprehension of reality.

In front of the altar he saw a group of people kneeling. They had their backs to him. There were seven in all. A man, a woman, four girls and a boy. The women were dressed in the fashions of pre-World War I. As the choir reached a powerful climax, they rose from the altar and turned. The priest and people looked on as Tsar Nicholas II, Tsaritsa Alexandra, Grand Duchesses Olga, Tatiana, Marie and Anastasia, and the Tsareivitch Grand Duke Alexis lit candles and left them burning in their receptacles. The congregation understood the miracle taking place in front of them instinctively and their hearts reached out to Nicholas and the others. They were praying now with the family leading them, a mighty unison of word, music and light. The aura of light around them increased in intensity with the prayers, eventually becoming as blinding as the noonday sun, before the family vanished, leaving behind them the singing of the choir and the feeling of the most intense love and radiant peace that anyone present had ever experienced. [17]

ETERNITY

Lydd Cemetery – Winter – Early Evening

"In memory of my very beloved Larissa Feodorovna, died July 18th 1926, aged 28 years, wife of Owen Tudor, 3rd King's Own Hussars."

Twilight. As the falling snow made the early evening light an eerie white, almost seemingly lighter than the day that was now passing, a tall fair-haired man in a long black overcoat stood up from his crouching position beside the now fading words on the stone. Casting one long last look at the inscription, he turned and walked toward the cemetery gate. The snow was now so heavy that everything was becoming obscure. Beside the gate stood a young woman, seen only in faint outline. As he reached her, they embraced and seemed to melt into one form. Then, as they turned away from view, in the last light from a street lamp, a small flash of gold light could be seen glinting from the lapel of her overcoat, which looked strangely out of place for the time, fashioned as of a century before, it was a brooch, two eagles locked together in an eternal embrace of fire and light. Then, suddenly, the two people, was it a man and a woman, or two women, in the blizzard, it was impossible to be sure now, disappeared into the brightness of the gathering night and were gone.

Prayer for the Departed, from the Russian Rite

With the souls of the righteous dead, give rest, O Saviour to the souls of thy servants, Nicholas, Alexandra, Olga, Tatiana, Marie, Anastasia and Alexis, preserving unto them the life of blessedness which is with thee, O Thou who lovest mankind.

In the place of thy rest, O Lord, where all thy Saints repose, give rest also to the souls of thy servants, Nicholas, Alexandra, Olga, Tatiana, Marie, Anastasia and Alexis, for thou alone lovest mankind.

Glory be to the Father...

Thou art the God who didst descend into hell and loose the bonds of the captives. Do thou give rest also to the souls of thy servants, Nicholas, Alexandra, Olga, Tatiana, Marie, Anastasia and Alexis.

Both now and ever...

O Virgin, alone, pure and undefiled, who without seed didst bring forth God, pray thou that their souls may be saved.

With the Saints give rest, O Christ, to the souls of thy servants Nicholas, Alexandra, Olga, Tatiana, Marie, Anastasia and Alexis, where there is neither sickness nor sorrow, nor sighing, but life everlasting.

Historical Note

This novel, *"Lost Eagle"*, is a work of fiction based on fact and extensive research. I happened on the story of Tatiana's rescue in 1994. The fact that the story was discovered by accident, whilst historian Michael Occleshaw was doing research for his book on British Intelligence during World War I, *"Armour Against Fate"*, is important. This is because it shows that this story, unlike other "escape" stories, was deliberately hidden away. In fact, as you'll see, an awful lot of trouble and energy has been expended in an attempt to make this story vanish altogether.

Part I of this book, *"Memories of Beauty"*, contains largely verifiable facts. The story of Grand Duchess Tatiana's rescue and her life with Owen Tudor in Lydd, Kent, related in Part 2 of this novel, *"The Isle of the Dead"*, has actually been in the public domain for the better part of the last five decades. No-one has realised it, because it was encoded in another fictional story. In 1957, Ian Fleming, one-time assistant to the Director of British Naval Intelligence, wrote a novel called *"From Russia with Love"*, whose heroine is actually called *"Tatiana Romanova"* – the very name of the Tsar's second daughter. After becoming very popular in the wake of an interview with President John F Kennedy in 1961 (see later on), it was turned into the second James Bond movie, starring Sean Connery as 007 in 1963. Did Ian Fleming's choice of name and character for his young heroine really amount to nothing more than a curious coincidence?

When I came to look more closely at the original book, I realised very quickly that Fleming, who as assistant to the Director of Naval Intelligence, had access to files closed to everyone else, had known exactly what he was doing in the writing of it. There are many references within the text itself that point to him knowing something directly about the real story.

First. In the very first page of the book he says, and I quote,

"Not that it matters, but a great deal of the background to this story is accurate."

That is the entire first paragraph of the "Author's Note". He then goes on to talk about the Soviet Spy Organisation SMERSH and the technical background to the story, not in the following sentence, which would relate this to his first statement, but in a whole new paragraph. The statement about the story's background and the technical statements in the subsequent paragraphs are **separate**.

Second. He opens the story on June 10th. Tatiana was born on June 10th 1897.

Third. Reinforcing point 2. We actually meet Tatiana for the first time in the story on June 10th. I repeat, the real Tatiana's birthday was June 10th 1897. Assuming a contemporary setting, we meet the fictional Tatiana on what would have been the real Tatiana's 60th birthday.

Fourth. Part two of the story opens on August 12th. The Tsarevitch Alexei, Tatiana's younger brother, and heir to the throne, was born on August 12th 1904.

Fifth. The Rosa Kleb character actually says in the text that the girl, Tatiana Romanova, is a direct relative of Tsar Nicholas II and therefore technically under suspicion as a possible reactionary.

Sixth. Tatiana is based in Istanbul. The cover story for "Larissa" is that she was a pork butcher's daughter from Istanbul (see below).

Seventh. When Bond and Tatiana escape from Istanbul disguised as a married couple, they spend their first full day married on August 16th. Tatiana and Owen Tudor married on August 16th 1923.

Eighth. While on the Orient Express, Bond's friend Kerim actually refers to Tatiana directly as "this Russian Princess you have in there."

Now one coincidence linking the real Tatiana to this story I can live with, maybe two. But *eight*? All of those references point to Fleming having a direct knowledge of the real story. But if Fleming did have knowledge of Tatiana's story, how did he stumble upon it in the first place? Intriguingly, the answer possibly involves Noel Coward.

The road to this realisation began when I saw a photograph on the mantelpiece of composer Sergei Rachmaninov's home at Lake Lucerne in Switzerland. It was inscribed to the composer with affection from Noel Coward, and dated 1938. This was the year Rachmaninov came to London to perform his Piano Concerto No.2 with Sir Henry Wood. Evidently Rachmaninov had been given the photo of Coward by him at that time. I already knew that Coward had lived on Romney Marsh a few miles from Lydd and wondered if he had ever met Tatiana. Following a hunch I discovered that Coward had written his first successful play "*The Vortex*" in a converted barn on Romney Marsh in 1923-4, the exact time when Owen and Tatiana moved to Lydd. This play was a great success in both England and the US. I also knew from a friend of mine who had done some detective work that Rachmaninov had visited Lydd in late 1924 while on tour in the UK. So it is entirely possible that he visited Tatiana then. Coward had already spent some time in the US from 1921 and may have got to know Rachmaninov there.

The other intriguing piece of this puzzle is that Rachmaninov, friend of Nicholas II and very probably one of Tatiana's teachers, and Noel Coward, had a mutual friend. Ian Fleming. Fleming also lived on Romney Marsh. Coward was a witness at Fleming's wedding in Jamaica in 1952. "*From Russia with Love*", was written in 1957. Is it possible that Coward was introduced to Tatiana by Rachmaninov and thereby got to know her story – which he later passed on to Fleming? Fleming had previously worked for Reuters as a journalist based in Moscow in 1933 and may have heard rumours about Tatiana's escape there. Later, as assistant to the Director of Naval Intelligence he would have been able to follow up what he had been told by Coward by researching in the files of SIS. What he found there could then have formed the basis for his novel – the story being a very obvious re-write of the facts of Tatiana's rescue.

An odd synchronicity here is that the sales of Fleming's books did not go well until, in an interview with Life Magazine in 1961, President John F Kennedy listed *"From Russia with Love"* as one of his ten favourite books (did he know the truth?). Sales promptly took off. Subsequently, *"From Russia with Love"* was made as a movie which became a worldwide smash hit in 1963 and has remained a movie icon ever since.

It should also be noted that on Rachmaninov's mantelpiece at his house in Lake Lucerne is a photo of the composer sitting with Tsar Nicholas II, in an obviously relaxed mood. It is a photo the composer's grandson treasures and has on proud display.

In *"From Russia with Love"*, the details of the fictional Tatiana's escape are of course transposed, but various shattered pieces of the real story remain intact, for instance, her escape by train, (Orient Express as opposed to Trans-Siberian) and having the fictional Tatiana based in Istanbul. The cover story for the real Tatiana appears to have been that she was a pork butcher's daughter from Constantinople (Istanbul). Also, the fictional Tatiana falls in love with James Bond – a naval commander - during the course of the story. The real Tatiana apparently fell in love with Owen Tudor, a dashing cavalry officer whose uncle, Admiral Sir Frederick Tudor, was in command of the Royal Navy's China Station during the First World War, through which Tatiana probably passed during her rescue, and was a friend of King George V. The fact that this case was so close to the Royal family could well account for a large part of the secrecy that surrounded it and continues to do so. The evidence that has been collated, by Michael Occleshaw in his two books, *"Armour Against Fate"*, about British Military Intelligence during World War I, and *"The Romanov Conspiracies"*, which deals directly with all facets of this story in detail from a very objective viewpoint, is quite overwhelming, especially in relation to all the documents about it that have mysteriously vanished without trace. As you study the history with an objective eye, it becomes clear very rapidly that there appears to have been deliberate suppression of documentary evidence.

This is useful for the historian on a couple of counts. First, it shows that there is a possibility that somebody has something to hide. Secondly, it prevents the story from degenerating into a rehearsal of a convenient fiction.

That a rescue of at least one daughter from the Imperial Family *did* happen is clear from the diary of Colonel Richard Meinertzhagen, CBE, DSO. He was a senior operative in MI0, a sub-section of what was then MI2 (c). In 1918 he had the responsibility of raising and direction of an intelligence service in Russia. Part of his duties involved frequent audiences with King George V to keep him updated with what was happening in his area of responsibility. So there is no question of the depth of his involvement in this case. He was also a meticulous diarist. His diary entry dealing directly with the escape of one of the daughters of the Russian Imperial Family is dated August 18th 1918. Part of it reads thus:

On July 1st everything was ready and the plane took off. Success was not complete and I find it too dangerous to give details. One child was literally thrown into the back of a plane in Ekaterinburg, and brought to England, where she still is.

He has no doubt whatsoever about the fate of the rest of the family, mentioning their murder on no less than three occasions in that entry. There is little doubt of this fact, although the precise details of exactly where and when the family actually died are open to question. The protocol of the head of the execution squad, Yakov Yurovsky, for so long used by historians as accurate truth, contains serious flaws when examined carefully, and there is eyewitness testimony, provided to Judge Ivan Sergeyev, in his investigation of the case in August 1918, that questions whether the family was still in the Ipatiev House by July 14th. This, and other related research, which is ongoing, has inspired the new account of the family's death which appears at the end of part 1 of this book.

Attempts have been made to cast doubt on Meinertzhagen's veracity over the years. However, many of these are based on a faulty reading of his psychology. Richard Meinertzhagen the man was, according to both his own son, and those who knew him, a very direct, uncomplicated man, who dealt in blacks and whites. Such people are rarely fantasists. Fakery would appear to have been alien to his nature. A case in point is the recent finding of the Forest Owlet in a very remote part of India. Meinertzhagen was a very keen ornithologist and claimed to have spotted this bird there whilst trekking many years ago. This was dismissed as a fantasy by those wishing to darken the colonel's reputation. Its recent discovery in the exact area he saw it in speaks volumes for his straightforward nature, and thus casts light on the statement made in the entry above.

Also important is the contribution of Lieutenant Colonel Nigel Watson. He was in the 3rd Hussars with Owen Tudor and also carried out intelligence work which brought him into contact with Richard Meinertzhagen. In the 1980's, two ladies from Lydd, a Mrs Bowler and a Mrs Daniels, were investigating the identity of Owen Tudor's first wife. They went to see Lieutenant Colonel Watson who confirmed – off the record, and after much interrogation - that Owen Tudor's wife had been called Tatiana, and that she was the second daughter of Nicholas II. When the historian Michael Occleshaw tried to confirm this with the colonel, he found him to be accompanied at his home by a rather unusual man who, in conversation, made remarks about Peter Wright, the Official Secrets Act and the responsibilities commensurate with signing it. Also, in this interview, the colonel denied that he had ever met "Larissa" at all, thus contradicting his own letters to Michael Occleshaw earlier on, in which he had stated that "Larissa" had very good manners. Mrs Daniels had stated that Colonel Watson had told her in their interview, that Owen Tudor's wife-to-be was beautiful. Something here does not add up. Owen Tudor's silence regarding his first wife, even amongst his own family, was positively deafening. Questions from researchers regarding her were always left unanswered. Most years on June 10th, he put flowers on her grave, the last time a few years before his own death in 1987. Grand Duchess Tatiana's birthday was June 10th 1897.

Also, on her death certificate, there is an odd mistake. Instead of being listed as *"Larissa F Tudor"*, which she should have been, given her apparent patronymic *"Feodorovna"*, she is listed instead as *"Larissa T Tudor"*. Is the otherwise meticulous Owen Tudor leaving a clue buried here? Does the *T* stand for Tatiana? On the gravestone itself, the surname *"Tudor"* is not attached to her two forenames, Owen Tudor being listed as her husband only at the foot of the inscription.

A couple of other curious facts surrounding "Larissa's" grave are that, first, when it was being dug, the local builder who usually lined the new graves with bricks asked if his services would be required. He was told no. The girl being buried was a Russian Princess, and she was being buried according to the rites of her Orthodox Faith. Second, in 1998, in the same week that the Russian Imperial Family were "buried" in St. Petersburg, "Larissa's" grave, which had been allowed to fall into disrepair, suddenly got a new set of railings and the stone was cleaned. All courtesy of a firm of London solicitors who have resisted all attempts to find out exactly who ordered it. To this day, flowers are regularly put on her grave, placed there by an unseen hand that has evaded all attempts to identify it. For a complete list of documents missing or suppressed in this case, please refer to Michael Occleshaw's book *The Romanov Conspiracies*, published by Orion Books in 1992.

But if this is true, how did Ian Fleming get away with revealing the story, even in code? Wasn't he risking prosecution under the Official Secrets Act? Well, no. The cleverness of Ian Fleming, who, it must be remembered, had access to Intelligence files that are closed to everyone else, was that he must have known he could never be prosecuted for this case. For, of course, to do so the government would have had to come clean. And that they were manifestly unprepared to do. And so, the story got out for all to see, in code, hidden in the story of a dashing British agent and a beautiful Russian girl called Tatiana Romanova from Constantinople.

Finally, although this case would appear to have been officially closed following the burial of the remains of the family in 1998, a team of scientists at Stanford University threw the identity of the bones into doubt in a new study in 2004 which called the earlier findings into serious question. Comparison of the DNA of the discovered bones with that of the Tsarina's sister, Grand Duchess Elisabeth, proved negative. These results have been published in peer-reviewed journals and been backed up by scientists in Holland and Japan. It should also be noted here that the Russian Orthodox Church refused to officiate at the burial ceremony in 1998. As Saints of the Church officials didn't want the faithful praying to the wrong bones. The issue, it seems, is far from closed.

Any objective study of this case will reveal that the documents which have been released and the conclusions reached so far are only those which point to a desired, possibly pre-determined conclusion. More research is ongoing, urgently needs doing and can only be welcomed in further attempts to lift the mist surrounding one of the last century's greatest mysteries.

Steven Ingman-Greer - February 15th 2013

Lost Eagle - Dramatis Personae

Grand Duchess Olga Nicolaevna – Oldest daughter of Tsar Nicholas II. Born at Tsarskoe Selo on the morning of November 15th 1895. Tatiana's closest friend and companion. Called "Olya" or "Olishka" within the immediate family. Officially murdered in the early hours of July 17th 1918 in Ekaterinburg, Siberia.

Grand Duchess Tatiana Nicolaevna – Second child of Nicholas II. Born at Peterhof on the morning of June 10th 1897. Called "Tanya" within the immediate family. Exact time and place of death are unknown.

Grand Duchess Marie Nicolaevna – Third child of Nicholas II. Born at Peterhof in the early afternoon of June 26th 1899. Called "Masha" within the immediate family. Officially murdered in the early hours of July 17th 1918 in Ekaterinburg, Siberia.

Grand Duchess Anastasia Nicolaevna – Fourth child of Nicholas II. Born at Peterhof in the early morning of June 18th 1901. Called "Nastya" within the immediate family. Exact time and place of death are unknown.

Grand Duke Alexis Nicolaevitch – Fifth child and only son and heir of Tsar Nicholas II. Born at Peterhof in the early afternoon of August 12th 1904. Officially murdered in the early hours of July 17th 1918 in Ekaterinburg, Siberia.

Emperor Nicholas II (1868-1918) – Emperor of Russia 1894 – 1917. The last of the Romanov dynasty which had ruled Russia since 1613. Officially murdered in the early hours of July 17th 1918 in Ekaterinburg, Siberia.

Empress Alexandra Feodorovna (1872 - 1918) - Grand-daughter of Queen Victoria of England. Wife of Nicholas II. Empress of Russia 1894 – 1917. Officially murdered in the early hours of July 17th 1918 in Ekaterinburg, Siberia.

Dowager Empress Marie Feodorovna (1847 – 1928) - Wife of Alexander III. Nicholas II's mother. The centre of the glittering "alternative court" during the reign of her son and one of the family's worst antagonists, especially in respect of Nicholas' wife, Alexandra, of whom she thoroughly disapproved.

Grand Duke Sergei Alexandrovitch (1857 - 1905) - Son of Alexander II. Uncle to Nicholas II. Governor General of St Petersburg. The man responsible for the massacre of civilian demonstrators in Palace Square on January 22nd 1905. Assassinated on February 17th 1905.

Grand Duchess Elizaveta Feodorovna (Ella) (1864 - 1918) - Wife of Grand Duke Sergei Alexandrovitch. Sister of Empress Alexandra. Following her husband's assassination in 1905, she took Holy Orders, founding her own convent, the Martha and Mary Convent in Moscow. Executed at Alapaevsk on July 17th 1918.

Grand Duchess George (1876-1940) – Member of the extended Russian Royal family, she was the second daughter of King George I of Greece and married to Grand Duke Georgi Mikhailovitch, a grandson of Tsar Nicholas I. Living in Harrogate from 1914, she founded four subscription-hospitals in the town for wounded soldiers between September 1914 and March 1916.

Emperor Alexander I (1777 - ?1825) - Son of Tsar Paul I. Grandson of Empress Catherine the Great. Tsar of Russia 1801 –

1825. Circumstances and facts of his death remain unclear to this day. Rumoured to have disappeared and become, like Rasputin, a "starets" or wandering holy man.

Grigory Efimovitch Rasputin (1869 – 1916) - Siberian peasant, shaman, mystic, seer and healer. Made many spiritual pilgrimages to the Holy Land and was a wandering "starets", or holy man. First met the Imperial Family in 1907. His cures of Grand Duke Alexis' haemophiliac attacks remain unexplained.

Prince Felix Yusupov (1887- 1967) – Cousin by marriage to the Imperial children. Heir to the richest fortune in Russia, made from fur trapping. One of the men behind the plot to murder Rasputin in 1916. Subsequently exiled by Nicholas II. The exile saved his life. He died in Paris in 1967, source of the many "mad monk" stories about his old enemy.

Grand Duke Dmitri Pavlovitch (1891 – 1941) – Cousin and sometime playmate to the Imperial children. Prospective suitor to Grand Duchess Tatiana. With Felix Yusupov, one of the men behind the plot to murder Rasputin in 1916. The likely crack-shot who actually performed the murder. Exiled by Nicholas II. Like Felix Yusupov, the exile saved his life. In increasingly frail health during the 1930's, he eventually died in Switzerland in 1941.

Anya Vyrubova (1884 - 1964) – Companion to Empress Alexandra from 1905 - 17. Arrested by the Provisional Government and imprisoned in 1917, she nevertheless survived the October Revolution. Took Holy Orders and died in July 1964 in Finland.

Pierre Gilliard (1879-1962) – Swiss citizen. He was French tutor to the five Imperial children from 1905-18. Followed them into exile in Tobolsk, he was finally prevented from following them to the Ipatiev House in May 1918. His intense loyalty to the Imperial family and love of the children is reflected in the books he wrote about them in the years following their deaths.

Sydney Gibbes (1879-1963) – English tutor to the Imperial children. Like Pierre Gilliard, followed the Imperial Family to Tobolsk, but was prevented from joining them in the Ipatiev House. With Pierre Gilliard, aided White investigators following the deaths of the family in July 1918. In later life became an Orthodox Priest.

Pyotr Stolypin (1862-1911) – Chairman of Nicholas II's Council of Ministers and Prime Minister of Russia 1906-11. Instituted agricultural and social reforms, which had widespread implications. Presided over the most successful period in pre-Revolutionary Russian history. Brought to an abrupt end by his assassination in Kiev in September 1911.

Alexander Kerensky (1881-1970) – Former lawyer and Minister of Justice in the Provisional Government following the February Revolution, he succeeded Prince L'vov as Prime Minister in July 1917. Evacuated the Imperial Family to Tobolsk in August 1917. Succeeded as leader of Russia by Lenin following the Bolshevik coup in October 1917. Died in New York in June 1970.

Leon Trotsky (1879 – 1940) – Born Lev Davidovitch Bronstein. Bolshevik Revolutionary and Marxist theorist. Leader of the October Revolution, second only to Vladimir Ilyitch Lenin. People's Commissar for Foreign Affairs at the time of the Treaty of Brest-Litovsk. In office until 1925, after which he found himself increasingly out of step with Stalin, who had seized control in the power struggle following Lenin's death in 1924. Was eventually expelled from the Communist Party and deported from the USSR. Fled to Mexico where he was assassinated by a Soviet agent in August 1940.

Sergei Rachmaninov (1873-1943) – Pianist, composer and aristocrat, widely thought to be the last of the great Romantics. He was a friend of Nicholas II's brother, Grand Duke Michael and conductor at the Private Opera in St Petersburg. Sponsored composer of the Imperial Family, his exile in 1917 as a result of an invitation to give a concert for the Swedish Royal Family probably saved his life. Lived in France, then Switzerland and finally the USA. He died in Beverly Hills California in March 1943.

Enrico Ceccetti (1850-1928) – Italian ballet dancer, founder of the Ceccetti method. He had a brilliant career in Russia, and was the originator of the roles of Carabosse and the Bluebird in Tchaikovsky's Sleeping Beauty. Later turned to teaching. His pupils included Nijynsky, Pavlova and Massine.

Emperor Yoshihito of Japan (1879-1926) 123rd Emperor of Japan according to the traditional order of succession. He was emperor from 1912-26. Prince Arthur of Connaught's mission to Japan in 1918 was to present the Emperor with an honorary field marshal's baton at the behest of King George V. It was this mission that was the likely cover for the rescue of Tatiana via Vladivostok and the Sea of Japan. Known since his death by his spiritual name, Emperor Taishō.

King George V – King of England 1910 – 36. Cousin and close friend of Nicholas II. Placed in an impossible position in 1917 following Nicholas II's abdication, he had to withdraw the offer of sanctuary to the family under pressure from the media. Likely source of a rescue attempt in 1918.

Prince Arthur of Connaught and Stathearn (1883-1938) –

Grandson of Queen Victoria and cousin to King George V. Governor General of South Africa 1920-23. His mission to deliver a ceremonial baton to Emperor Yoshihito of Japan in July 1918 at the behest of King George V is the possible cover for the rescue of Grand Duchess Tatiana.

Prince John (1905-19) – Youngest son of King George V. Suffered with epilepsy. Regarded as an embarrassment by King George V, he was kept out of the way and effectively incommunicado for his entire life. Corresponded with the Imperial children, who were very fond of him.

Admiral Sir Frederick Tudor – Head of the Royal Navy's China Station in 1917, close friend of King George V and responsible for Siberian refugees passing through Japan. Tatiana possibly went through his hands after her rescue in July 1918.

Lieutenant Owen Tudor – (1900 – 87) - Nephew of Admiral Sir Frederick Tudor. Married the mysterious and untraceable Larissa Feodorovna Haouk in London on August 16th 1923. After her death on July 18th 1926, never mentioned her or wrote of her ever again, even to close family members. Rose to the rank of Lieutenant-Colonel and commander of his regiment, the 3rd King's Own Hussars in the field in 1941.

Colonel Richard Meinertzhagen – Operative in MIO. Organiser of the rescue attempt which apparently extracted one of the imperial children from Ekaterinburg on July 1st 1918. Also a keen ornithologist. First to spot the Forest Owlet in a remote part of India. This sighting has only recently been verified. Received DSO. Refused a knighthood in 1951, but accepted CBE in 1957.

David Lloyd George (1863-1945) – Prime Minister of Great Britain 1915-22.

Footnotes

1 Author's Note:

From time to time in the last 80 years, visitors to Peterhof have seen a tall young lady in an Edwardian travelling cloak walking in the grounds. She is sometimes seen in the gardens, sometimes in the forest and at other times is seen walking by the sea. She seems to be part of a re-enactment and talks pleasantly to the people she meets, but when they go to ask her deeper questions, she is found to have mysteriously vanished, leaving behind a faint scent. What is odd is that no two people report the same scent. Some say it is a scent of Jasmine, others that it is a scent of Roses. Her identity is a mystery. Those who have seen her do not remember her face, only her gentle, serious and noble manner, as if she were someone from a bygone era.

2 Author's Note:

This photograph, alluded to in this entry by Grand Duchess Tatiana, can be seen reproduced in the memoirs of Pierre Gilliard, Thirteen Years at the Russian Court, facing page 240.

3 Author's Note:

At this point, several entries to the diary appear to be missing. In the original copy, there are pages which have very obviously been torn out. Suffice it to say that the most significant absence of entry is for August 14th 1917. On that day, the family left Tsarskoe Selo forever.

4 Author's Note:

After a gap, the diary picks up again in January 1918 during their captivity at the governor's house in Tobolsk, Siberia.

5 Author's Note:
As before, there is another gap here in the narrative. In the original copy, pages are missing. Some of the remaining pages have been singed, so the diary was obviously placed near a heat source at some point in its history. The narrative picks up again during the family's captivity at Ekaterinburg. They reached here in two phases. First, the Tsar, Tsarina and Grand Duchess Marie went on in March 1918, followed by the others nearly a month later.

6 Author's Note:
The volume Tatiana refers to in this entry mysteriously survived her attempt to destroy it. Inside, one quote of Rasputin's that is underlined by the Grand Duchess reads:
"Love is Light and it has no end. Love is great suffering. It cannot eat. It cannot sleep. It is mixed with sin in equal parts. And yet it is better to Love…If Love is strong – the lovers happy. Nature Herself and the Lord give them happiness…All is in Love, and even a bullet cannot strike Love down."

7 Author's Note:
The only known fact about the fate of the Imperial Family is that none of them was seen alive or recognised as such again with complete certainty after July 4th 1918…

8 Author's Note:
Amorel Meinertzhagen crossed the Atlantic from Canada on board the Canadian Pacific Ocean Service Ltd. Vessel Corsican, arriving in London on August 8th. She occupied cabin 14. In cabin 13 was a young Canadian woman called Marguerite Lindsey, aged 22, and described as a masseuse. Also on board was Miss Henrietta Crawford, a War Office Matron. On disembarkation, all trace of Marguerite Lindsey disappears. Her given address was false and there is no trace of the birth of Marguerite

Lindsey in the records of Canadian births, marriages and deaths. All this flew in the face of very strict entry requirements for the United Kingdom in 1918, which would never have allowed for the entry of a person who was so untraceable. Her identity would appear to be a cover. Also, it is worth noting that Tatiana's age in 1918 was 21, just one year younger than the apparent age of "Marguerite Lindsey".

9 Author's Note:
Tatiana did not realize that her letters to Dowager Empress Marie were intercepted by British Intelligence. The letters sent to her in return were very clever forgeries, giving, however, some notion of what she was doing, so as to appear authentic. Even the handwriting was cleverly forged. Dowager Empress Marie, whom British Intelligence regarded as a serious security risk, was told that her family was safe and sequestered at a monastery in Poland. She died in 1928, two years after Tatiana, never having seen her son or his wife and children again. Given her attitude towards them, particularly towards the Tsaritsa, this will probably not have troubled her conscience much.

10 Author's Note:
Several pages of the diary appear to have been torn out at this point. The narrative resumes in June 1920.

11 Author's Note:
This was to be the last time that Tatiana saw her cousin. She was not to know it but what had passed between them represented the final end of their era. A world died in that room, in those few minutes, as the fate of the final member of the House of Romanov was sealed.

12 Author's Note:
It would appear that whilst in the act of playing, Tatiana was

unfortunately recognised by a member of the shop staff who was an Anti-Bolshevist and Russian Royalty Supporter. He informed the editor of the Manchester Guardian, a close friend, who, out of courtesy to Buckingham Palace contacted King George's private secretary and asked him a question he was unable to answer officially. This was the beginning of the end of Owen and Tatiana's freedom.

13 Author's Note:
This entry is blank, although Tatiana had obviously intended to write in here, something prevented her. A clue is provided by the following slip of paper, found in the diary at this point.

14 Author's Note:
There are no diary entries for the rest of December 1923 or early part of 1924. It would seem that the Grand Duchess was either too ill or too distraught to write. It forms the only major blank in the sequence. The diary does not begin again until June 1924.

15 Author's Note:
The plane Tatiana saw seems, from her description, to have been a Spitfire. The Spitfire prototype did not fly until 1936.

16 Author's Note:
It is a matter of public record that Larissa Feodorovna Tudor, first wife of Owen Tudor, died of pulmonary exhaustion, brought on by spinal caries and tuberculosis in the early afternoon of July 18th 1926. Strangely, her entry in the Public Record lists her as Larissa T. Tudor, not Larissa F. Tudor. Owen never spoke or wrote about his first wife. Letters on the subject, even from family members, were ignored. Most years, on June 10th, he put flowers on her grave, the last time, a few years before his own death in 1987. Grand Duchess Tatiana's birthday was June 10th 1897.

17 Author's Note:

Since the year 2005, an increasing number of churches and cathedrals have been built all over Russia dedicated to Nicholas and the family. The Cathedral on Blood, built on the site of the Ipatiev House, was consecrated on June 16th 2003. It is an integral part of the deep spiritual revolution that is sweeping through their beautiful country and converting new hearts to Love, Beauty and consciousness of the Creator with every day that passes. In Russian Orthodox thought, Nicholas II, his wife and children are living people, who are joined with us in continuous prayer and supplication for the redemption of Mankind and the regeneration of the Earth.

Select Bibliography

Edwards, Sue. *No Resting Place for a Romanov*. Sue Edwards, 1998

Massie, Robert K. *Nicholas & Alexandra*. Pan, London, 1972

Massie, Robert K. *The Romanovs - The Final Chapter*. Jonathan Cape, London 1995

Occleshaw, Michael. *Armour Against Fate – British Military Intelligence During WW1*. Pan, London, 1989

Occleshaw, Michael. *The Romanov Conspiracies – The Romanovs & The House of Windsor*. Orion Books, London, 1992. (*This book has an exhaustive bibliography, which is perfect for researchers interested in the subject.*)

Prince Michael of Greece. *Nicholas & Alexandra – The Family Albums*. Tauris Parke Books, London, 1996

Townsend, Carol. *Royal Russia*. St Martin's Press, New York, 1995

Further Reading
Occleshaw, Michael. *Dances in Deep Shadows – The Clandestine War in Russia 1917-20*. Constable Publishing, London, 2006

**TOP HAT
BOOKS**

Historical fiction that lives.

We publish fiction that captures the contrasts, the achievements, the optimism and the radicalism of ordinary and extraordinary times across the world.

We're open to all time periods and we strive to go beyond the narrow, foggy slums of Victorian London. Where are the tales of the people of fifteenth century Australasia? The stories of eighth century India? The voices from Africa, Arabia, cities and forests, deserts and towns? Our books thrill, excite, delight and inspire.

The genres will be broad but clear. Whether we're publishing romance, thrillers, crime, or something else entirely, the unifying themes are timescale and enthusiasm. These books will be a celebration of the chaotic power of the human spirit in difficult times. The reader, when they finish, will snap the book closed with a satisfied smile.